KINGS REIGN TRILOGY

BOOK ONE

"THE HOUSE OF KING AND RAINBOW"

KINGS REIGN TRILOGY

BOOK ONE

"THE HOUSE OF KING AND RAINBOW"

Copyright © 2024

All rights reserved. No part of this book may be reproduced or transmitted in any form or by any means, electronic or mechanical, including photocopying, recording, or by any information storage and retrieval system, without written permission from the publisher.

This is a work of fiction. All characters, locations and events in the narrative - other than those based on family history - are products of the author's imagination and are used fictitiously. Any resemblance to real persons, living or dead, is entirely coincidental and not intended by the author. Where real historical figures, locations and events appear, these have been depicted in a fictional context.

Dedication

This book is dedicated first to my family, starting with my loving wife, for without her holding me down; I wouldn't have had the peace of mind to write. It is said that you don't know the true protection and strength of your home until it's been through a storm. Well, I have been through a storm. The protection and strength that my beautiful, loving, and dare I say, perfect wife has displayed throughout the storm has me "Thanking God" for her every day. Erica, publicly I want to thank you, I know I am not the easiest person to deal with, let alone love, but you somehow do. Thank you, for in my absence, you give loving support and care to our four little angels whom I love dearly. "Thank you." I also dedicate this book to my mother, JoAnn; my in-laws Pat and Tommy, and my sister Nichelle and thank you to Alvin, my big bro. for stepping up and filling my shoes while I was away. Also, thank you to all those brothers that are still spending time in the belly of the beast, Hank, the unit's Thomas Payne, "If you are afraid to offend, you can't be true." Do believe me when I say Hank was always "true." Also thank you to Chris, our unit book critic and all-around good guy, and to one more Brother whom without his words of experience, and his caring attitude toward his surrounding and the brothers around him, incarceration would have been miserable. Thank you Stew. Finally, to the Bros on the Peterburg compound, peace, love, and blessings. "Keep your head up."

Hello, I am Saint "A BOSS" and one of the most hated and revered motherfuckers in San Diego. I am my father's son. Yes! I am that Nigga that other Niggas hate, but wanna be at the same time. There are Niggas out there that wanna be me so fucking bad they dick get hard at the mention of the name "Saint King", a bad Motherfucker. I love my life but wouldn't wish it on my worst enemy. I tell this tragic life ending story with the hopes that no matter how glorified pushing dog food, stacking racks, and fucking bad ass bitches may appear to be that y'all lil-nigga-wanna-be's out there will take another road. Trust me when I say the glorified road is a dead-end road to prison or a Crypt.

I tell this story as I lay here at the Presbyterian Hospital in an ICU bed with tubes running everywhere and more bullet holes in me than in a pin cushion. This shit is real! My brother Hakeem is dead, and the Doctors are saying a nigga is on his way out. When I heard this, I closed my eyes to shot a quick prayer to the man upstairs. No sooner had I said amen, my thoughts were interrupted by a "click"

"click" and a baritone voice saying, "Nigga your next fucking prayer you can tell your mother fucking maker face to face!"

I have always heard that at the moment of pending death, your life flashes before your eyes. I used to think that was some bitch ass Nigga bull shit, but trust me, in that minute, my life flashed before my eyes. It first had me asking myself, "How the fuck does a Nigga go from an under and post grad degree from Berkley at California, with the whole world in front of him, to an ICU bed and a Nigga with a Nine pressed against his Temple. This is some glorified shit for yo' ass." My life flashed back to when I was a boy growing up on the south side of Emerald Hills in one of, if not the worst, areas in San Diego.

I grew up with my Pops William Saint King the second, which of course was his father's name and now my name, making me William Saint King the third. Everyone calls me "Saint". My grandfather was known as "King". My father was known by everyone but my mom, as "Will". My Pops was a hell of a man. He stood six foot four and was about

230 pounds with dark chocolate skin. That Nigga could wear a suit, Tom Ford, Brioni, it didn't matter the brand, he wore them and looked good doing it. He almost wore one better than me. Pops looked like one of those Niggas on I.G. with over six hundred thousand followers. Pops was a Black American that spoke with a slight French English dialect because his father was from Cameroon, Africa, and he spoke French.

My father got respect in our area. He ran the whole south side, a street Mayor of sort, but his touch reached out through the whole city. As a young kid, being around him, I didn't really know what all that meant; I just knew no one fucked with my Pops. I also grew up with my Mom Brenda Ann King, a short fair skinned, almost white, Black woman. I am told my mom looked like her grandmother who was Puerto Rican with white skin, which explained the fair skin. She grew up in Englewood California. My Mom was a beautiful woman that didn't say much, but when she did speak thunder roared, and the earth shook. Even my strong-willed boss of a father even moves to her bellows. Then there was my best friend, my Nigga, my younger brother Hakeem. Back in those days, Hakeem and I were the opposites of each other. I was quiet, shy and about my books, but Hakeem, he was straight bout it, bout it, if a Nigga was looking for an ass stomping, Hakeem was willing and always able to give it to them. Hakeem would go to a fool's ass at the drop of a dime. If he couldn't beat you by throwing hands, he would pick up something and crack a Motherfucker across the head. I remembered back when I was Twelve and Hakeem was ten and we were attending East Union Middle School. This school was full of all types of Niggas. Black Niggas, White Niggas, Brown Niggas, and a lot of Niggas that couldn't talk English good. It was a California school, the second largest school system in the nation. So, when I tell you we had two thousand students at East Union we had two thousand students. Now, imagine two thousand kids trying to fit in wherever they could. It was a recipe for gangs active, drug dealing, bullying and Niggas that just didn't give a good damn.

One morning, I had to walk to school alone because Mom was giving Hakeem a good ole fashion tongue lashing about his fighting at school. See over the past few weeks of school, I had been avoiding four of the biggest Niggas in the whole motherfucking school. These Niggas was big bullies and I somehow got on their line. Normally, Hakeem and I walked to school together, and they wouldn't bother me for some reason. So, I only had to avoid them in the hallway. Hakeem's classroom was way on the other side of the school, so I usually walked the halls by myself. It was easy to avoid them in the halls cause the school was so big. However, this one morning, there was no Hakeem, and those Niggas was gonna be on my ass. I got thrown off my game of trying to avoid them by the voice of this hella fine ass girl. She was 5 foot 4 inches with mocha color skin and an ass on her oh my God! I'm telling you, what that ass was all that. Man, I hope she didn't get that ass from her momma cause if she did her family went hungry cause, there was no way her daddy worked. That nigga stayed home all day watching her mom's ass. She was the prettiest motherfucking girl that ever walked the halls of East Union. I couldn't believe she was even speaking to me. I didn't know she knew who I was.

This fine ass motherfucker name was Dash. Dash usually sat three seats behind me in Homeroom. Other than a small scar on the right side of her chin, that she had gotten from putting in some hand work on a few bitches who crossed her path, she was picture perfect. Dash had the heart of a lioness. Damn, that girl was just too pretty to be able to throw hands like she could. I respected it though.... cuz in this jungle they called a school, to survive you had to be able to throw hands. However, because of her, I lost my attention on the bullies, "Smack", "Smack", "Smack", "Ha", "Ha", "Ha". I cried out, "Leave me the fuck alone!" One of the bullies was hitting and kicking me as his co-bullies yelled out, "He ain't gon fight back, his scared bitch ass." All of this was happening in front of Dash; she just looked on as they taunted me.

I had to say something to not look so much like a pussy in front of Dash. I yelled back to the bullies, "I ain't no pussy!" I know, I know, that statement sounded just like one a pussy would make. I told the bullies, "I just don't want to fight! I want to go to class and go home! That's all." They left me alone and I went into the classroom. Dash and I took our seats, but one of the bullies came into the classroom, stopped at my desk, and leaned over it until he and I was face to face. "If you don't fight me, I am going to bust your ass every day until you do, like today when the last bell rings." After saying that, he picked up my homework up off my desk, ripped it up and then flipped me and my desk over. As he walked over to his desk, he said, "After school! After school, yo' bitch ass is mine. Nigga yo' can run but you can't hide." Dash helped me up from the floor and whispered in my ear, "Saint, what are you going to do? All four of them will jump you." "Ya! I know! But one more thing I know Dash." "Ya what's that, Saint?" "That nigga watches too much TV. 'You can run, but you can't hide', really?" Dash laughed. When the bell rang, it caught me by surprise. I looked up at the clock and it sure was three-fifteen already;

that was the last bell. "DAMN! Three-fifteen got here quicker than a motherfucker". I headed to the other side of the school building to my lil bro. Hakeem's classroom so we could walk home together as we always do.

As I got closer to his classroom, I could hear Hakeem's teacher, Ms. McAfee, scolding him. I didn't go into his classroom. I just stood out in the hall and listened. "You are an intelligent young man, Hakeem but your aggressive behavior has to stop. I am going to give you one more chance Hakeem. One more and I mean, just one more. Any more incidents of you fighting or hurting another student as you did yesterday and it won't be just after-school detention, you will be expelled for the rest of the year. Do you understand me?" Hakeem replied, "Yes Ms. McAfee." "Now get your books and go right home. Also, try to do some homework for once."

When Hakeem walked out of the classroom into the hall, I didn't notice him at first because by then my mind had gone back to my bullying problems. The four kids that were harassing me were Black kids.

When is this black-on-black fighting going to stop? I thought to myself. "Lord, I bet there's no chance it can happen today, is it?" I thought this while shaking my head. "Whatever their reason is for picking me to bully on is about to blow up in their faces." When Hakeem yelled my name, "Saint! Hey Saint!" I snapped back into focus and said, "What's up lil bro!" "Nothing! What's up with you?" "Nothing, lil bro, but I did hear Ms. McAfee giving you hell." "Ya, didn't she?" "Ha, Ha, Ha. Let's go lil Bro." As we walked down the hall toward the side exit door of the building, we noticed broken glass all over the floor of the hall with a brick lying in the middle of the broken glass. I said to Hakeem, "Some damn fool Nun' thrown a brick and broke out the window next to the door." We walked around the broken glass and left out the building through the side door. Hakeem and I walked toward the School's Courtyard we made it almost to the center of the Courtyard when we were met by four big niggas. They stood right in front of us. They were my bullies, and you could tell by their stance that their intention was not only to make me fight them, but to fuck me up.

Ignoring them, Hakeem and I tried to walk around the niggas, but they encircled us. This drew the attention of the few students that were still on campus. They came running over so they could have a better view of what they thought was about to be a beatdown on Hakeem and me. The crowd of kids who had gathered got closer and louder as the bullies commenced to whopping ass by swinging and kicking on me. The first blow that was thrown landed dead into my jaw. I immediately tasted and smelled blood. Looking around, I saw Hakeem break and take off running back toward the side door we had just exited the building from. I thought to myself, "My lil bro left me here alone to fight these four bullies." I was doing the best I could but was getting more than I was giving. I was no match for these big motherfuckers. I couldn't believe Hakeem picked today of all days to listen to our mom and his teacher, Ms. McAfee about not fighting anymore. These motherfuckers were delivering the ass kicking of a lifetime. They were beating my ass like I had slapped one of their mommas or something. The kids that were standing around cheered on the ass whipping I was getting.

Then from nowhere, one of the bullies cried out, "Ouch ahhhh!!" and fell to the ground holding his bleeding forehead. Then I heard, "Bam!!!", "Oh yo' motherfucker my eye! My eye!!" When I raised my head from the fetal position I had been beat into, I saw one of the bullies run away toward the building holding a fucked-up eye. Now there were only two bullies left. They still were landing some hell of blows with good foot-hand combinations they had going on. I looked around and to my left there stood my lil bro, Hakeem with a bloody brick in his right hand. He hadn't run away because he was scared, he had run back into the building to retrieve the brick we saw lying in the hall in the middle of the broken glass as we exited the side door. Hakeem smacked one of the two bullies that was left right in his fucking mouth with that brick. Blood and teeth went everywhere. I went to work on the other one. We were now kicking some pure ass, but the backlash from that ass kicking we were now giving to the bullies, was a different story all together. The bully that ran off holding his fucked-up eye ran straight to the principal's office. He lied about everything that was going on; he made it seem like Hakeem and I were the aggressors. When the principle arrived on the scene, the bystanders scattered. The principle saw Hakeem with a brick in hand putting in work on the biggest bully, and me giving Nike bottoms to the face of the other one. I was trying to leave the fucking Nike Swoosh imprint on that Motherfucker's forehead. I am sure, to the principle, the scene looked like a battlefield, there was blood and teeth laying all over the Courtyard, and according to the lying fucked up eye boy, Hakeem and me was the one that started all this shit. The two bullies that were still there getting their asses torn out the frame looked like two scared kids trying to unsuccessfully defend themselves as they bled and cried. The scene plus school policy prompted the principle to call the police. The principle was the only adult still at the school, so he had a hell of a time gathering us all up by himself. It was so difficult because Hakeem was still trying to kill the bully he had hold of. The principle finally took us to his office where he called our parents. I looked over at Hakeem and his facial impression was blank as though nothing just happened. On the other hand, I was scared as hell and was about to shit in my pants knowing that the principle was calling our parents. East Union middle School is known for their gang fights, drug dealers, and its high ethic population which usually causes a simple school fight to be a full-blown big deal where the police was concern. The Police arrived with their sirens blaring as if a nigga nunn caught a body. Two white officers burst through the door of the principal's office with their hands on their gun. The two officers came in on set and wishing a Nigga would. Principal Owens quickly intervened by saying, "Officers, Officers! There is no need for all of this. Please take your hand off your guns. These are children, officers. They only had a school yard fight." The officers looked around the room and one of them walked toward Hakeem, he grabbed Hakeem's arm, he said, "Boy who were you fighting and what gang do you belong to?" Hakeem pulled back from the officer just as Principal Owens jumped up to stand between them. "The kids' parents have been called and they are on their way." The officer tried to get around Principal Owens to get to Hakeem but couldn't, he then demanded the principal to stand back out of the way. Principal Owens replied, "No! I am not backing away." Principal Owens even gave the officer a slight push. That push may not have been that slight. Principal Owens is not a small man. He looked like he may have played football back in the day. Six foot Two, Two Hundred and Seventy-five pounds a big black, red eyed man. He looked like he was able to hold his own.

After Principal Owens pushed the officer, the officer told Principal Owens too, "Put your hands behind your back." As the officers went to handcuff Principal Owens, he told him, "You are under arrest for impeding and aggressively interfering with an officer in the act of his duties." "Now what kind of nonsense is this?" Principal Owens yelled. As the officers continued in their attempt to handcuff Principal Owens, the office door swung open and a tall silhouette stood in the doorway, fully erected with shoulders back wearing the hell out of a well-tailored suit that fit perfectly on his slim body frame. His face was stern like he didn't take no shit. The stern-faced man asked, "What's going on in here?" When Hakeem and I heard the stern-faced man's voice, we felt somewhat at ease because we knew who the man was. The Officer quickly replied, "Why? Who the hell are you? We are here trying to do our job and investigate an assault and attempted murder case." "Say What?" The stern-faced man said while stepping into the office. His forehead wrinkled and his jaw line tight from him clinching his teeth. The stern-faced man moved towards the officers. One of the officers pulled his gun and pointed it in the stern-faced man's face. The stern-faced man became visibly angry. The other kids that were in the office with us moved to one side of the office out of fear because the officer was now swinging his gun around the room. He was doing this as the other officer called for backup. "Officers under attack!" the officer yelled into his radio. No one in the office knew that the stern-faced man was me and Hakeem's Pops, but more importantly, the officers didn't know they were pointing a gun at "William Saint King" San Diego most connected man.

After some minutes, more police cars rolled in; it looked as if it was a police officer down situation. Meanwhile, my Pops started to verbally express his anger toward the racist cops. When it seemed as though things would get uglier, the Chief of police walked through the door. The Chief immediately scanned the room to assess the situation, his eyes came to a halt when he made eye contact with my Pops. With his eye fixed on Pops, the Chief asked, "What's going on here?" His officers quickly replied, "Well Sir, we were called to this address about an assault and a possible attempted murder. "Stop! Stop! Stop!" yelled the Chief. "Why the hell is Principal Owens in handcuffs? What the fuck! God damn it!" the Chief yelled. The Chief moved closer to my Pops. Pops didn't part his lips, he just stood there with that stern look on his face. "Take those cuffs off Principal Owens and you two officers meet me outside in the hall," the Chief demanded.

Once the officers took the cuffs off Principal Owens, they followed the chief into the hall and away from everyone else. I leaned over to Hakeem and said, "The Chief, Ain't that Mr. Parker, the man that comes to our house to meet with Pops in Pops office?" Hakeem

 nodded his head "yes". "Chief Parker, what's going on?" The two officers asked the Chief frantically as they stepped into the hall. The Chief said, "Let me ask you two a question. How long have you been in this district?" The two officers said, "Chief, we just transferred into your district." "So, officer Knotts and Officer Sanders, how long have you been on the job?" asked the Chief. Officer Knotts said, "Two years Sir," and officer Sanders said, "One year Chief." "So, you mean to tell me I have two new ass wipes in my district and not long on the job? Both of you fools are lucky to still be alive. Do you know or ever heard of the name William Saint King?" "Chief you mean the King from the King family?" "Yes fool! What fucking King you think I'm talking about?" "Chief?" "Yes, Sanders." "Chief, so all the things that people have said about the King family are actually for real. Chief, I always thought that was scenes from a gangster movie or a tall tale." "Well, Sanders it's not, they are real, and he is real and standing in that fucking office."

"Shit! Shit! Shit! You guys don't understand the shit storm y'all have caused." Officer Knotts asked, "Chief, what is he doing here?" "I don't know Knotts, but it can't be good. Listen, you two don't worry about all that right now. I need you two to go back in there and apologize to everyone in that office. Then go back to the station and wait there for me! Go! Now get out of my face and go now!" Both officers said, "Yes, Chief. We'll go now Sir." Officer Knotts and Sanders did as they were told. They stepped back into the principal's office and apologized to everyone and the officers gave a direct apology to Pops.

When the officers said the name 'King', the principal's head snapped up; he had a confused look on his face. With that stern look and his teeth clinched, Mr. King, my Pops, stepped toward the two officers and said, "You can keep your fucking apology. You two motherfuckers were up here on some type of racist bullshit and if you didn't know King Reign Supreme you will find out today." As Pops moved closer to the two officers, my mom walked through the door and saw what was about to happen. Mom yelled out, "William!! William!! William Saint King!" Oh Shit! Mom used Pop's full name. Whenever Mom uses our full name, that meant she meant business. At that very second, Pops came to a dead stand still. He looked up. Mom grabbed Pops by the arm, pulled him close to her, and whispered in his ear, "William, go home. Let me handle this. William, I got this!" Pops turned and left without saying a word.

The chief saw what had just happened and ordered all his officers to leave the school. The principal was thrown off by the fact that William King was in his school, and in his office. Only close family and friends knew that William Saint King was Hakeem and my father. My Mom, Hakeem and I go by our mother's mother birth name, "Autry" to hide the fact that we are the family of one of the most connected and dangerous men in all of San Diego, if not all of California. By this time, all the boys' parents were in the principal's office. The Chief met with the parents and told them, "I will be appointing Officer Wright to further investigate the fight but based on the statement taken from the boys and other eyewitnesses, at this time there will be no criminal charges filed." The principal told the families, "I am glad that no criminal charges will be filed, but there were a number of school discipline policies on student conduct has been violated." Everyone talked for a while and concluded that no one was going to press individual charges. The principal said to the group, "A separation of these boys is appropriate, and suspension will be put in place as well." The four bullies got transferred to a different school. Then the Principal said to my mom, "Mrs. Autry, your two boys will be suspended for ten days. Hakeem's ten-day suspension will be out of school suspension due to the number of fights he has gotten into this year, and Saint's ten-day suspension will be in school suspension."

My Mom, Hakeem and me left the principal's office and nobody said a word. Everyone was quiet as hell even in the car on the ride home. Hakeem and me would look over at each other every now and then but we dared not mumble a word. When we got home and stepped through the door, we were met by Pops. Hakeem and me started to tremble in fear from not knowing how Pops was going to react to today's events. Pops immediately said, "Okay, who wants to go first? Somebody tell me what happened at that school today?" I was the first to speak out, "I tried to avoid them Pops. I did just what Momma has always told us to do." "Okay, so what do you have to say for yourself Hakeem? And I'm guessing you were the one with the brick, Right Hakeem?" "Yes Sir, but Pops, it was too many of them. They were ganging up on Saint. Pops, I had to do something." Pops put a hand on Hakeem's shoulder and said "Yes Hakeem, as you should have. You ain't did nothing wrong. Always stand up for yourselves and never leave each other to fight a battle alone. I am glad that both of you are alright. Always know this, I love y'all and I will always be here to look after you know I have eyes everywhere." While Pops talked to us, Mom never said a word. She waited until we were finished talking, before she said, "Hakeem, you and Saint go ahead upstairs and do your homework and chores so your dad and I can talk." Yes, Ma'am."

Hakeem and me ran upstairs and started doing our homework and talking. Hakeem asked me, "Why do you think Pops don't want people to know that he is our dad, Saint? Do you think that he is ashamed or embarrassed by us?" "Naw! I don't think that Pops is a real important man. Didn't you see how everybody showed him so much respect at the school?" "Ya Saint, everybody except those two white police officers." "Ya but Hakeem, they came back and apologized to everybody, that was because of Pops.

Still though Hakeem, I wish that I knew what kind of work Pops really do. Also, Hakeem, what I really didn't understand was why did that Chief Parker acted like he didn't know Pops." "Me too, Saint." "WELL! Come on Hakeem, let's finish our homework and chores so we can go outside before dinner time."

Meanwhile, Mom and Pops were talking in the front room. They became pretty loud. They were so loud Hakeem and me quietly walked halfway back down the stairs to see and hear what was going on. "William, I don't understand why you went to that school today. Anyway, how did you even know what was going on up there?" "What do you mean, Brenda? Those are my sons. When Little Joe, my right-hand man that I have keeping an eye on my sons, call me about what was going on, I went to the school." "William, no one is questioning the fact that they are your sons. Hell! One looks just like you and have that little sexy walk of yours and the other one has that hot ass temper of yours." "Brenda, I am tired and completely over hiding the fact that you are my wife, and those boys are my sons. Brenda, y'all are carrying someone else's last name. Y'all are "King" damn it! And King Reign Supreme, not no fucking Autry and I don't mean that in disrespect to your mom's family last name, but ya'll are my family. Those boys are old enough to know who I really am and what I do to support and protect this family. My family! They need to know why I vanish for days and sometimes weeks at a time. Damn it Brenda, they need to know what it means to be a "King". "But William, I thought we decided..." "Oh no! Hell No! Brenda, Hell No!!! It wasn't 'no we' that decided. It was you that decided all this crazy low budget shit we got going on around here. From the last name, where and how we live, to where the boys go to school. We make more money than daddy Grac and Reverend Ike put together but live like we are the Evans. (For you Bougie ass motherfuckers, the "Evans" is a 'Good Times' reference, best Black-American show of all times) How long Brenda? How long do you want me to keep them in the dark?" "William, as long as it takes. I don't want this family, as you say, 'my family', to end up like my parents and brothers and your parents and brother. The Marsh and the Kings were untouchable, yet I lost them behind some bullshit, William. I be damn if I am going to lose you and my boys over some gangster bullshit."

"Brenda, that's exactly my point. Yes, I lost my father, mom, and brother just like you did, but that was because our fathers didn't understand that you must grow your organization from the inside out. If our fathers would have brought me and your brother up in the organization and taught and groomed us to be hitters who would drop a motherfucker without a second thought or even, if our fathers had family watching their backs and their family's backs, they would still be here with us today. Hell! Brenda, our fathers weren't even real hitters themselves. They never put any real work in." "William, I am so afraid of losing you and the boys. Y'all are all I got." "Brenda, baby, if you want me to pull back baby I will, and we can go on living just fine right here. We don't have to go anywhere." "Well, William don't go that far because after what happened today at that school, we just might have to move into another house and school district. Listen William, I do understand where you are coming from. Your sons need to know their father and what it means to be a "King". It's not like I can stop it anyway. I saw that today; those boys are their father's sons." "Ha ha ha. Yo' right! Brenda my boys kicked some ass today, didn't they?" "WILLIAM! Shame on you…. But yes, they did!" "Ha, Ha, Ha Brenda my sons" " Stop it William, yo' know yo' not right! So, when are you going to talk to the boys?" Hakeem and me ran back upstairs once Pops and Momma started laughing and kissing each other.

A few days into our suspension, without Hakeem at school; it just wasn't the same. I couldn't wait to get home to see what Hakeem had been up to all day. Once the last bell rang at three fifteen, I darted home. Just as I got there and called out for Hakeem, Pops walked into the house and started yelling for Mom, "Brenda! Brenda! Where are you babe?" "Right here, William. What's all the yelling about?"

"Brenda, you and the boys grab a jacket. We are going for a ride. Babe, we are going to look at some houses. Do you have any idea which area or neighborhood you want to move to?" "William, as far as my concerns, it's all about our boy's safety." "I gotcha on that Brenda Ann." "William, wherever you want to move us to is just fine by me. The only thing I have a problem with is..." "Brenda, don't. Please don't even finish that statement cause we have been through all that over a thousand times." "Well, boys I guess your dad is a mind reader. William, are you a mind reader? You must be cause I always hear you completely out so that you can make your statements or points clear and plain. So will you please allow me to finish my statement so that you can understand completely and clearly what I am trying to say to you. Instead of you trying to predict what I am saying?"

Pops could tell that mom meant business because whenever she gets upset her nostril flairs out and sweat accumulates on the bridge of her nose. He quickly apologized to her. "Okay Brenda baby.

Please calm down. I'm sorry for cutting you off. I should have let you finish your statement. Babe, what were you trying to say?" It took Mom a few minutes to completely calm herself. Then she said, "Nobody knows about me and the boys being your family. How safe will we be once it gets out that we are?" "That's it Brenda? That's all you had to say? Wow, Brenda, you just wanted to act like a woman today." (emotional) Then Pops laughed. Mom gave Pops a soft playful punch in the arm and said, "Stop playing, William." Pops said while laughing, "Sorry babe, just joking. But for real, Brenda, I got your concerns but know that I want nothing but the best for us and I love you and my sons, and with that, no motherfucker will ever lay a hand on my family, Brenda. I allowed you to convince me to move our family to that neighborhood and let the boys go to East Union Middle School. I knew that school was almost like being on a street corner selling drugs with it having some of the most thuggish kids around going there. It was all part of a bigger plan to groom my sons. I needed them to experience what it's like to come up hard, cause if I would have just given them everything they wanted or asked for, then they wouldn't know how to scratch."

"Okay William. So, are you going to teach the boys self-defense?" "Yes, I am, not only that, but I'm also going to send them to take MMA classes and learn about firearms. Don't worry Brenda Ann, I got this. I am not your father or my father, as much as I loved them both, they got caught slipping." "Okay William, Okay. I don't want to think about them." "I got this Brenda." When they were done, we left the house and rode around for hours looking at all types of homes until it got dark. When we got back home Pops called a family meeting. Everything was explained to us. We were moving to another house, Hakeem and me would be going to another school district, and we will be learning self-defense. Pops gave us details on what he wanted us to focus on in our training. "Hakeem, you are headstrong and hot tampered definitely going to be the one everyone needs to watch out for. So, not only will you be taking MMA classes, but you will also be taking weapons training. Saint, you are more of a thinker, and you pay attention to detail. I want you to stay in those books hard, learn to pay attention to your surroundings and assess everything. Saint and Hakeem, we will be spending a lot more time together. Finally, you guys will no longer be using the last name Autry, but using your rightful name "King", and boys, I want you to know that now and forever that your Pops and you both are "King" and that King Reign Supreme." Me and my brother's eyes lit up as we looked at each other. We were happy about spending more time with Pops.

A few months later, we packed to move into a four-bedroom house not even five blocks from Skyline Boulevard in East San Diego. Me and Hakeem's new school will be Weddington Middle School. Pops had started us in training before we moved. It was a lot of discipline and patience training. Pops told us that he wished his father would have taught him in the same fashion as he was teaching us. "Boys, I am starting you guys at a young age so you can perfect your skills," he said one day as he dropped us off for training.

On the day that we were moving, Pops called me and Hakeem into his office; the room hadn't been completely packed up yet. "Boys, sit down because you are going to have a short training before the movers come to take us to our new home." As we sat down, the doorbell rang. Pops went to the door. Then walked back into his office. Behind him was a pasty, Chucky, white man. I looked at Hakeem and Hakeem looked at me. It was Chief Parker. Pops said, "Hey Parker, have you met my two sons, Saint and Hakeem King? Oh! I'm sorry Parker why! Sure, you have met them right. It was at East Union school in the principal's office the day I was there. I'm sure you remember that day, don't you Parker?" The Chief looked at Hakeem and me and turned white as a sheet of notebook paper. He turned to Pops and said, "Will, I am so sorry. I had no idea they were your boys. King wasn't the last name that the principal used when referring to the two boys." "Parker, I need to address two problems right here and now in this room before we talk about the reason I called you here," Pops said with that stern look on his face, that look never eased as he continued to talk to the Chief. "First of all, Parker, did you just call me "Will" like we are fucking friends? You fat greasy pig, you work for me. We ain't friends, you fat fuck. My name to you is Mr. King. Let me hear it, Parker." "Yes Sir, Mr. King." "Next, if I ever hear you call my sons 'boys' again, I will cut your mother fucking tongue out your fat pork eating mouth and hang it on my rear-view mirror. Now for the reason I called you here, the two officers at the school…" "Who, Mr. King? Are you talking about Knotts and Sanders?" "You know which two racists' motherfuckers I'm talking about. Before the sun goes down today, I never want to hear about, run into, or ever see these two cracker mother fuckers again. You can choose, you make sure I don't, or I make sure I don't, but if I make sure I don't it will be two officers and fat fuck Chief of police chopped up and put in a shoe box and placed on their family's doorstep. Now, get your fat sloppy Joe eating ass out of my office and house."

As the Chief left, Hakeem and me looked at each other and didn't say a word. Pops said to us, "Today's lesson is over, now you boys go make sure you have all your stuff packed up for the movers."

Three years have passed, and I am now in my sophomore year at Forest Hills High School. Hakeem is in his freshman year. Pops' training has us ready for any type of physical and mental confrontation. In situations, I would always remain calm, while Hakeem quickly went to work on whoever or whatever got in his way. Pops never let anyone watch us train, so we never trained outside. Pops had set up a complete gym in our basement. As time went on, we grew taller and bigger. The basement gym became too small to workout in. So, Pops took Hakeem and me to Hornet Nest Park to train during the week there were never many people there. Pops knew we needed more space to move around because our training now was getting harder and much more painful. He would strap forty pounds of weight to our back and make us run and jog until he said it was enough. Hakeem would always drop out ahead of me, that's because I was smart about it. I preserved my energy so that I could do more if Pops demanded us to do more, but when we go to the shooting range; no matter how hard I tried, Hakeem always outshot me. Hakeem was natural, he hit the targets dead center every time.

These few years have changed Hakeem and me totally. Pops main words to us was always, "King Reign Supreme and mind our own business. Stay away from situations where you don't have a nickel in that quarter!" Pops was strict with us, but he was teaching us to stick together no matter what, plus how to hold our own. One Saturday afternoon, at about two o'clock, Pops decided to give Hakeem and me the rest of the day off from training. Pops told us that it would be okay to go to Mission Beach Roller coaster. The sun doesn't go down until around eight thirty, so we had plenty of time before it got dark. Pops gave us some cash and dropped us off. He said, "It's three thirty now. Call me around nine o'clock and I will be here to pick y'all up." With that, he drove off. At that point, Hakeem and I felt a form of freedom that we hadn't felt in a long time. When Pops got out of sight, Hakeem and me did what teenagers with money in their pockets would do, "wild the fuck out". We brought all kinds of food, especially sweets. We ran on and off the beach, up and down the boardwalk. As we were coming out of the taffy shop with a handful of candy, we looked up and saw a group of girls walking toward us. As they got closer, Hakeem said, "Damn Bro, look at that fine ass girl right there with those long braids and that booty in them jeans; oh my God! She looks like that rapper girl, 'young Miami'. Damn she so fine." As they passed by us, I said to Hakeem, "Wait! Wait, I think I know that girl." "Ya! Right big Bro." "Naw! I do, watch this lil bro." I ran up behind the girls and tapped one of them on the shoulder, she turned around. "Dash! I knew that it was you." She quickly said, "Nigga who yo'!" "Dash!! It's me Saint!" "Oh! shit! Saint, it is you. Wow Nigga, I know one thing, yo' ass need' watch how yo' pull up on a bitch. I almost cut your ass." I looked down at Dash's hands in her right hand she held an open box cutter. I shook my head. "I'm sorry Dash, I was just happy to see you. What's been up with yo, I haven't seen you since we moved from the old neighborhood?" "Nothing, still in the same old neighborhood, so every day I'm trying to survive. What you been up to Saint since yo' family moved on up like the 'Jeffersons'." "Naw! Dash nothing like that." By that time Hakeem had stepped up beside me and said, "Wow Saint! She is pretty!" We all laughed. "Dash, you remember my little brother, don't you?" "Ya Saint, I remember him. Hakeem, right?" As soon as Dash said Hakeem's name, Hakeem blurted out, "You gon' be my girlfriend." All the girls laughed at Hakeem's statement. Hakeem said, "Laugh if y'all want. I'm dead ass matter fact lil ma'. Give me your phone number so I can call you." "Little boy, you better get on and find a toy to play with." "Ma, you not but a year older than me. Any way you can be my first older woman experience." Dash smiled as the other girls laughed. Hakeem said, "Ok that's cool lil momma, but you are gon' be my girlfriend, know that!" Dash smiled once again and said, "I tell you what! When you grow a mustache, yo' call me." "A mustache?" Hakeem said as he touched his top lip. "Yeah! That's what I said, a mustache." Once Dash said that she then turned her attention back toward me and asked, "What y'all getting into?" "Nothing, where y'all heading?" "We going to the roller coaster. Cum'on, let's hang". "Okay Dash, let's go." Hakeem and me went to the Coaster with the girls. We were running, laughing, and having fun on the way to the Coaster. As we were all waiting in line to ride the coaster, three young guys ran up and got in line a few people behind us. After some seconds, an older man walked up to the three young guys yelling and enraged. He said to the three young guys, "I know you saw me and my wife walking. Y'all ran into us. Y'all Lil motherfuckers almost knocked us down and you broke my wife's glasses." The three young guys laughed and continued talking, ignoring the older man. This made the older man get louder and closer to the young guys as he aggressively verbally expressed his anger. "You little bastards don't hear me talking to y'all? Y'all almost knocked us down and you broke my wife's glasses!" One of the young guys stepped up to the older man and said, "First of all old man, who are you calling a bastard and a motherfucker, and on top of that y'all slow asses should've moved into the fucking old people lane somewhere." One of the other three young guys stepped up to the old man as well and said, "If we did break that old ass bitch glasses, then we did her a favor, now she can't see your old, wrinkled ass."

The older man saw this wasn't going anywhere, they were very disrespectful boys, and he didn't want any trouble with them. So, he turned to walk away and said in a low whisper like voice, "Y'all better be glad it's three of y'all lil punk motherfuckers or I would be kicking somebody ass and knocking them down." The low voice that the old man used wasn't low enough. The three young guys heard him, and they quickly pulled up on him. One of the guys said, "What did your old ass say?" Before the old man could respond to the young guy, one of the other guys yoked the old man right in the side of his head. Then another one of the young guys joined in on an old man beat down. The old man's wife came running over in a panic begging the young guys to stop and pleading for someone to help her husband. By this time, the only people that were still in line for the coaster ride was Hakeem, Dash and her four girlfriends and me. We all stood in line and watched the beat down until it was our turn to ride the coaster. Just before we could walk up to get on the ride, one of Dash's girlfriends said, "Saint, Hakeem. Y'all not going to help the old man?" Hakeem replied, "We don't have a nickel in that quarter." He then looked over at me, I said, "Right lil bro." We moved on ahead in the line to get on the coaster. As we were boarding the coaster, Hakeem looked back over his shoulder and said, "You are right, that old man do need some help. Those three guys are beating the breaks off that old man." Hakeem and me got on the coaster with the girls and had a ball. Once the ride was over, we all walked back up the boardwalk to get something to eat and talk. We were having so much fun that time just got away from us. It was right at Nine p.m., I called Pops to let him know we were ready then I let Hakeem know it was time for us to go. I said my goodbyes to Dash and her girls. "It was great hanging with you and your girls." "Ya Saint, it was. Hi Saint, listen these girls are not only my girls, but we are teammates too. We all play softball together. We have a softball tournament coming up next weekend at Jaycee Park. You should come and bring yo' little brother with you. He is kinda cute like a little puppy dog." "Bet Dash, I know Hakeem and me are normally in training, but I will ask my Pops if we can come." Hakeem said, "Yes we will be there because Dash I'm comin for you. You are going to be my girl." "Lil boy, I nun told you! And don't nobody come for me unless I call for them!" "Oh ma' you'll call for me. You already said I'm cute like a puppy dog. Well puppy dogs do grow up to become Big Dogs. You are going to be my girl Ms. Dash! so, know that." I laughed at them both. We all said our goodbyes again and then split up. As Hakeem and me walked back to the designated pickup spot, he couldn't stop talking about Dash. "Hey Saint?" "Yes, Hakeem?" "Why don't you like Dash?" "I do like her, but we are just friends." "That's all y'all are, Saint?" "Yes, Hakeem that's all we are." " Okay then Saint, y'all stay just friends then. Cause one day, she is going to be my girl." "Ha, Ha, Ha!" "What's funny Saint?" "Nothing at all Hakeem." "You don't believe me, do you Saint? Watch and see, she gon' be my girl." "Okay, Okay! Hakeem time will tell. Pops should be here in a minute, but before he comes, I want to ask you a question that I have been wanting to ask you for a long time." "Yeah! Saint what is it?" "Do you remember three years ago when you flipped down that hill that was behind our house, you fell and got that big scar on your leg." "Yeah Saint, what about it?" "Nothing really, but for some reason I felt like something else happened other than what you told Pops and Mom. I was sure that that big Nigga Darrly Rush had beat you up and took your lunch money that day." "Yeah, Saint that is what happen, but I am older now and I bet he wouldn't try that bullshit now." "So, I was right then, it was that big motherfucker, Darrly Rush." "Yeah, he was much bigger than me. He threw me down on the ground and made me eat dirt and grass in front of everyone, and then he kicked me down that hill. Anyway, that was four years ago, not three. I will never forget that day, but I tell you this, I am not scared of any motherfucker now. I wish a Nigga would try me now. I am hoping one day I run into that Nigga Darrly Rush, not only am I going to kick his ass, but I'm going to kill that motherfucker." "Well Hakeem, we don't live on that side of the town no more, so you don't have to worry about him again. I'm sorry for bringing it up Hakeem, but I just had to know what really happened that day." "That's okay Saint, but today I don't care how big anybody is, especially that Darrly Rush. As I said that nigga right ther' I will kill." "Okay, okay Hakeem, calm down, plus here is Pop, come on let's go."

As we walked towards the car, I could see how upset reliving that incident made Hakeem, but there was nothing Hakeem could have done with that big bully. At the time, Hakeem was eight and Darrly Rush was sixteen years old. I am sure that incident is part of the reason for Hakeem's aggressive behavior, especially with anybody he feels poses a threat to him. I mean, he is a firecracker and will pop off in a heartbeat. Now I know for sure why my little brother is the way he is, and I know most of all, as a big brother; it's my job to look out for him. I put my arms around Hakeem's shoulder to reassure him that he had a big brother, and we are in this thing they call life no matter how fucked up it is. We are in it together to the end. Pop looked over at us walking toward him with our arms around each other. Seeing how close his two sons were made him happy. This was something Pops liked to see. He has always repeatedly said, "Together we are unstoppable." He kept on smiling at us until we got into the car. "I'm glad to see that y'all had a good time. I want you guys to know you have done better than I would have ever hoped with your training. So, I will let you go out more often as long as you always got each other's back. Let's get on home, your mother is being a woman today boys." "Emotional, right Pops?" We both said at the same time then laughed. "Ya, your mom was scared that something may have happened to you because you didn't call earlier." "We are okay, didn't anything happen. Pops, do you think that Hakeem and me can go to a softball tournament next weekend? It's going to be at the softball field at Jaycee Park. Hakeem likes a classmate of mine." "What! Hakeem you got a crush on some little gal?" Pops laughed. Hakeem quickly said, "Pops, she's not a little girl. She is fourteen years old." You could tell by how Pops shook his head that it seemed funny and cute that his boys were now old enough to start paying attention to the girls. Pops had a little smirk on his face when he asked Hakeem, "If she was to kiss you on the lips Hakeem, what would you do?" "Kiss her back," Hakeem blushed. All of us laughed. After a few minutes, Pops said, "Hey, hey, boys, seriously you boys can go to the softball tournament, but I need y'all to always stay away from the craziness out on them streets. If you don't have a nickel in that quarter, then you ain't got no business in it or around it, period!" Pop was adamant about what he was saying, so we paid close attention to him. He ended by telling Hakeem and me how proud of us he was. "I am so proud of you boys. I have a surprise for both of you when we get to the house and don't ask what it is because I'm not telling you until we get home." That conversation went on all the way home as we were trying to guess what the surprise could possibly be. When we pulled up in the driveway at home, Mom was standing in the doorway with a look of ease in her eyes. She was happy to see us and that we were okay. We got out of the car and went into the house. Mom asked Pops, "Did you tell them yet William?" "No Brenda Ann," Pops said. Then he told her, "I waited until you were all here together so that it would be a family meeting." "What's going on Momma? Hakeem asked. "Hold on. Your father will tell you both in just a minute." "We didn't do anything wrong, did we Mom?" I asked. "No, of course not. Tell them William." Pops called us all into the front room and said, "Okay boys, there is some business that I got to handle, and I will be gone for a few days. This will happen soon boys. The surprise is that both of you are going with me." Hakeem and me both screamed,

"Ya, that's great Pops. Where are we going?" "Boys, we will be going a number of places but there are some important things you both need to know and understand. Your Mom has felt that you boys are too young to fully understand who I am, what I stand for and at what levels I will go to protect you, my family.

"Boys, I feel that you are now at the perfect age to know, to learn and to understand my business and the business that our family died over." "Pop, are you talking about you and Momma's parents?" "Yes, Saint I am, but not only your grandparents but your uncles your mom brother as well as my brother." "Pops, can you tell us what happen to them?" Mom spoke up quickly, "No! Saint, you don't need to know that. William no! Don't tell them, please don't." Pops said to Mom, "Brenda Ann, baby, I understand how you feel, and I respect it, but for one we can't keep it from them forever and the other thing is, we can't make the same mistakes our fathers did by trying to shelter their kids from a business that very much impacts their kids' life. Plus, Brenda Ann, they need to know about our fathers so that they can understand the reason and purpose of all the training and me being so strict and hard on them." "Okay William, as much as I hate it, but you are right," Mom said with tears in her eyes. "Yes Pops! Please tell us, we want to know." Hakeem and me both said. "Yes, guys! I am sure you want to know. Okay boys, I need you guys to listen to me closely," Pop said while looking Momma in the eyes. Then Pops began to tell us the mistake that their parents made.

"Your mother's father, James Rainmond Marsh "Rainbow" and my father William Saint King "King", were bosses of the largest drug organizations in San Diego. It was an organization that spanned from San Diego to Tampa Florida. The thing is, when you become that big and on top, there is always somebody looking to pull you down. King and Rainbow were best friends and had been that way since they were children. King's father and Rainbow's father, my grandfather and Brenda Ann's grandfather, your great grandfather grew up together in a small poor village just outside Cameroon Africa. Not only did they grow up together, but they were also best friends and when they became old enough, they left Central Africa Region and came to America. After getting to America, they found wives. William's father married a Black woman from America, but James's father married a woman from Cuba which caused chaos for James's father when it came to dealing with his wife's family. With all that, the two men were able to stay close friends. Eventually they both had sons. Their sons grew up as best friends just like their fathers did. Both families were poor with next to nothing. As William and James got older, they would go out after school and sometimes even skip school to do odd jobs. They mostly sold newspapers, bottled water and orange slices at the off ramp at Brookshire Freeway and Eighty-five South. They worked hard trying to feed themselves and help their fathers support the rest of the family. Day in and day out, William and James were at the Eight-five South and Brookshire off ramp. The two boys made a promise to each other, "No matter what they had to do, they were somehow going to be rich or die trying." On one extremely hot summer day, while selling bottles of water at the off ramp, a big black Lincoln continental with Chrome Spoke Rims, gagster white wall tires, and a wheel kit on the back pulled up and stopped for the traffic light that was at the end of the off ramp. There was a young guy with full gold fronts driving the car with a tall cool-looking man with the biggest Afro that William had ever seen sitting in the passenger seat. The driver let his window down and yelled, "Lil Nigga, bring me two bottles of water." William didn't have but one bottle of water left in his ice bucket, so he yelled to James, "Hey James! Bring a bottle of water to the Black car." Williams and James got to the car at the same time with a bottle of water in hand. As they reached the bottles through the window to the driver of the car, the man in the passenger seat leaned forward, pulled his expensive looking sunglasses down his eyes and looked at them. He said, "It's hot as a bitch out there, ain't it lil Niggas? I've seen y'all lil Niggas out here every day, hustling. I like that. Do y'all lil Niggas want to make fifty dollars each? If yo' do y'all come to fourth ward at nine o'clock tonight. Tell Jeff, the big Nigga at the door, y'all ther' for 'Black Mike'."

"William and James were there early. There was a big Fifty-foot nigga standing at the door. He looked down at them and asked, "What the hell yo' lil niggas want?" They said, "Black Mike, he told us to come." The Fifty-foot-tall nigga Jeff let them in. William and James walked into the front room and stood in the doorway just in case they had to make a quick move. Black Mike walked into the room carrying a box; he gave the boys the box and told them where they needed to take the package to. Black Mike said to them, "Lil Niggas, tis' shit here is gold. Yo' heard me lil Niggas. It needs to be there by Twelve mid night, yo' heard me?" The boys took the package and walked out the front door. The boys thought they knew what they were getting into, but William knew that they really didn't know. So, when they got out in the hall, he stopped to talk to James about what they had just gotten themselves into. William was the thinker, so he came up with a plan to make sure they delivered the package and was safe doing it. On the way to deliver the package, they noticed someone was following them. As William had planned, in case they felt unsafe or if someone was going to run up on them, they got to the closest corner which was the corner of Durant and Franklin Street as fast as they could. William went one way and James went the other. The package that they were to deliver, William had stuck it in a paper bag that he picked up as they were walking just before they split up. William stuffed the paper bag with the package in it behind a row of trash cans that was lined up against a building. Then he ran as hard and as fast as he could to circle the block and get back to the trash can with the package hidden behind them. When he saw the dark shadow that was behind them earlier continue to follow James, William retrieved the package and delivered it by Mid-Night then quickly headed out to find James. William went to the pre- planned meeting place and found James there waiting for him. They were pleased with themselves, not only was the package delivered but it was delivered on time and most of all their plan worked. The next day, they went back to get their Hundred dollars from Black Mike. When the Fifty-Foot-tall Man that stood at the front door of Black Mike's house let them in, they went into the front room where Black Mike was sitting playing cards and smoking a joint with some other big men. After a few minutes of being in the front room, Black Mike noticed William and James standing there. He was the first to turn around to look toward them and he said, "Lil Niggas." As he spoke, the other men in the room looked up at where James and William were standing. Loudly and in a panic, James yelled out, "That's him, him right ther' William. That's the man that chased us last night. I'm telling you William, that's him." Black Mike quickly said "Calm down lil Nigga, yes! That's the Nigga that followed y'all lil asses last night. This is Que, one of my Lieutenants. I told him to keep an eye on my shit and also put a scare in y'all lil Niggas to see if y'all lil motherfuckers had any heart." Que stood up, walked up to James and William and said, "I don't know how y'all lil motherfuckers did it but y'all got the shit to the drop." Black Mike said, "I knew I was right about you two lil Niggas. Do y'all want a lick as my chore boys? That means getting coffee, sandwiches, wash my car, and making package deliveries every now and again. You lil Niggas will be making real nigga bread or do you lil Niggas wanna go back to that hot ass off ramp to making water bottle money?"

They both became Chore boys for Black Mike. After a short while of working for Black Mike, William and James were walking up the block from the corner store and met some guys standing around outside of the store. They were giving William and James a hard time. As they got Halfway back up the block, Black Mike's car pulled up beside them. It was Black Mike and Que. Black Mike yelled out the window, "What's up lil Niggas? Is everything good?" "Ya! It's all good just getting some shit from them Niggas down the block at the store," William replied. Black Mike asked, "Lil Nigga, do you motherfuckers know how to throw hands?" William and James said, "Yes, I guess we can fight." Que looked at them and laughed. "They guess they can fight! That's funny as hell. Well, are y'all lil Niggas strapped?" "Hmm?" "Strapped! Do you got a gun or even know how to use one?" "No." "Damn Lil Niggas." Black Mike jumped in and said, "Que for now on when you and the boys go to the shooting range, take the lil Niggas with you. Teach them how to strap up and how to use a heater. I want the lil Niggas to be able to drop a fool on the first shoot." Over time, William and James trained and became good at using all types of guns. They got to the point where they became known to be strapped. They were chore boys for about two years until something happened that made Black Mike start to look at them totally different. What had happen was, Black Mike's house was hustling sugar that was supplied by the Mexicans. The Mexicans was fronting Black Mike's house with all the sugar he put on the streets. Somehow, some front cash got hit at the drop just before the Mexicans got to the drop to pick up their money. It was over Fifty Thousand dollars, and the Mexicans was looking for their money or as many niggas of Black Mike's that they could kill. William and James were at the stash house breaking down the sugar to be taken to the trap houses when Black Mike and Que pulled up to the stash house. As they got out of the car, all hell broke loose. "Bang!", "Bang!", Bang!" It was the Mexicans, and they weren't there for no coffee or sandwiches. William and James could hear nothing but bullet shells hitting the concrete. Que went down first. Black Mike was hit but made it inside the stash house. There was blood everywhere. Black Mike looked around and he only saw William and James. Black Mike said, "Fuck, it's just you two lil Niggas. It's the Mexicans out there and those motherfuckers are coming." William and James had been working in that stash house for over two years, so they knew every inch of the house. Most of all, they knew where the guns were hidden, the AR 15's, the Street Sweepers, Dracos, Bulldogs, Tek 9's and AK 47'. They both went and grabbed as many guns as they could, and then helped Black Mike get to one of the rooms next to the back door. Then they hunkered down like they were soldiers in the trenches shooting Vietcong. They were dropping

Mexicans as fast as they came through the door. William had the front door and James the back door. William and James got out of there that night with Black Mike in tow. From that night on, Black Mike never called them lil Niggas again. They became known as Black Mike's Niggas, a member of his house. Over a number of years under Black Mike's wings, William and James learned the game inside and out. They could move work like it was second nature. They were now able to take care of themselves and put food on their families' table. William even bought himself a 1971 Ford LTD with keystone rims, quarter inch white wall tires, mud flaps, curb finders, and it even had the fuzzy rearview mirror but the beef between the Mexicans and Black Mike's house continued, which got in the way of everybody making money. One of the things William and James quickly discovered was that the time spent shooting at the Mexicans and the Mexicans shooting at them left no room for work being moved, and if there's no sugar hitting the streets then nobody is making money. With this, James and William knew it was time to pull away from the house of Black Mike and build their own house. They knew the first thing they had to do was to find their own sugar factory to supply them. William had the idea about James's contacting some of his mom's family members that were still in Cuba. James talked to his mother that night and learned that some of her family members made money by doing charter boats for deep sea fishing. These charters left out of Treasure Island Florida once a month.

"Treasure Island is on the gulf side of Florida where you can stand on white sandy beaches and with the naked eye look right over into Cuba. James and William contacted James's mother's people to arrange a deep-sea fishing trip. They also had other hurdles to overcome. They somehow had to come up with the bread to make that move. James's mom's people told them that each fish they catch would cost them twenty thou'. They wanted to hit the streets hard, so they knew they needed to catch at least four fish. But again, where do you come up with that kinda bread? William came up with a plan that he knew James was not going to like.

"On the way to the stash house that morning William told James the plan. William said, "James, Black Mike's house is warring with the Mexicans right! So, if someone ripped their cash drop during their front payment and reup with the Colombians they would think it was the Mexicans that hit them." "Yeah, William they would, but what are you getting at?" "James, what I'm saying is we are going to rip black Mike's cash drop. Not only will Black Mike blame the Mexicans, but he won't have the money to reup. So, that means we will bring Black Mike's house crashing down around him, allowing us to take over his territory." James paused and just looked at William for a minute then said, "William that's some dirty low-down shit." "Ya, James it is! But this is a dirty low-down game. James dirty as hell. Who taught us this dirty ass game anyway and how the shit is played? Black Mike, right?"

So, William, hatched a plan on how they were going to rip Black Mike's cash drop and make it look like the Mexicans had done it. William picked James up the next morning, as always. He drove them over to the Mexican's hang out spot. They parked close enough so that the Mexicans knew that they were there, but not close enough that the Mexicans could grab them up. They stopped the car, got out and stood in the front of their car leaning against the front bumper with each one brandishing a Forty-Five. Once the Mexicans noticed them, William threw two or three shots up high in their direction. William and James quickly jumped back into the car and sped off heading straight back to Black Mike's stash house, where all Black Mike's goons were standing around outside. William and James sped down the block toward them with the Mexicans not far behind. William pulled the car into the driveway of the stash house and they both jumped out of the car running toward the stash house pointing back behind them yelling "The Mexicans!!! Look! look! The Mexicans!!!!" The Mexicans stopped their car just down the block from Black Mike's stash house. Black Mike's goons stood out in the driveway daring the Mexicans to come and get some, each one of the goons was brandishing their guns. The loud noise caused Black Mike to come outside and ask, "What the fuck is going on out here?" William quickly spoke up, "It's those Mexicans; them motherfuckers trippin. They chased James and me all the way over here." The goons chimed in and said, "Ya, them motherfucking Mexicans are trippin bad. I want them to bring their refried bean, Taco eating ass on down the block so I can put one in them." "Look at them motherfuckers they won't come any closer. Them Motherfuckers don't want no smoke." After about twenty minutes of the Mexicans sitting in their car playing loud ass Music and racing their car engine, they took off in the other direction doing burning outs. When Black Mike saw them leaving, he said, "Naw!! Them motherfuckers didn't want no smoke. Anyway, niggas we got to get ready to handle this business tonight. BoBo, oh shit. I'm sorry Nigga I forgot; I meant David. Grow up with tis' Nigga watching Go, Go, Speed Racer and the whole Nine and BoBo was always his name. Now the Nigga got hair on his balls. His name 'David." "Y'all motherfuckers kill me. David, Nelson, and Jeff, y'all Niggas good foe' tonight. Y'all Niggas are running point on this drop, we can't have no fuck ups. Y'all know them Columbian Niggas ain't fucking around about their bread. Plus, this is my brother Ricky's. I meant Rick, damn another one of them niggas got grown they changed their name that Nigga know goodin damn well his momma named his ass Ricky Lee. Anyway, it's his connect and he put me on. After we pay for the work, they fronted me plus buy some new work, I won't have to go to the Columbians through Rick. They will deal with me direct. That way I can get my brother off my ass and out my pocket. That Nigga taxing the hell out of me for any work the Columbians front me through him. So, motherfuckers, no drinking, popping pills, or using blow. None of that shit. I need y'all head in the game. That go for the rest of y'all motherfuckers too. I need y'all at them trap houses tonight waiting for that work to drop." One of Black Mike's goons yelled to him, " Hey Mike, that means no blazing up either." "No nigga, you crazy as hell, no blazing up! Matter of fact, some motherfucker fire one!!... Not! Blaze up! That Nigga nun' lost his fucking mind. Alright Niggas, tonight I see y'all after the drop. I got something I got to handle first. Donnie, Nigga fire up that Joint yo' stingy ass trying to hold back the weed." James and William had learned Black Mike's plan for the drop and that he was not going to be there. Their plan of getting the Mexicans to chase them to the stash house had worked perfect. Now Black Mike and his goons are all thinking that the Mexicans were still tripping with Black Mike's House. That night, James and William waited around the corner from Black Mike's stash house for his goons Daivd, Nelson, and Jeff to show up. His goons were to pick up the cash from the safe in the basement of the stash house then head to the drop. William and James waited for over an hour when they showed up. They pulled into the driveway and got out of the car. The three goons went up the steps in front of the stash house. David and Nelson went inside, Jeff stood outside at the front door. James and

William watched the goons take their position, two goons inside to get the money and one goon outside at the front door. So, now it was time for William and James to put their plan into play. William drove slowly toward the stash house and pulled up in the driveway behind the goon's car. Before William and James could get out of the car, Jeff pulled his strap and stepped toward the end of the porch. "Who the hell out there? And I am going to ask but once." William and James swung their car doors open quickly and jumped out. "Jeff! Jeff! Man, it's us! William and James!" "Niggas step forward and keep your Motherfucking hands where I can see them and I'm telling yo' motherfuckers, if you even scratch yo ass, I am going to empty into yo' bitches." William and James walked toward the steps slowly with their hands out at their side. They moved carefully around the cars so as not to excite Jeff's trigger finger. When they got closer to the bottom step, the porch light shone on them revealing who they were. Jeff yelled, "Oh it's you two Niggas the 'Siamese Twins'." Some of the guys called William and James that because they were always together. William shouted out, "Ya! It's us. Black Mike told us to get some baggies for the corner boys earlier and because of that shit with the Mexicans we forgot to get them. Jeff, you know the corner boys them niggas been talking shit." "I gotcha on that, them corner boys like to talk shit, but y'all Niggas know you shouldn't be here when we making a move. Y'all Niggas know Black Mike would have all our asses if he knew y'all was here." "Jeff, I know man, but Black Mike going to have James and my ass if we don't get them corner boys their shit. Come on Jeff man, it won't take us but a few." "Ya! Yo' right about Black Mike, he would kill you two motherfuckers if he knew y'all didn't give them niggas there shit. Come on in and get the Baggies and get the fuck gone." William and James went up the steps into the house once inside, William slowly moved toward the basement door while James took a stand on the hinge side of the front door. Looking back to make sure James was in place behind the front door, William went down the stairs into the basement, Slowly and quietly, he walked up on David and Nelson with their back turned toward the door counting money. The safe's door was still wide open. William walked up on them with his Forty-five in hand and he took three pulls of the trigger. David and Nelson bodies dropped to the floor like a sack of potatoes. Once Jeff heard the gunfire coming from the basement, he hit the front door. It flung open, hiding James behind it. When James saw Jeff run past him heading toward the basement door, he fired twice, putting two bullets into Jeff's back. Jeff didn't fall, he went down on one knee and then the other knee as he began to crawl. Walking up behind him, James popped one right into the back of his head. Jeff dropped like a big ass grizzly bear. "William! William! You good down there?" "Ya! you good up there" " Ya! I'm good up here. I'm coming down." When James got down to the basement, it was quiet and eerie. This caused him to freeze in place; he could only hear the noise of dogs barking next door and in the far distance was the faint sound of empty aluminum cans in a bag rattling. William called to him, grabbing his attention and putting him back on point. James walked over to William and saw that William had stacks of bills in both hands and there was still more money inside the open safe. There was more money than either one of them had ever seen. James became frantic and said, "William, what are we going to do? I didn't expect there would be this much money. Black Mike and his goons are going to hunt us down and hand us each other's nuts and I don't know about you William, but I don't want to hold your bloody nuts in my hands." "Dawn James, Calm down. Ain't nobody nuts going to get cut off at least not our nuts. James, nobody even knows that we are here or that we've been here. Remember, we planned this to a tee. Black Mike, is going to think it was the Mexicans that came to get some get back for their Amigos that Black Mike and his goons killed." "Ya! William, I know, but this is a lot of money. It's got to be a billion dollars in here." "Ha. Ha. Ha. James it ain't no billion dollars. It's only a few thousand. So, let's get this money and get the fuck out of here." They got all the money from the table that David and Nelson were counting, plus the money from the safe and they left the stash house as fast as they could. As they ran out of the house and down the front steps, that faint sound that James heard of rattling cans became clearer and louder. They quickly jumped into William's car and headed down the block and away from the stash house. When they got halfway down the block, James finally saw where the sound of cans rattling was coming from. There was a bark blue 1974, two door Chrysler Cordoba, with Tee tops parked on the curb with a pretty ass girl sitting in it on the passenger side of the car. The car's stereo was blasting so loud the bass coming from the speakers made the sound of aluminum cans rattling in a paper bag. As they passed the car, the girl looked over at James. James also looked over at her. They both stared each other down until William and James drove past and out of sight.

They went back to William's house where he lived with his father, mother, and younger brother. It was late so they came into the house as quietly as possible so as not to wake anyone up. But as they walked into the living room, the light popped on. It was William's father. "Papi, yo' still up?" "Yes, William I couldn't sleep for some reason." "Is anything wrong PaPi?" "No William. I just couldn't sleep tonight. What are you boys up to?" "Nothing PaPi. We were out working, and it got late before we knew it., So James decided to stay the night here." "That's good Son. William, what are you now, twenty? twenty-one?" "Twenty-three PaPi." "Twenty-three really? Wow! How time flies, but okay Twenty-Three, William, I know you are at the age where you want your own place, and I am sure you will be moving out soon. But I want you to know you are always welcome here. This is your home. Son, I am proud of you; how you have always pitched in to help your poor old PaPi out. If it wasn't for your help son, I don't know what we would have done. Thank you, Son. And James, I know your father feels the same way about you, he's always bragging on you, saying 'my son James this, my son James that', he is so proud of you as well. Alright boys, let me go back to bed before your mother wakes up and comes looking for me." "Okay PaPi. Bonne Nuit," William said to his PaPi. "Bonne Nuit oncle," James whispered. William looked at James and said, "Come on James, let's go to my room." "But William, your little brother is in your room. Did you forget you share a room with him." "Naw!! I didn't forget. I'm going to bring him to the couch in the living room." "Okay cool." William picked up his little brother and carried him out into the living room and placed him on the couch and covered him up with a throw that was hanging over the back of the couch. William gave his little brother a kiss on the forehead and headed back to his room where James had poured the money out all over William's bed. They spent the rest of the night counting money and planning. They counted money until they fell asleep. The next morning, they got up and did what they normally did, which was to go to work. As they turned onto the block of Black Mike's stash house, they saw yellow police tape everywhere. There were Police officers, Crime Lab vans, and the County Coroner's Van all filling the driveway and front Lawn of the stash house. The po- po was running in and out of the stash house like it was a Krispy Kreme Donut shop with the hot light on. Over on the side was Black Mike and his guys. Black Mike was pacing back and forth shaking his head and yelling at everyone in sight. He was freaking out saying, "I know it was those Mexicans, them motherfuckers got all my motherfucking money." One of Black Mikes goons shouted out, "Ya! And they killed David, Nelson, and Jeff." Black Mike looked over at him, "Fuck them Niggas. I want my motherfucking money back. Y'all niggas get in y'all mother fucking car and all y'all motherfuckers met at The Trap house on Lewis Avenue, and I mean, right fucking now!" They all scrambled like roaches when the lights are turned on. They all headed toward their cars. William and James ran and jumped back into William's car and William drove to the Trap house as fast as he could. When they got there, things were already heated. Black Mike was still outside talking to some man that he called Willie Ray. Willie Ray was one of Black Mike's brother Rick's goons. It is said that a goon is a man hired to terrorize or kill his opponents. Willie Ray by that definition was a real goon. This man was terrifying; he was bigger than "mean Joe Green" and didn't have a smile nowhere close to his face. I bet he has never smiled a day of his life. Willie Ray told Black Mike he was there until his brother Rick got there to see him, and that it would be a good idea for Black Mike to be there when Rick got there. Black Mike yelled out loud, "Fuck Tis' big Nigga right here. Cum'on guys let's go inside." Black Mike and his goons went inside of the trap house, so did James and William. Rick's goon Willie Ray, stayed outside at the front door. Black Mike started to shout at everyone, "Tis' shit is all fucked up. Them motherfucking Mexicans took it all, the Columbians front money and reup money. Fuck me! fuck me! Tis' is fucked! I got to get those motherfucking Columbians they money back. I need y'all Niggas to hit the streets and see what y'all can find out. Curtis you and Jermine, I need y'all two Niggas to go and pull all the cash from the Trap houses and corner boys. I need y'all two motherfuckers to go into those

Corner Niggas pockets and get every penny they got. Fuck it, even snatch the motherfucking gold fronts out of them Nigga's mouth. If a motherfucker got it, I want it. William and James, I need y'all two Niggas to go back over to the stash house and see what the po-po talking about. I know it was them Mexicans. Them Niggas going to pay. I know it was them. William and James, y'all Niggas hurry up back here and the rest y'all Niggas hit them fucking streets. I don't care if it takes all day and night. Bring me something back." William and James walked out of the trap house right by Rick's goon that was still standing out in front of the house. As they passed him heading for William's car, the goon moved from the front door of the house to farther out in the yard where he could see both the front and back of the house at the same time. When William and James got in the car and pulled out, James asked, "What we gon' do now? We not gonna go back, right William?" "Yes, James we gon' go back!" "Say what! we are?" "James, calm down. Look, we can't just not go back. If we did that and they find out it wasn't the

Mexicans, they will turn their sights on the two Niggas that got ghost in the middle of all this shit. We got to stay and make sure this whole thing falls on the Mexicans." "Ya! William, I guess you are right. So, what are we going to do?" William looked at James, laughed and said, "First, what we going to do is go to Denny's' for a 'Rooty Tooty Fresh and Fruity' cause I'm hungry than a bitch, then we going to go back to further place a target on the head of them Mexicans." They sat down in Denny's, they ate, and laughed until they felt they had been gone long enough. They then asked the server for their check. The server was a bad ass redbone with a gap between her legs like she had a catcher's mitt down there. James left a tip, and they both went to the front counter to pay the check. The man behind the counter said, "That will be fourteen dollars." They both reached into their pocket at the same time to get the money to pay the check. William came out first and he only had three dollars in his pocket. James pulled out his money and he had only two dollars. Both stood there in front of the counter with a line of people forming behind them as they checked the rest of their pockets for more money, but between them both they only had five dollars on a Fourteen-dollar check. They both looked at each other. James thought back to the tip he left for the redbone server. He quickly ran back to the table and grabbed the ten-dollar tip he had left. As he grabbed the money up from the table and turned to go back to the counter, he ran smack dead into the redbone server. She had seen him pick up the tip money from the table. She shook her head; James dropped his head as he stepped around her and ran back to the front counter with the ten dollars in his hand. William grabbed the money from him, quickly added up everything and paid the man behind the counter. As they were exiting the restaurant, William handed a dollar change to James. "Take this back to the table for a tip." James stared at William, snatched the dollar from his hand, put it in his pocket and said, "Fuck you, William." As they exited the Restaurant doors James gave William a playful push and said, "Man, why you ain't got no money?" William playfully pushed James's back and said, "Nigga why don't you have any money?" James laughed and said, "Damn! We ripped the biggest drug dealer on the Southside for over two hundred and fifty thousand dollars and neither one of us had Twenty-four dollars to pay for our food and leave a tip. How fucking embarrassing!!" William gave James another playful push and laughed, "If you weren't trying to impress that waitress with a ten-dollar tip, we would have had enough to pay the check." James laughed and said, "Fuck you! You just better come up with a good ass lie to tell Black Mike about what the police had to say about those Mexicans." They got into William's car and headed back to the Lewis Ave trap house. When they got there, Willie Ray was still standing out in the front yard like a good watch dog. They both got out of the car and went into the house where they saw a nervous acting Black Mike pacing back and forth smoking a joint. Black Mike looked up at them and said, "Damn it. It took y'all Niggas forever. What did the motherfucking Po- Po say?" William paused for a second before he said, "The police said that a witness saw something unusual for that area, it was a low rider car playing what sounded like loud Hispanic music leaving the area late last night." After William told Black Mike this, Black Mike hit the roof and started to incoherently yell and shout, "I knew it, I fucking knew it was them no English talking motherfuckering Mexicans. I'm first gon' get my fucking money back, then I'm gon' get some get back for my Niggas David, Nelson, and Jeff! Cum' on, let's go find my Niggas so we can ride down on them fools." Black Mike headed for the front door with William and James reluctantly behind him. As Black Mike reached out for the doorknob, the door swung open. It was Black Mike's brother Rick and his goon Willie Ray and two other gigantic Niggas. They all stepped into the Trap house. Black Mike's brother, Rick stood in the middle of the doorway. "Where y'all Niggas think y'all going?" "Nigga who you supposed to be, but if it's any your business, I'm headed out to get my Niggas so we can go peel back the wig on some motherfuckin Mexicans. Why the fuck you want to know?" "What the fuck you mean why I wanna know? Nigga did you forget that you are into the Columbians for over hundred and seventy Thousand dollars for the shit they fronted you, by the way they are my connect that I put you." Black Mike yelled at Rick. "Ya!! NIGGA, I know all this shit. Them Columbian motherfuckers gon get Da' money. I'm on the way out right now to get them Niggas money." "Black Mike, you were supposed to do that cash drop last night. What you think, this is a fucking game? Black Mike, I told you when you asked me for this put on you was going into the lion's den and one motherfuckin misstep, and the lion would eat your monkey ass up. I told you the Columbians don't play about their money or about being disrespected. And they feel like you have disrespected them and they can't let anybody go around thinking it's alright to disrespect them." "I hear you, Rick, but you tell them motherfuckers to give me a few days. I will have Da' money." "Black Mike!! You not hearing me! Last night was when you should have made that drop. This put my ass on the line just like yours. Three hours after your guys didn't show up at that cash drop, I got a visit by Five Columbians that made me go for a ride with them, they took me to another dozen Columbians wanting to know why the disrespect. Black Mike, as always, you nun fucked up." Black Mike stood up and waved Rick off. "Nigga, please I'm not worrying about no fuckin Columbians. These are my streets. I'm Black Mike. I run all tis' shit up and around here." "Black Mike, yo' bitch ass don't get it, do you NIGGA." Click, Click, Click, Click. "Nigga, you see these four heaters on your ass?" "Rick!! What the fuck? We are brothers!" "Ya! Mike, we are brothers. That's why your ass shouldn't have left my ass out naked blowing in the wind. Black Mike, you didn't even bother to oversee the drop. Naw! Your ass was somewhere cross town getting your dick sucked." "Rick, come on man, we can work this shit out. Let me talk to the Columbians." William and James stood quietly in the corner like two church mice as Rick and Black Mike continued to go back and forth. Black Mike was at the point of pleading with Rick. "Look, look bro. I promise I can get the money back."

"Mike, how are you going to get their respect back? I told you Mike, it's not all about the money. It' about you disrespecting them." "Rick, you can't do this, we are brothers. We have the same mother and father, the same fucking blood run through our veins. Come on Rick, listen Rick man. I can make this right. I can find the motherfuckers that ripped me for the money and get it back." "Black Mike, don't worry about finding out who took the money. The Columbians will do that and make their life a living hell before they kill them, bro. That statement you made about you making it right, why do you think I'm here with my boys? It's so you can make it right." "Ricky Lee!! Please don't do this. Ain't we our brother's keeper?" "Nigga this ain't no movie. This shit is real life." Bang! Bang! Bang! Rick and his goons empty their clip into Black Mike, as he went limp and drop to the floor. Rick's focus then turned toward the two Mice in the corner, William and James. Rick asked, "Who you two Niggas that I'm getting ready to fucking lay down?" James fearfully answered Rick, "Mr. Rick, Ricky, Ricky Lee, Sir. Whichever one is your name. Me and William have nothing to do with this shit. We are just chore boys, Sir. That's all we are. Mr. Sir, if you let us go, we will be gon' Sir." "What did yo' Niggas see happen here tonight?" "Mr. Sir, nothing, Sir! We ain't seen nothing happen here, Sir. Matter of fact Sir, we ain't never been to this house or street Sir." Rick pointed toward the front door; "Yo' motherfuckers get the fuck out of here before I change my mind." William and James ran out of the house without looking back. They jumped into William's car and headed down the street like a bat out of hell. James was sweating and breathing hard. "William, pull over to the nearest bathroom so I can clean myself," James said, with his voice trembling. William looked over at James and began to laugh. "You laughing William, ain't bull Shitin, you need to pull over quick as hell." William laughed even harder.

A few weeks had passed since Rick shot and killed his brother, Black Mike. James and William had bought their airline tickets to Tampa Bay Florida. James was a little apprehensive or better yet scared as hell about flying. This would be the first time that William or James had ever been on a plane. They called for a taxi to take them to the San Diego International Airport. The Taxi dropped them off at the United Airline Curbside baggage check. They checked their bags and paid for the one overweight bag that William had. They got their tickets and itinerary then headed inside. They looked at their itinerary, then checked the departure arrival board and saw that their flights were on time. William kept talking to James as they sat at their boarding gate to keep James's calm and his mind off the long flight. When they finally boarded their flight, about halfway through the flight, James became more nervous. He started talking his ass off about nothing. He talked for the rest of the flight and seven hours later, they landed at Tampa Bay International Airport. James was still talking while they were taxiing up to the gate. Once their plane reached its arrival gate and they disembark they made their way out through the Airport to baggage claim, where they were to meet James' family member and pick up their checked bag that had two hundred thousand dollars in it. They had arrived a day ahead of their scheduled fishing charter, so that they could arrange for their drive back to San Diego with the four fish that needed to be put on ice. James' family member was waiting for them at the luggage carousel. William grabbed his bag from the carousel then he and James walked over to meet James family. They were able to pick him out from a description they received with the details on the deep-sea fishing charter. James walked up to him and said, "Hello Dee." "Yes, I'm Dee, are you James?" "Yes, I am, and this is my friend William." Dee asked, "What you guys wanna do first? Go to the hotel or what?" William said, "Dee we have a shopping list of things that we need to get." Dee said, "Okay, so I will take you both to the hotel and we can talk about the shopping list you have." "Okay, bet," William said. William, James and Dee exited the airport and got into Dee's 1970, two tone Cadillac Seville and they went to the hotel. Once William checked him and James in, they all went up to the double room that William and James were to share.

"William, James, tell me about the shopping list you have." William spoke, "Well Dee, we need to buy a work van, coveralls, building materials like, wood, Sheetrocke, and a toolbox, and two heaters." "Okay William, we can do that. I tell you what, you guys take a nap for a few hours while I run down the heaters then I'll be back to take you to get the rest of the stuff." "Okay cool Dee. See you in a few hours." Once Dee left, James looked at William with a confused look on his face. He said, "William, I don't understand. Why do we need a work van, coveralls, and building materials?" William said to James, "James, let me ask you, who would most likely be stopped, two niggas in a car traveling out west or two niggas in coveralls driving a work van with building materials in the back?" James answered, "The two Niggas traveling west in the car." "That's right James, that's why we need the van, coveralls and building materials. I'm going to take a quick nap until Dee comes back." About two and a half hours later, a knock on their room door woke them up. It was Dee with some guy. William let both in. Dee said,

"William, James, this is my Nigga 45. 45, these my kin folk, William and James. Guys, this is your gun man. We call him 45, because he sells everything but 45's." William and James bought two 9 mm's from 45. After buying the guns, James said, "45, I'm sorry, but I got to ask. Why don't you sale 45s?" "Cause of my old lady, that crazy bitch busted me in the ass with a 45 all cause she caught me in the hoe next door house and ever since then, I shake whenever I get close to one," 45 replied. Dee jumped in and said, "Alright then! Let's get out of here and go shopping." William, James, and Dee went shopping for the other stuff on their shopping list. When they got back to the hotel, William asked, "Dee, how does the fishing charter work?" "It's easy; the charter supplies everything you need, fishing rods, and hooks. You just bring a tackle box of fish bait. You feed the fish with the bait, and you catch the fish. Of course, the more bait you have, the more fish you catch, but don't worry it's all good, y'all family. I tell you what William, I'm going to come back tonight to get you and James. We gon' hit the city and turn up." "Okay bet, see you tonight." Five hours later, at about eleven o'clock, Dee came back and picked William and James up. They headed for Ybor, one of the hottest party destinations in central Florida. When they got there, people were everywhere. Dee did a head nod out the car window to all the niggas and threw the peace sign to all the bitches. Dee knew everyone and everyone seemed to know him. Before getting out of the car to walk up to all the clubs that lined both sides of the street, Dee looked back at William and James and said, "Y'all with me in my town, if anything jumps off and any pulling out needs to be done, I'll do it. Yo' Niggas just chill and have a good time pull some bitches look at them, straight cornbread, fatback, and collard green feed, they ain't like them skinny anorexic bitches y'all got in California." William and James laughed. Women and Men alike gravitated to Dee like a moth to a flame. Dee's energy was off the chart. Almost every club had a long line to get in. The club that James and William followed Dee up to had the longest line. The line went down the block and around the corner, but

Dee walked up to the big security guy standing at the door. He slapped him five, whispered in his ear and a few minutes later, some big booty girl was escorting them to a table. As soon as they got to the table, several women in mini shirts and knee-high boots on came over and started dancing all up on them. When William and James thought they had seen it all, they looked up and there were four women with Daisy Dukes on walking toward their table. Each had a bottle in their hand. Eight bottles of liquor. Four bottles of Crown and four bottles of Gin with sparklers coming out the top of each bottle. This was some shit you hear about but never see. No matter how impressive the events going on around them were, James looked bored out of his mind and William just kept looking at his watch as though he was ready to go. William and James came to town for one reason and one reason only, that was to get some fish and go back home and cook it up. William and James liked women and pussy just as much as the next guy, but they were about their business and their business was to transport four fish back to San Diego.

Dee picked up on the fact that the party scene wasn't their thing. So, they left the club and Dee dropped William and James off at their hotel and told them he would see them in the morning to drive down to treasure Island. At seven o'clock the next morning, Dee was out front of the hotel waiting for William and James to come out. After about thirty minutes, they came out. They all got into the work van that they had bought the day before and headed to Treasure Island. It was a long ride, but a nice one. Once they were on the charter boat and about forty minutes out, each person on the charter was called to meet with the charter organizers one by one. It became James and William's turn to bring their tackle box full of bait to the lower Deck of the boat. The organizer, which was James's mother's family, wanted to know all about James and his mother. They talked for hours; later that day, they had a supply chain and a Tackle box with six fish instead of four, all for one hundred and twenty thou and a stern warning, "You don't cross family. Snitching is a cancer, and cancer has to be eradicated." William,

James and Dee got off the charter. William and James felt satisfied and empowered. On the way back to Tampa, Dee told William and James that they are now family. If at any time they needed him, he was only a call away. They finally got back to Tampa and said their goodbyes to Dee and went their way to check out of the hotel and head back to San Diego. William and James drove back as two carpenters with coveralls on in a work van full of building materials heading to remodel a house. They made great time getting back to San Diego. The trip only took them four days. They were so eager to get started that they went straight to the house that William rented before leaving on their trip to Tampa. They had work and a supply chain now, so it was time to gather up some corner boys to move their work. They gathered the boys that didn't move over to Rick when he took over Black Mike's house. According to Rick, Black Mike supposedly left town in a rush. Almost all the corner boys knew James and William. So, it wasn't hard to get them to move their product. William told James that their product was going to be better, more readily available and that they would sell theirs pure and let the buyer step on it as they saw fit. They will not tax the corner boys for the corners that they are going to take over for them. "William?" "Ya James." "You know that means we will have to go to war with Rick and his goons." "Ya! James. I'm sure we will and if he or anybody pushes us, we will push back hard. Over the next several months, William and James were selling sugar like it was water in the desert. All the corner boys were coming to them for all their sugar supplies. Everything was going great, and everybody was getting money, until something that William and James anticipated eventually happened. Back when, they only had a few corners around the city, there were no problems. But now, that they had over half the corners in the city the wanna be gangsters and thugs started comin for them. This unsettled William. "Damn it, James! We got to change the way we operate, them streets out there ain't kind. Them motherfuckers out ther' bustin our niggas over the head, I mean they hittin hard. James! Our corner niggas, if they ain't shooting them up they rippin there, our shit, showing us no respect and their disrespect is costing us money. Starting today, James, these very fucking minute, we gettin' rid of these Sunday school boy attitude we have. This lookin out for this motherfucker, lookin out for that motherfucker stops. We must go back to the attitude we had when we decided to rip Black Mike's stash house. When we had to do what we needed to do to get money. Pushin motherfuckers in our way out of the fuckin way." "I hear yo' William. What's the plan?" "The first thing we gon' do is call Dee to come here for a visit and the next thing motherfuckers gon' stop and tats calling us by our government name. If a motherfucker don't wanna give us respect, then we gon' take it. From the ashes rose "King" and "Rainbow" Two no shit takin motherfucking drug dealers." Later that week, Dee and three of his boys came to San Diego. King and Rainbow went to meet them for brunch at their hotel. They walked into the restaurant which was in the lobby of the Marriott in Sea Port Village, they stopped at the host, told her their guests was already in the restaurant. The host asked, "Is it three big guys with this one gorgeous looking man?" "Yes, ma'am, that sounds like them." The host pointed towards a table over in a corner, King and Rainbow walked over to the table. It was Dee and some monsters sitting there. William noticed that Dee was as fascinating and charming here in San Diego as he was in Tampa. At the restaurant, women were falling all over him. A six-foot five inch, 250 pounds muscular Nigga with dark skin, with dreads down his back and dressed in designer from head to toe. The scent he wore had to be Givenchy Gentleman EDP and draped from a button on his shirt was a pair of off-white designer sunglasses, which had to hit that Nigga for at least three Gs. Dee loved money, women, partyin, and most of all fuckin a Nigga up if they got in his way. This was the very reason William called him to San Diego; there was some niggas in the way. As William and James approached the table, Dee stood up to greet them. "What's up fam? These my Niggas Jay, Devis and Davon. Niggas this is my fam, James and

William." Rainbow quickly corrected Dee, "Naw! Dee, my name is Rainbow, tis' here is King." "Okay then fam, these motherfuckin Niggas here, but I like it!! So, talk to me fam. Why y'all got a nigga across the world? I know y'all Niggas cakin as many fishing trips y'all Niggas been on. So, talk to me. What's good, King?" "Respect! Dee, these Niggas out here are some disrespectful motherfuckers. They show Rainbow and me nothing but disrespect, hittin our corners, shootin up or runners and ripping our shit. Dee, Rainbow and me got to change the way we been doin business and start layin some motherfuckers down." "I hear you fam. I was wondering how long it would take yo' motherfuckers to stop all that 'we are the world, kumbaya' bull shit. Fam, lookin out for motherfuckers in this game gotcha ass handed to you. So, talk to me fam. Who the motherfuckers need to be taught some manners. I got the best and baddest motherfuckers in the game right here waiting and wanna teach a motherfucker." "Cool Dee, let's hit them streets." Everyone got up from the table to leave. As they walked out of the restaurant into the hotel lobby area, a woman ran up to Dee. She tapped him on the shoulder and said, "Sir, excuse me, but I had to tell you. When you passed me, you smelled so good it made my cochee jump." All the guys laughed and said, "Damn!!! Nigga." "Fuck y'all motherfuckers. Don't hate the player, hate the game." Over the next two weeks Rainbow, King, Dee, and his goons were giving etiquette lessons all over the city. Dee was rippin Niggas shit and flushing it down the toilet or pouring it into the gutter while he made them watch. Dee would tell them, "Nigga, I don't want yo' shit. I want you and your motherfucking Niggas to learn to stay the fuck out of my pocket." Dee also would cut a Nigga's thumbs off and he would say, "The only difference between humans and animals are opposing thumbs. So now motherfucker, what you are, a FUCKING ANIMAL!?" Dee had some serious issues, but he got his point across. Although the party scene wasn't Rainbow and King's thing, but since it was the last night for Dee and his goons in San Diego, and them knowing Dee and how he liked to turn up. King booked a table at one of the honest clubs in San Diego, The Fluxx. It was always packed with hustlers, Rappers, local celebrities and all type of bitches that would go to any length to get next to all the who's who that were in attendance. King hired a stretch limousine for the night. He and Rainbow went to pick Dee, Jay, Devis and Davon up from their hotel in the stretch limo. Dee and his boys walked out of the hotel and into the limo like they were walking the runway during fashion week in New York. Those motherfuckers were straight GQ. They rode for about fifteen minutes before the driver pulled up to the VIP door of the club. They all got out and looked around, to King and Rainbow the shit looked unreal, people were everywhere. They were walked to their VIP table by women that had to be models. As soon as they got to their table, women swamped them. The women were up on them like they were movie stars. Dee, Jay, Devis and Davon acted as if it was no big deal, like it all was normal and something they were used to. But Rainbow and King were in awe and amazement yet stand offish. Bottles came to the table but everyone in their VIP was already turned up. The music was extremely loud so King leaned into Rainbow's ear and said, "Bro, this ain't me. It's hard to get with this shit." As soon as those words left King's mouth, he saw what he knew was an Angel. She walked with the grace of a ballet dancer and slight era of hood. She had a short bob haircut and looked like she jumped out of a two live crew video. King was sure of one thing that night. "I just met my baby momma." The Angel King saw walk across the room to a group of girls. She had King's full attention to the extent that he didn't hear Rainbow talking to him. "King! King! Nigga, what's wrong?" "Nothing Rainbow, but did you see that Angel that just floated past us?" "Where, King?" King pointed over toward the group of girls. "Rainbow, look over in the corner, the one with the short haircut with those other girls." "Ya, King, I see her. Wait a minute, I have seen her somewhere before. I don't know when or where, but I have seen her somewhere, anyway, just send a few bottles of Dom over to her and her girls." "Hmmmm! Ya Yo' right! I'll do that." Everyone stayed in turned-up mood for the rest of the night, even Rainbow loosened up just a little. The lights came on in the club indicating it was time to go. Everyone was gettin their shit together to leave, that included a half dozen fine ass bitches that Dee and his boys were takin back to the hotel with them. King was lookin around for his Angel who he had lost sight of in the crowd. So, he headed toward the exit door. He had just taken a few steps when he got a tap on the shoulder. A low sweet voice said, "Hey you!" King turned around in anticipation to see who had this heavenly sounding voice. He saw that it was his Angel and that she was standing right there before him. He couldn't think of what to say so he repeated what she said. "Hey you." "Zoey." "Excuse me!" "Zoey, that's my name." "Oh, okay then Ms. Zoey. I am King." "Yes, I know who you are Mr. King." "Oh, you do? And may I ask how it is that you know who I am?" As Zoey started to answer King's question, a big commotion started at the exit door, and it drew their attention. It was Davon having words with a nigga that pulled up on him because he said that his girl kept lookin over at him. Rainbow quickly intervened and said, "Bro, look here, we are not here for all that. We are leaving, you and your girl have a good night." This seemed to have enraged the guy even more. He yelled back at Rainbow, "Nigga I know you didn't just put my motherfuckin girl's name in your mouth. Mother fucker, don't you know me, and my boys will fuck yo' punk ass up?" The enraged guy had two other big niggas standing behind him. King asked Zoey for her number. Zoey said, "No not right now. But I will get in touch with you." King said to her, "Yes you do that young lady. I'm sorry, but I have to go right now." King rushed to get to the exit door where Rainbow was going back and forth with the enraged guy. Rainbow continued to try to calm the situation, he said, "Listen Bro, you drunk I don't know your girl, so I didn't use her name. Plus, this is not something we want to do here right now." "You pussy motherfucker. Now you telling me what the fuck I wanna do?" The guy moved his right hand up and behind him toward his waistline. By the time King got to the exit door, Rainbow had already popped one in the enraged guy's knee. The party crowd scattered. The shot dropped the guy down to one knee. As King walked up his Nine in hand, he close muzzle tapped the enraged guy in the top of his head. "Let's go. It's time to move your asses," King yelled to everyone with him. The limo driver pulled up and they all jumped into the limo with the girls. Not a word was said about what had just happened. Everyone acted as if nothing even happened. They continued with the turn up, like that shit was normal. The only ones who were concerned were King and Rainbow. When the driver pulled up to the hotel, Dee and his boys, followed by a number of girls, hopped out. Dee said, "Fam, I am fucked up right now, but we'll talk in the morning before me, and the boys get to the airport." "Cool Dee. Y'all niggas don't get into anymore shit tonight." "I hear you fam. The only fightin I'm doin the rest of the night is to beat this pussy right here up." "Alright Dee have at it, in the morning then," King said while shaking his head. "Dee, Rainbow and me will be here at ten to take y'all Niggas to the airport." The limo driver pulled off from the hotel and King looked over at Rainbow and again he shook his hand. "Long fucking night." "Ya King, it was." "Rainbow, you good?" "Ya King, I'm good." "Rainbow, listen bro. When we pull out on a fool, right, wrong, or indifferent, we don't shoot to hurt or lame. We shoot to dead a motherfucker and anyone with them. Don't give a motherfucker a chance to get some get back or tell what happened. Cause what happened is what we say happened." "I gotcha King." "But Bro, ya' good right?" "I'm good King! But let's stop this bitch and get something to eat. I'm hungry as hell." " I hear yo' on that. Driver swing by Denny's." The limo driver pulled into Denny's parking lot. King and Rainbow got out of the Limo and went inside. They stopped the host and asked for a seat for two. The host took them to a table, she told them their server would be right with them shortly. After the server came to the table, she said, "Good morning. What can I get for you?" King and Rainbow looked up from their menus. When Rainbow saw the server, he paused due to embarrassment. The server said, "Oh it's you two again. Do y'all have money this time or do I have to pay for y'all meal again?" King laughed out loud as he gave her his order. Rainbow was melting in his seat, he said, "Just bring me a glass of water." Rainbow had lost his appetite. This was the redbone server that he took back the tip he left her to pay his and King's check the last time they were in Denny's. Rainbow was still embarrassed from their last encounter, but wanted to get to know her so when they were done, he decided to leave a tip with his name and number to see if she would call him. When the server came back to the table as they were about to leave, she said, "I'm gon' wait until y'all pay the check before I clean the table and get the tip, just in case." King was laughing his ass off. "Rainbow, I like her, she's funny as hell." "What the hell ever King. Niggas bring yo' ass on, and let's go that shit ain't funny." The limo driver dropped them both off They went right home and straight to bed. They only had a few hours of sleep before they had to be back up to take Dee and his boys to the airport. King and Rainbow were up and at Dee's hotel at ten o'clock that morning. Each of them Niggas filed out of the hotel like they had a full night of sleep and rest. King said, "Rainbow, looka here at thes' Niggas! You and me hurting trying to operate on a few hours of sleep, but these Niggas her' probably didn't go to sleep and they act like it don't phase them." They all got into William's car and Dee said, "Fam, how y'all feelin this morning?" "Like shit." "Fam, all you need is a good shot of Crown, you'll be good." "Hell no! y'all Niggas crazy." "Naw! Fam, this what we do.... fam! I wanted to let you and Rainbow know, that was some good ass lookin last night. Y'all Niggas did what you had to do. No, yo' did what you supposed to do. Real nigga shit! This y'all city If you pull out on a fool you drop that motherfucker straight dead his ass. Fam, for life niggas." Dee held up a fifth of Crown Royal and took a big swig. King and Rainbow respected what Dee had said to them, "Fam, for life." They made it to the airport, dropped Dee and his boys off and all said their goodbyes. Then King and Rainbow headed back across town to go home to get some sleep. On their way home, King's and

Rainbow's pagers went off; it was a nine one-one page. They both grabbed their pagers to look at the number. It was Qwan at the Icemorlee street Trap house. King immediately pulled the car over to a pay booth to use the phone. He called Qwan. Qwan, answered on the first ring. "Hello! Hello! Mr. King, is this you?" "Yes, Qwan. What's up?" "Mr. King, someone just hit the house." "What did they get, Qwan?" "Mr King, them Niggas didn't take anything. They shot one of our cooks in the leg and told us to give you and Mr. Rainbow a message." "Ya, what was the message?" "They said, 'We see you' Mr. King that was all they said, fucking we see you" "Okay Qwan, you handle everything there and we'll be around later." "Yes Sir, Mr. King." King hung up with Qwan and walked back to the car. "What's up King?" Rainbow asked. "Some bullshit, some Niggas send us a message by hittin our Trap house and shot one of our cooks." "Fuck, really King?" "Whoever the motherfucker was they said, 'We see you.'" "What the fuck?" "Ya, I know Rainbow. We got to keep our head on a swivel."

Rainbow and King went a few weeks without having any problems, but they knew it was time to hire their own goons. They went shopping to find the biggest and baddest niggas they could find. They reached out to Dee, and he told them about some two niggas that just moved to the California area because the city they were working in got hot. They had to drop a nigga that had family ties with the Haitian mafia. Dee told them that they were true motherfucking, no shit taking hitters. King and Rainbow broke bread with the men and was very impressed. So, they brought the two hitters into the house of King and Rainbow. One, JT he was a six-foot six-inch Nigga that didn't talk much, and the other one Zo he was six foot five inches and all about his business, but he also was a jokester. Zo and JT were now the door keepers of the house of King and Rainbow. It wasn't long before JT and Zo proved their worth. King, Rainbow, and their two goons were out checking on their corners when they noticed that there were some other niggas slinging on their corner. Rainbow and King pulled up on the Niggas. "Hey!! Lil Niggas, who told you you can sling shit off my corner?" "Tis' Rick's corner, he took from some Niggas tis' morning." "You tell that Nigga Rick, he don't get nothing from the house of King and Rainbow unless we give it to him. So, you lil motherfuckers get the fuck off my corner. And so that you remember what I said, give me everything you got. Call this a tax and you go tell that nigga Rick to come see me if he got a problem with it." As King and Rainbow were talking to the corner boys, and JT and Zo sat in the car not far away making sure King and Rainbow's back was covered. JT and Zo saw a young nigga walk up on King and Rainbow from their blind side. The car's windows were down so JT and Zo could hear the guy loudly say, "Nigga, what the fuck you two motherfuckers doing fucking with our boys?" The guy said this while holding his shirt up showing off his waist band that had a Smith and Wesson in it. Before King or Rainbow could react to the young nigga, JT jumped out of the car. He came up his left side and popped one in the back of his left knee, by then Zo was on his right side and he popped one into the back of the young nigga's right knee. JT said, "Boss, are we teaching lessons today?" Rainbow responded, "Hell No! Dead this fool. Our lesson teaching days are over." "Cool Boss!" Zo said after putting one dead center of the young nigga's forehead. King took his taxes from the boys and said, "Yo' lil niggas! Go tell Rick I don't fuck with him or his, so, don't he fuck with me or mine, but if he decides to be stupid and want to battle with the house of King and Rainbow, instead of every body's pocket gettin fat let him know it will be a FUCKING WAR! Now take y'all lil dusty asses off my corner." King looked over at Rainbow and said, "Tis' what the fuck I'm talkin bout niggas gettin laid out! Ha. Ha. Ha! Let's roll out."

Over the next months, other than the occasional tightening a fool up, things ran smoothly with the house of King and Rainbow. The house of King and Rainbow was making money and taking over more and more corners. Their sugar was the best everybody wanted it for their candy shop. King and Rainbow were growing in the game and was getting noticed. One early Morning Rainbow was getting ready to leave his new downtown penthouse apartment to meet King; he made his way through the apartment to the front door when his home phone rang. He turned and went back inside to answer it. He answered the phone and said, "Ya' Nigga! I'm on the way." "Hello, excuse me?" It was a female's voice and Rainbow could not place it at first. He said, "Hello?" Then the female voice said, "Wow! That's how you answer the phone?" "No, it's not. I'm sorry I thought you were someone else." "Okay, well do you even know who this is?" "I am sorry, I just can't place the voice." "Hmmm okay. Then I tell you what. I want to go out with you, so you think hard about who this might be and if you figure it out, you will know where to come pick me up tonight at seven o'clock." "Do I not even get a hint?" "No but you will get my name if I see you at seven tonight." "Okay. This is interesting." "Yes, it is, isn't it? Goodbye." "Bye, I'll see you tonight at seven." "We'll see, won't we?" Rainbow hung up with who thought herself to be a mystery, but Rainbow clearly knew who she was. He went out the door and to his car to go meet King, JT, and Zo at the stash house. It was the middle of the month; they had a load of fish coming in at the end of the week. King and Rainbow made it a habit to go around personally to check on their operations just before fresh fish came in. Their low-level workers liked seeing Mr. King and Mr. Rainbow coming around to check on them. They knew when they came, if things were running well, they would give them some exact bread. After running around all day, they made it back to the stash house. Rainbow told King he was going home to lay it down. King said, "Nigga it's early, you sick or something?" "Naw, to be honest, old girl from Denny's hit me up this morning." "Naw! Nigga you bullshitin." "Naw, she did she called. I'm going to pick her up at seven at Denny's." "Alright then, go handle your business. I'll stay around here for a while. One of the runners is bringing some cash in tonight." "King, you need me to stay with you?" Naw, I got it. Go meet your girl and have fun." "Cool, because I really want to go." "Nigga, I knew that your bitch ass nose is open already." JT and Zo both said, "Goodnight, Boss, have a good time." Rainbow left the stash house and drove home so that he could get ready for his date, while King, JT and Zo waited at the stash house for the Runner with the cash drop. Rainbow made it to Denny's just before seven o'clock. He got out to open the car door for her. She got in and reached over to open the driver's side door for Rainbow to get in. When Rainbow saw her do this, he said to himself as he shook his head, "Hmmm, yes." When he got into his car, he said to her, "Thank you." "You are welcome, and I see you figured out who was on the phone." "Ma', there was nothing to figure out. I don't just run my number to anyone." "That's good to hear because I don't just call a number that's left for me on a bill or otherwise." "Well then, let's start with your name." "It's Debra Ann Autry." "Okay Ms. Debra Ann, tell me the type of food you like, and do you have a favorite restaurant?" "No, not really. I will go wherever you would like to take me, not Denny's." Rainbow laughed at her comment. They talked and talked like they knew each other all their lives. Rainbow took

Debra Ann to Beef and Bottle off South Boulevard, a quite elegant restaurant, with a nice wine selection. They ate, they drunk, they talked, and they laughed until it got late. They enjoyed each other's company so much that they didn't realize the restaurant had closed and they were the only customers still left in the restaurant. The staff was cleaning up around them; the wait staff had even cleaned the dishes from off their table. Rainbow or Debra Ann didn't even notice it had been done. They finally left the restaurant after been politely put out by the Manager. Rainbow drove Debra Ann back to her car at Denny's "Well, we are here, and I had the best time." "Yes, so did I, James Rainmond." "Ha. Ha. Ha." "What are you laughing at?" "You calling me James Rainmond, nobody does that. But it sounds cute when you say it." "James Rainmond, James Rainmond, James Rainmond. You like that?" "Yes, I do, Debra Ann. I can't believe the night is over already." "I don't either, James Rainmond and I hope that you don't find me to forward or think this is something I always do, but can we go to your place for a night cap?" "No, I don't find you forward or think that it's something you do all the time and yes, we can go to my place for a night cap." When they got to Rainbow's condo, he turned on the eight-track player and popped in an eight track of Billy Ocean. As the song 'Caribbean Queen' played, James went into the kitchen and opened a bottle of Merlot while Debra Ann sat on the couch in the living room. James took the bottle and two glasses back to the living room to Debra Ann. He sat them down on the coffee table. "Dance with me," Debra Ann said. With the lights low and the music soft, they danced looking into each other's eyes. He moved his head close to hers until his lips were on her moist perky lips. As they danced and kissed, Rainbow felt his dick take a mind of its own. His dick was throbbing so hard that it felt as if it had its own heartbeat. Debra Ann could feel the bulge in his pants pressing up against her. After a few minutes of holding each other close, she reached up and released her spaghetti straps from her shoulders, dropping her dress to the floor. She was wearing no bra, her mellow sized perky breasts bounced freely as she wiggled a bit as she danced. She had a phat round ass adorned with silk black panties. She took Rainbow's hands and placed them on her firm ass as his tongue licked her erected nipples. Still in rhythm with the music that was playing, Debra Ann began to grind on Rainbow's seconds from exploding bulge. His right hand moved from the finest ass God nun ever made to between her creamy thighs with a pussy that was bursting with so much juice that he literally had a puddle of her fluids in the palm of his hand, it was leaking through her panties. Rainbow danced Debra Ann right into his bedroom and onto his king-sized waterbed; he began to kiss every inch of her body. He even sucked the wetness out of her silk panties. He knew that she was about to climb the wall by the way she was moaning and tearing at his clothes, at that moment, Rainbow whispered into her ear, " Debra Ann, can we just hold each other until the sun comes up tonight? As bad as I want you, and I do want you, but I want you to know I have nothing but respect and a deep affection for you. I don't want our animal lust to mess that up." She nodded yes and they both laid together the rest of the night.

Jalenn, one of King's runners came about Mid-night with the cash drop. King took the bag and sent Jalenn on his way. King counted the drop as JT and Zo watched his back. He put the cash in the safe and said, "Let's get out of here." They all walked to the door and Zo opened it. Right outside of the front door was Jalenn, King's runner. He had been pistol whipped bout to death. King anxiously asked, "Jalenn, who did this?" "I don't know Mr. King, he just told me to tell you and Mr. Rainbow, 'We see you.'" King still frantic, said, "What the fuck, it got to be that motherfucker, Rick. Let's get Jalenn somewhere to get some help."

The next day, they all met at the stash house. King, JT, and Zo filled Rainbow in on what happened with Jalenn. King felt like what was done to Jalenn was a shot over the bow which was an act of war. King said, "We are going to react in kind. A Nigga for a Nigga. That big nigga Willie Ray Rick's Lieutenant gotta go. Maybe if we cut off Rick's right arm, he'll know he fuckin with the wrong Niggas. Tonight, that big motherfucker Willie Ray will lay down." "We gotcha Mr. King." "Me and Rainbow will be with y'all niggas. I want that nigga Rick to know who did it."

That night, King, Rainbow, JT and Zo rode around Rick's tuff trying to catch that Nigga Willie Ray slipping. After three hours of looking and waiting for that big motherfucker he hadn't shown his head, Zo said, "That Nigga Willie Ray's bitch dance down at the strip club on Old Pineville Road. She got that Nigga Willie Ray twisted. He's there to pick that hoe up every night that she works." "Let's go down there then." "Okay Boss." They all rode down to the strip club to see if Willie Ray's girl was working that night. When they got to the club, King told JT, "Run in and see if she is in there." JT jumped out of King's 1979 Cadillac Eldorado convertible and went inside. He walked around the club for a few minutes, not only did he see Willie Ray's girl, but Willie Ray's pussy whipped ass was sitting up in that ditch. JT rushed back out and jumped into the passenger seat of the car. He looked back at King and Rainbow and said.

"Boss, that Nigga Willie Ray is sitting up in there with his bitch." "Cool! Zo pull this motherfucker over into the parking lot, so we can wait for that Nigga to come out." Zo pulled the El-dog into the back of the parking lot under a broken streetlight. They anxiously waited for Willie Ray to come out of the club. Two hours passed and the club began to close. Security started walking the dancers to their cars. Willie Ray finally walked out with his bitch. They walked across the parking lot and got into a car that was parked facing the club. "Zo! Zo! Pull up behind that motherfucker," Rainbow shouted. Zo pulled up and blocked the car in as they tried to back out. With the club building in front of them, Willie Ray and his girl couldn't go anywhere. Immediately, JT jumped out of the front passenger seat and headed for Willie Ray's car's passenger door where Willie Ray was sitting. Zo quickly sprung from the driver's seat heading for the car driver's door. JT ran up on Willie Ray and snatched his bitch ass from the car. King and Rainbow climbed out of the back seat of the EL-dog and Rainbow yelled, "Zo get that pussy shaking bitch out too." King walked up to Willie Ray who was being held by JT with a Nine pressed against his temple. King asked Willie Ray, "Nigga, do yo' remember me?" Willie Ray said, "Fuck you Nigga." "JT, get this motherfucker's attention please." JT popped one in the back of both of Willie Ray's knees. Hitters would shoot Niggas in the back of the knees because it caused an extreme amount of pain without killing them, but King liked it because he wanted a Nigga to bow to the King, also it most definitely got a motherfucker's attention. King said to Willie Ray, "Now that I have your attention, I'm going to ask you again, Motherfucker, do you remember me?" "Ya! Nigga, I remember you. You that Nigga Rick let go at Black Mike's the night Rick dead him." "Why is your mother fucking boss Rick fucking with the house of King and Rainbow?" "Ain't nobody fucking with y'all niggas. I don't know what the fuck you talkin bout." "Ya! yo' don't know, hmm! Then Nigga you'll never know. JT, dead this fool." JT popped one dead center of his forehead. This had become the house of King and Rainbow's calling card. Then King turned his attention to Willie Ray's girl and said, "Give the message of what you just saw to Rick. Plus tell him Mr. King and Mr. Rainbow said, "Every time I have to fuck with him because he has fucked with me, the dick only gets bigger and harder.' Let's go. Let's get the fuck out of here." They all went to the car, all but Zo. Before Zo let the pussy shaking bitch go, he said, "Call me girl, since you don't have a Nigga no more." "Zo! If you don't come, get yo' dumb ass in this car and drive..." "But boss, this bitch is fine as hell." "Yo' stupid." Everyone laughed as they pulled off.

As time went on, the house of King and Rainbow grew bigger and became more powerful. Rainbow had been seeing Debra Ann for a while; they moved in together. King still hadn't found that one woman; he knew he wanted to be in her life and her in his. Until one nice California afternoon, King was driving home with the car window and top down. The O'Jays were playing on his eight track. He was thinking, grooving, and talking to himself, "These Niggas in these streets going to learn." At that very moment he had a mental interruption, his car started to hesitate. king removed his sunglasses and started looking around the car wondering what it could be. When he looked down, he saw that his low fuel indicator light was on. He shook his head, he was livid. He threw his sunglasses over into the passenger seat and said, "Damn it! First, I got to teach that damn Zo's crazy ass how to put gas in my motherfuckin car. I'm gone kill that Nigga." King pulled into the nearest corner store that sold gas. He jumped out to go inside. Since he had to stop away, he decided to go into the store to get himself a V-8 with the gas. He got the V-8 and headed up to the register. He asked for gas on pump three then paid for them both. King walked out of the store back to his car to pump his gas. As he got into the store's parking lot, he saw there was someone leaning against his car, but he couldn't tell who it was because he was seeing whoever it was from a distance plus facing the sun. He threw the V-8 down and slowed his walk; he took a wide turn to walk past his car. He now was walking back up toward his car with the sun to his back. It was a female leaning back on the driver's door. As he got closer, he couldn't believe his eyes. He moved even closer to the car and said to himself, "I know it's not; it can't be." But it really was its that girl Zoey, the Angel, his future baby momma. He was somewhat confused. Where did she come from and how did she get here? Most of all, how did she know so much about him? King stopped at the back of his car with his right hand on the Nine-millimeter that he wore in his waist band, he peeked around the back corner of his car on set just in case he had to pop off on a motherfucker King wasn't above sending a Angel to hell. King said, "Hey You" "Ha. Ha. Hey you," Zoey responded. "What are you doing here?" " I saw you going into the store as I was driving by, so I thought I would stop and say Hi. Hi." King laughed at her cuteness. "I hope that wasn't a problem." "No! Of course not, believe it or not, you just made my day" "I'm glad I did." "Mrs. King, I meant Ms. Zoey, what are you up to?" Zoey smiled at his cute on purpose slip of the tongue. She said, "I'm not up to anything, as I said, I saw you walking into the store, and I just wanted to say Hi." "Well, then come have an early dinner with me." "I can't right now, but I tell you what, how about tonight? You come to my place and let me cook you dinner." "Cool Ma', I'm with that." Zoey gave King her address and the time to come to her apartment then she left. King got into his car smiling from ear to ear, he pulled out into the street and his car started to hesitate again when he pressed the gas paddle. Looking down at his fuel hand, he saw that the light was on, still, and the gas hand read empty. "Damn! I forgot to pump my gas!" King yelled. He had to turn around and go back to the corner store to get the gas that he had already paid for.

King got to Zoey's apartment that night a few minutes early so he could sit in the car to get himself together before going in. King had been nervous about coming to Zoey's all day. After sitting in the car for about twenty minutes, he walked up to the building slowly and nervously like he was a young schoolboy. He talked to himself trying to give himself a pep talk, "Alright King, get your shit together Nigga. You been around beautiful women before. Plus, Nigga, you are William Saint King, that nigga. Okay. I'm good. I'm cool." He walked up to door that had A- 2 on it, which was Zoey's apartment number. He knocked on the door and it seemed like Zoey had been lying on the door because she opened it faster than mofo. King froze and he immediately began talking to himself. "Damn King. You can't do this. This girl right here is so fucking fine. King, get your punk ass together." Zoey said, "Hey. You." That broke the ice for King, he laughed and said, "Hey You." He wasn't so nerves anymore. Zoey invited him in and said, "You look nice and damn, you smell good, is that Faberge Brut you are wearing?" "Yes, it is, but let's talk about how good you look and smell." "Thank you, King. Would you like a drink?" "Yes. Wine please." "Okay Wine... a man after my own heart." "You have a nice apartment. Wow, that dinner smells good." "Thank you, dinner should be ready in about twenty minutes. I will get the wine for you King, but if you don't mind, I'm going to have a short cocktail instead of wine tonight." "No! No! Please, I don't mind at all."

Zoey lit two big black suede scented candles that were sitting on the coffee table. Then she walked to the kitchen for the drinks. King watched her every step as she left the room. He couldn't believe how amazing Zoey looked in that short fitted black cocktail dress. It was a V cut back out with the point of the V stopping just above the crack of her ass and it was an ass you could bounce a quarter off. To King, the apartment got hot suddenly. He didn't know if it was him or a combination of the candles burning and her cooking, he didn't know what it was, but he most definitely knew it was hot as hell. He was minutes away from sweating out his clothes. King looked around the room, frantically looking for something to occupy his mind. He saw a record player console against the wall over in the corner. He got up and walked over to the console to check out Zoey's record collection. She had a nice collection of forty-fives and Albums. He saw a Betty Wright album "Danger High Voltage". He put the Album on the record player to play just as Zoey came back into the room with a bottle of Moscato, a bottle of Remy

Black, a wine glass, and a glass of ice for her Remy. She had it all on a nice silver tray. Zoey laid the tray down on the coffee table where she poured a half glass of wine for King. As he walked back to the couch to sit down, Zoey handed him the glass of wine. She then sat down right next to him on the couch. King said, "I hope you don't mind that I messed with your record player?" "No! Of course not. Anyway, tonight you can mess with anything you want." "Are you not going to have your cocktail before all the ice melts in that glass?" "Yes, I will. I just wanted to sit right here with you for a moment, if that's okay?" "I'm fine with that ma'. So, tell me something. When I first met you that night at the club, you said you knew who I was. How is it that you know me?" "King, do we have to talk about that right now? I just want to sit here and look into your eyes." "I am good with that. I want to look back into your deep blue eyes too until I drown." "King, may I kiss you?" "William." "Hmmm!" "William, that's my name. William Saint King." "Now I want to kiss you even more." Zoey moved closer to King. She then leaned forward until her lips were barely touching King's lips, then she whispered his name softly, "William, William, William." Her whispering his name that close to his lips made his lips vibrate slightly, causing it to tickle his lips. As she continued, he noticed that his slacks began to get tight in the crotch area as his manhood started to feel heavy. Now his thoughts and feelings were running wild. King knew one thing for sure, he had to get that damn wine glass out of his hand before he crushed it. Leaning away slightly, he reached over to the coffee table to sit the wine glass down. As he laid the glass on the table, Zoey put her hand on his thigh. His manhood went into autopilot. It grew thicker and heavier. Without any warning, Zoey's lips covered King's whole mouth, with her tongue going in and out of his mouth. While doing that, she maneuvered her hand to King's crotch and began to gently message it. King's manhood began to claw at the inside of his slacks like it was a wild beast trying to get free. Zoey obeyed it. She slowly freed the beast by zipping King's slacks down.

Once she had his fly completely open, the beast jumped out looking for a territory to conquer. King only knew that the beast had been released because he felt a slight breeze. She kept King busy up top with her lips all over his mouth. At that very moment something happened that almost stopped King's heart from beating. Once Zoey had the beast released, King didn't know how, he didn't know from where, but King felt a big gob of something cool and moist on the head of his dick. This made King jump and abruptly turn his head from Zoey's lips to look down to see what was going on. Zoey had grabbed a hand full of Vaseline from the Vaseline jar that appeared from thin air but was now sitting on the silver tray with the Wine and Remy bottles plus the glass of ice that was on the top of coffee table. She was going to work with that gob of Vaseline on the head of King's dick. In a state of drunken passion, he thought to himself, "Oh my God, Lord Jesus Christ in heaven. What the what is this woman trying to do to me?" Right then if she had asked him, "Who yo' momma?" not only would he have said, "You' my momma", but he would have said it with tears running down his face. King knew this had to stop and this had to stop right then because if it did not stop immediately, not only was he about to unload a massive load in her hand, but also in her ears by telling her the three big words that a man should never say to a woman first, and most definitely, not on the first date. But those words were about to spring from his mouth faster than a nigga in an interrogation room facing thirty years. King quickly put his hand under Zoey's chin to turn her head toward him so he could look her in the eyes and get her attention. "Zoey! Zoey! Baby, looka here, you have to stop this." "But why? William, you don't like it?" "No, No, baby that's not it. I just need you to stop. Besides I want to get to know you." "How do you want to do that?" He got close to her ear and said, "You just lean back and relax, I'll show you how." King began to nibble on her ear lobe, then he made his way around to her mouth. He used his tongue to softly lick her lips, separating them. He engaged her tongue in a slow dance with his tongue. King sucked her tongue into his mouth and continued to suck it with light pressure. When he heard her moan, he let her tongue go, kissed her chin and asked, "You okay?" "Yes," she moaned out. With a slightly moist tongue, he went down her neck to her shoulder blade. He kissed her shoulder as he gently inched her fitted cocktail dress up and over her head. Immediately, his innate ability to nurse on breast took over. He sucked and caressed her erected nipples like a hungry newborn baby would. His moist tongue slid slowly to her navel. While at her navel, King said, "Since we are using props around here, let me accommodate you with a prop of my own." King's thoughts had gone to the glass of ice that Zoey brought in on the Tray. He reached over to the coffee table and grabbed a cube of ice out of the glass. He put the cube in the center of Zoey's navel. She gasped as the coldness from the ice cube kissed her skin. "Relax baby. Relax you started this," King said. As he started moving the ice cube around her flat, well-toned stomach with his tongue. He moved it until the ice cube melted leaving a pool of water on her stomach that King sucked up as if he was a wet vac. He then moved down to her pelvic region, licking every inch on the way down. He picked up one of her legs, lifting it as he gently kissed and sucked it. Her body's reactions and her voice were driving him mad. "William, you are going to make me make a mess on this couch," Zoey said to him. Due to his inexperience with women, King didn't fully understand what Zoey meant but he said, " Okay, if you mess it up, I'll buy you another one." King picked up her other leg and placed her feet on each of his shoulders revealing a pinkish hue. Calling what he was looking at a "pussy" would do it an injustice, but a "pussy" is what it was and oh my what a hell of a "pussy". King once again reached for the glass of ice and turned it up filling his mouth with as many ice cubes as he could hold. He then went little man in the boat hunting. His plans were to go, find, and give it his undivided attention. As his cold lips touched that little boat rider, she jumped and moaned, "William, I told you, you gon' make me make a mess." Still befuddled, King continues licking and sucking her clit into his ice-cold mouth.

She groaned loudly pushing her feet into King's shoulders lifting her hips, "Oh God, I told you." She squirted all in King's face soaking him and her couch. King sat up with Zoey's fluids dripping from his face and he said, "Okay then." He went right back at it; he had that little man in the boat right where he wanted him, and his little boat had taken on water. He continued to cold tongue wrestle with him as he grabbed Zoey's ankles holding her feet in place on his shoulders. Zoey couldn't do anything, but squirt and plead. "Yo' motherfucker, please, please, oh my god please, William, I will do anything please. Oh my god, William, I can't see. I'm serious William, I'm going blind. I can't take it anymore." King knew at that point he was putting in work and he was not about to let up, so he said, "No Baby, not yet. I want to get to know you by tasting all your juices." By this time, King's hundred fifty-dollar shirt was drenched. Zoey could barely talk, she could only say, "Oh my god, I'm done Please! Please! William." "Relax baby, I just want to taste just a little more. Don't you want me to know you?" King snatched his soaked shirt off, snapping all the buttons. He then jumped out of his slacks as Betty Wright played in the background. "Tonight is the night I'm going to make you, my woman." In the air was the smell of food burning. King was now completely naked. Zoey began to come back around, and she yelled, "Oh my food William, it's ruined." "Baby, don't worry about the food, we'll go out to eat." "Okay then, come on let's get ready to go." "No! No! Not yet give me a minute Zoey. We have not finished talking yet. There is still more I want to know about you." "No! William. Not now, I can't take no more." "Baby, Baby, just tell me one more thing I promise." "Okay William, just one more William, you promise?" "Yes baby, one more." King reached for the glass of ice one more gain Zoey quickly said, "No William, not the ice I can't take that no more." "mmmmmmm" King's mouth was full of ice so he couldn't talk. He could only mumble, "Relax baby." He took both of Zoey's legs held them together as he placed her feet in the middle of his chest. He then put his left arm over her knees locking her feet against his chest.

With his right hand, he took one ice cube from his mouth and placed it between her already wet dripping pussy lips. He grabbed hold of his throbbing dick and pushed the ice cube up and down her pussy lips, while with his ice-cold mouth, he sucked her toes. Once the ice melted, King inserted his dick into her wet cold pussy going in and out, just head deep only. Zoey yelled, "William, William, please." "What's wrong baby, you want all of it?" "Yes! Yes! All of it. Give me it all please." King pushed his hard thick dick into Zoey, softly, gently until he felt the boundaries of the back of her pussy walls. He pushed up against it with force and stayed right there on the back wall pushing in and out. Zoey screamed in pure pleasure. "Yo', motherfucker, you got me. Oh my god I'm." As King felt his missile about to explode, he pushed hard against her walls again as he yelled, "Shit, oh Damn." King pulled his now unloaded missile out of her dripping hot pussy. Zoey began to shake, and there was a gash. She squirted completely, soaking the couch. King slowly laid Zoey's legs down and sat at her feet looking down at her with a smile on his face. When Zoey finally stopped shaking, she opened her eyes and looked at King. "Hey, you, I thought we were going to get something to eat?" King said to her, with a slight smirk on his face. "I hate you!" Zoey said as she tried to sit up. King extended his hand out to her, "You need some help." "Hell no! Not from you, stay away from me," she said as she knocked his hands away. They both laughed.

The next evening, King went to meet up with Rainbow, JT, and Zo at the stash house. When he walked into the stash house, Rainbow looked up and said, "There's that nigga, where you been all night and day? I been calling and paging yo' ass since yesterday afternoon." "I'm good; ran into somebody that had me out of pocket for a while." Zo immediately said, "Oh hell, boss nun run into some fine hoe." King stepped toward Zo, "Watch yo' fucking mouth. She ain't no hoe!" "Sorry boss! Just joking." "Naw! you good... matter of fact Zo, I would be busting yo' monkey ass fo' not putting gas in my car yesterday, but if it wasn't fo' yo' fuck up I wouldn't had run into her while stopping to get gas'. So, nigga you shouldn't push it." "Boss, I'm sorry. I got busy and forgot to stop for gas." Rainbow and JT wanted to know who this girl was that got King tight like this. JT asked King, "Hey boss, who had you all out of pocket. She got to be fine as hell." "Ya JT, she is. I met her in a club last year sometime. Rainbow, you remember her don't you. The girl I sent the Champagne to." "Ya, King I do remember that. That was back when Dee, and his boys was in town. and ya! She is fine, but I still say I've seen her somewhere other than the club that night. A nigga don't forget a face especially a face that is as fine as she is. Anyway, JT and Zo what time is that load of fish supposed to be here tonight?" King also switched back to business as Rainbow did. King said, "Ya! What time." "Boss I'm not sure now because they should have been here an hour ago," JT replied. King angrily said, "Ya, really fuck! Let's go hit the streets to see what's up with that. Them niggas got Fifty blocks of our shit." They all got into Rainbow's 1980 Cadillac Brougham and Zo drove them down the route that the runners should have taken. King, Rainbow, JT, and Zo were the only ones who knew about the fish delivery, time, date, and the routes as it normally changed from one delivery to the next. The runners never got the routes until the fish is picked up by them. They continued to drive the route looking for their runners, they were almost at the fish pick up spot when they saw Jalenn's car sitting on a side street. King yelled out, "Look there! What the fuck! Zo get over there." Zo pulled the car up close to Jalenn's car. King jumped out of the car before Zo brought it to a complete stop and he went straight to the trunk of Jaleen's car. He opened it and saw that the lock on the stash box hidden in the trunk had been shot open. He first was relieved because he thought his shit was still in the box, but upon further inspection he noticed that twenty-five blocks were gone. King was furious and he expressed it forcibly and loudly. "What the fuck.... HOW!!!? How in the hell did this happen? We are the only fucking ones that knew about this delivery and the route they would take back to the stash house." Rainbow was looking around inside and outside of Jalenn's car while King continued to go off back at the trunk. "Fuck! Fuck! Rainbow who, how 750 thousand dollars' worth of shit motherfuckin gon'?" Right then Rainbow said, "King, look at this shit here." Not only were there two bodies in the car, but a message had been scratched on the hood of the car, "We see you." With this, they knew who hit their load but "how" was still the question. This message made King even more furious. "That Nigga Rick, Ricky, whatever the fuck that Nigga name is. That motherfucker nun fucked with the wrong somebody. Zo don't that Nigga Rick got a Trap house over off Statesville Avenue?" "Ya! Boss he does." "Okay, then this is how this shit gon' to go down. Y'all niggas gon' to drop me and the shit off at the stash house, while I bust it down and now stretch the shit out. Rainbow, you, Zo and JT go over to that Nigga Rick's spot. Y'all motherfucker dead every motherfucker in that bitch. If there's a rat crawling around that ditch, dead that motherfucker too!!" They all jumped in the Bro-ham and dropped King and the shit off at the stash house. Rainbow and the boys headed to Rick's Trap house. They slowly drove up the block that the trap house was on, Zo stopped the car in the middle of the street down from the trap house, so they would have a clear view of the Trap. While they were preparing to go in to handle some work, somebody walked out of the front door of the Trap with a large bag. It was a female, as she got closer, Rainbow shouted, "Wait a fucking minute. I know damn well it's not. It can't be, but she looks just like that fine bitch from the club that got King twisted." Zo turned to the back seat where Rainbow was sitting and he said to Rainbow, "What the hell Boss? Are you sure?" "Yes! That's her. I know it is." "So, what we gon' do Boss?" "Right now! We gon' go in here and drop every motherfucker in sight in this bitch." Rainbow and his goons kicked the front door in, they gauged everything and anything that moved. They then headed back to the stash house. When they got back, King was still there breaking down and stretching product. When they walked through the door, King spun around with a gun in hand, "Oh shit!

It's y'all fools. Did y'all send a clear message to that motherfucker Rick?" "Ya! Boss, it was a clear message, but boss if not now you know eventually, we got to cut the head off that snake that nigga Rick." "Ya King, Zo is right, we gon' have to take out Rick." "Y'all are right, but until tonight that nigga Rick only been having a pissing contest with us, an all-out war with him is not what we want right now. You can't make no money in the time of war, but his day is coming. He's going to stick his head up at the wrong time and we are going to take that motherfuckers head completely off." Rainbow agreed with King, he then told Zo and JT, "Y'all Niggas go ahead and go, we are good here, but ride by the Traps and check on them niggas before y'all head in for the night!!" "Okay Boss, if you sure y'all good." Rainbow nodded his head. Yes" Zo and JT left. Rainbow turned toward King, he asked him, "You good?" King said, "No! I'm not. I do not understand this shit. How them motherfuckers knew about that delivery and pick up point, but better yet, how the fuck did they know the details of the route? Rainbow, it was only us four that knew that shit. Do you think JT or Zo is back dooring us?" "No, King I don't. But King, let me ask you this. Do you know where your girl was tonight?" "No, I don't, but rainbow what the fuck that got to do with this shit we got going on here?" "King, I saw your girl leaving Rick's Trap house with a large bag in her hand when we pulled up. King, you have to think that she is either a runner for Rick or she has a hell of a drug habit. So, I have to ask you, did you talk to your girl about our business?" "Hell no! What kind of question is that to ask me, NIGGA!! Yo' know me better than that. James Rainmond Marsh, are you sure it was her you seen?" "King, I saw her with my own eyes, it was her." "Damn!!! I hope on all I love... you know what? Never mind. Come on Rainbow. Let's get the fuck out of here. I got to make a run." "King, you need me to go with you?" "Naw, I got this." "King you sure?" "Naw, I'm telling yo' I'm good." "Alright then, handle your business."

King headed out straight to Zoey's apartment with anger and fear in his heart at the same time. He had no idea what he was about to find out or what he would do if in fact she was working for Rick and playing him. He talked to himself all the way across town. "Is that why she knew who I was when I first met her at the club? What the fuck! This shit can't be happening. Damn! Damn!" King had real feelings for Zoey. He felt he possibly loved her. When he arrived at Zoey's apartment and walked up to her door, he hesitated for a few seconds to give his heart the opportunity to leave his throat. He could also feel butterflies in his belly. Once he got himself together, he knocked on her door. Zoey quickly opened the door once she looked through the peep hole and saw that it was King. "William, hey I'm surprised but happy to see you, come on in." "Hey Zoey, how are you tonight? Listen Zoey, I'm sorry for coming by so late, and not calling first. I was out riding and had you on my mind and wanted to see you." "Oh please, that's okay, you can come by anytime. William, you know I really enjoyed you the other night. I was hoping to hear from you again." "Yes, I enjoyed myself with you as well. Zoey, it's been my intent to call you after the other night, but I got busy at work. Speaking of work, I thought I saw you earlier tonight over off Statesville Avenue." "No William, I wasn't. It wasn't me that you saw. I been home all evening, actually I been sitting here with a glass of wine thinking about you." "Ya, what about me were you thinking?" "Well, I was hoping you knew what happened the other night was about you and the way I felt when I first saw you at the Club. Most of all, I was hoping that you don't think me some naive jump off trick. Especially when I tell you that I know it has only been a few days, but William, I love you." "Hmmm, I got to go now." "William, what's wrong? Was I wrong and out of line telling you how I feel?" "No Zoey, you are good, it's all good, and we are all good. I just need a minute before I respond, that's all. I promise we will talk tomorrow." King gave Zoey a peck on the lips and got the hell out of there before his emotions took over, but what Zoey didn't know was that King felt the same way about her. King went home and straight to bed; he was to meet Rainbow for an early morning meeting at Denny's.

The next morning, Rainbow got to Denny's before King. He went on in and was seated by the host. By the time the server brought back the cup of coffee that Rainbow ordered, King was walking toward the table. King's head was down as if he had alot weighing him down. Rainbow noticed this so he waited for King to sit down and make his order before he asked him, "Bro, you, okay?" "No Rainbow, I'm not bro. we took a big hit last night. Neither our pockets nor our reputation can stand another hit like that one. Rainbow that was a hit to the tune of over a half of a million dollars gone just like that. Listen bro, for now on, the only ones that will know about our delivery, drops and routes will be you and me." "King bro, what about Zo and JT? How are they going to feel now that we are leaving them in the dark on everything?" "I don't give a good god damn about them motherfucker's feelings. As much money as we pay them niggas, they feel how the fuck we tell them they feel. Rainbow bro, listen,

I know how you are, I got that, but I'm going to ask you what Black Mike always asked us, 'Do you want to go back to that hot ass off ramp selling bottled water?'" "Bro we ain't never going back there, neither will our kids ever have to. JT and Zo is meeting us here. I called them this morning, matter a fact, I just saw Zo's car pull up into the parking lot. I will tell them Niggas how it's going to go down for now on!" Zo and JT parked and walked into the restaurant. The host led them to King and Rainbow's table. They both sat down, and King greeted them. "What's up?" Rainbow asked JT, "How was everything at the Trap houses last night?" "It was all good Boss. We need to do a cash pickup from them on Friday. Oh ya, I forgot all except for this fain hoe I had to throw out of the Icemorlee Street Trap." "What the hell happened?" "This fool Zo the fain was given ten-dollar head jobs. Zo told her ten dollars was too much for fain head, so he gave her seven dollars. When the fain finished he took five dollars back from her talking about she owed him some change for that sorry ass head job. She was trying to whoop this Nigga's ass." They all laughed as King began to lay out the new business plan. Once King finished, JT and Zo left leaving King and Rainbow behind. "So King, what about it?" Rainbow said. "What about what?" "King! Why was your girl leaving Rick's Trap house?" "It wasn't her you saw. It was somebody else." "King, it was her and for another thing, I know I've seen her somewhere else before." "No, the hell it wasn't!! Rainbow drops it. You don't know her or have you ever seen her before." King quickly got up from the table, he was frustrated and upset. He walked toward the exit door without saying another word to Rainbow. King knew in the back of his mind that Rainbow saw who he said he saw, he even knew that Rainbow possibly had seen her somewhere else before. His heart ached at all the pending possibilities of where that may have been that Rainbow had seen her before.

Time had passed; the house of King and Rainbow had become a major enterprising force, moving product up and down the West Coast. The last message the house of King and Rainbow sent Rick must have been well received because other than some small beefs with rival corner boys, things were running straight ahead. Niggas were making real money. Rainbow and Debra Ann got married and they were expecting their second child. King and Zoey have been going strong for a while. Rainbow, although for King's sake, is always respectful toward Zoey, but he still doesn't trust her. He never has many words for her other than 'Hey and Bye,' plus he couldn't get over the fact that he had seen her somewhere before. This conundrum continued to nag at him.

Overall, everything with the house of King and Rainbow had been going good until the night that JT and Zo were late for a cash drop at the stash house. They both were to meet King and Rainbow there at nine o'clock. At about eleven o'clock, JT showed up with a bullet in his shoulder and driving Zo's car. Zo was in the passenger seat with his right arm completely cut off. JT came into the house out of breath and bleeding everywhere. When King and Rainbow saw him, they became frantic. King began to yell, "What the fuck happened JT? Who did this shit?" "I'm not sure Boss, but I think it was Rick's boys. Zo is in the car, those Niggas cut his arm off then killed him. While another one held a gun point blank at my shoulder. Once they killed Zo, they shot me and said, "Tell your boss we still see you. A right arm for a right arm." Rainbow shouted at King. "This is about that Nigga Willie Ray, Rick's right-hand man. King, we need to get JT to the hospital or a medical center some fucking where." "Fuck that right now. Where the fuck is my money JT?" "It's in the car. They didn't take any of it. It's all in the stash box in the trunk." "Okay. Okay. Rainbow, you take JT to get some help. I'm going to drive the car and Zo across town and leave it there. Rainbow, when you drop JT off, meet me back here." Rainbow left to take JT to the medical center while King went out to Zo's car to get the money out of the stash box. He opened the trunk and saw that the stash box had been opened. The lock was broken. King opened the box, and he jumped back. "Damn! Them sick motherfuckers." They had put Zo's arm in the stash box on top of the money. King took the money out and put it in the safe of the stash house. He then drove Zo and his car to dump it. King took it to an empty lot and then set it on fire. The car blazed up as King stood and watched Zo and the car burn. The blaze drew a crowd to watch the car burn. Shortly, the police and the fire department arrived. King stood watching with the rest of the on lookers. It was almost like he was in some type of trance. He began talking to himself. "The house of Rick is going to burn down just like Zo and this fucking car is burning. Slow with everyone watching until that motherfucker burn to ashes." Then he took a cab back to the stash house. Rainbow had already gotten back to the house from dropping JT off at the Medical Center. When King walked through the door, Rainbow said, "Damn! That took you a minute." "Ya, I had to do some thinking. Hey Rainbow, you do know that it's time to end this cat and mice shit with Rick, right? Tonight, when I get home, I am gon' make a call to Tampa to get one of Dee's goon squads out here." "King, I'm with that but damn, Dee's goons them Niggas crazy. They like cutting Niggas body parts off." "Ya, Rainbow they are, but that wasn't no girl scouts that did that shit to Zo and JT tonight." King went straight home; he got on the phone with Dee. "Hello Dee, this King." "Fam, what's up in that fuck up time zone you live in? I haven't been on time for nothing since I been back in Tampa." "Nigga, yo' crazy. Dee look here, we got some Niggas pushing up on us tight. They took out one of our boys and fucked up the other one. I need the whole fucking city of San Diego to know what the price is for fucking with the house of King and Rainbow." "I feel you fam, but me and my hitters down here schooling some hard to learn motherfuckers what side of the street to walk on, but I have these two funny eyes looking motherfucking Hitters out of the NC that I fuck with, but fam, I must warn you before I call them. These are two don't give a damn motherfucker I have ever worked with. You only call these two motherfuckers when not only you want to dead a motherfucker, but if you hate a motherfucker and want them to suffer before they die. Those two hardcore motherfuckers will make a Nigga beg to die before they drop them." "Ya! Ya' Dee, those are the two motherfuckers I want." "Alright then fam, I will set it up. Oh, did I mention these motherfuckers are twins and one is a girl?" "A girl? What the fuck Dee? Are you sure they can handle this job?" "Fam, I told you I fuck with them, didn't I? Besides that, don't let the hips fool yo'." King said, "Cool Dee." He hung up with Dee and laid back on his bed with a thousand and one things going through his mind. His deep thoughts rocked him to sleep.

It's been three weeks since JT and Zo got shot, and it's also the day the twins hit town. King and Rainbow were going to have a meeting with them later that night once the twins get settled. King and Rainbow went to Capital Grill where the Twins wanted to meet. When they pulled up to the restaurant, they felt underdressed, and somewhat intimidated by how upscale the restaurant was. Rainbow said, "Damn King, I lived in San Diego all my life. I had no idea this restaurant even exists."

"Ya, bro, me neither." Pulling up to the valet, the well-dressed valets opened the doors of Rainbow's Bro-ham on the driver's side and passenger side at the same time, greeting both King and Rainbow. They directed them inside to the host. As they got to the door of the restaurant, they heard someone yelling. "Boss! Boss!" They turned to look. It was JT. Rainbow had invited him along to meet the twins. When he got closer, they greeted each other. King asked about his shoulder that was still in a sling before they all walked in. "The White party please," King said to the hostess. "Mr. White is having drinks at the bar Sir. If you like, follow me." The host escorted them to the bar where Tony and a group of goddesses were standing. The women looked like they came right off the pages of Hustler or Playboy magazine. Standing in the middle of these beautiful women was a tall Nigga, six foot five. He had a large muscular body frame, brown skin with curly hair. Right then, King understood Dee's earlier comment, "Them two funny eyes looking motherfuckers". This Nigga's eye was a funny color; when you look at him in the face his eyes draw your attention. This Nigga and John Belk, the owner of Belk Department Stores had to be best friends. He had on every brand name Belk sold; Prada shoes, Gucci slacks and belt, Fendi watch. Even the shirt and jacket were bad as hell. You didn't have to tell this motherfucker he was a bad nigga. He knew it and displayed it. King called out to get Tony's attention. "Tony, hey how are you? I'm King. This is my partner, my family, Rainbow, this Nigga here is JT, our right-hand man." "I'm Tony White aka 'The Twin'. Let's go find my twin so we can chop it up." They all walked toward the cigar lounge, when they reached the center of the lounge area, Tony stopped to scan the room for his twin. He saw his twin outside on the lounge's patio. He pointed, "There on the patio." They all walked out to the cigar lounge's patio. Tony walked up to where his twin was sitting and said, "Hey, sweetheart, pardon me, if you don't mind, I need to talk to my twin for a minute or two." There was a girl sitting on the arm of the patio chair talking to the twin. When she got up, all eyes were on this statuesque chocolate bombshell as she sashayed past the guys. Tony called the guys to grab their attention. "Niggas." They turned their heads back to Tony and Tonya. They saw Tonya and their mouth fell open and their tongues hit the floor. Neither Rainbow nor JT had any idea that the twin was a woman. JT quickly said, "A woman." Tonya paused; she looked at him, took her Cuban from her perky lips and said, "No Nigga, a hell of a woman! Get that straight!" Tonya was hella fine. She was smoking an eight-inch Cuban cigar. There's nothing sexier than a bad ass woman puffing on a cigar. Tonya was sitting there showing off the most prefect set of legs they had ever seen. They were long and thick going up to even thicker thighs. The Versace cocktail dress she was wearing left nothing to the imagination. She had her beautiful toned legs crossed. She was bouncing the top leg up and down with an open toe Versace stiletto dangling from the tips of her well pedicured toes. The long black lace front she had on had to cost a grip. Her Carmel skin tone set that wig off. "Damn, if she didn't have those funny color eyes too." King thought to his self. Tony introduced everybody. "This is Tonya White aka the other Twin." "Ha, Ha, Ha, funny Tony," Tonya said. "Tonya this is King, Rainbow, and JT." JT's mouth and brains was no longer in sync after seeing Tonya. He kept blurting out stupid shit. During their introduction, JT blurted out, "Damn! ma' yo' so fine, will you marry me?" They all laughed but no one made a comment. They all pulled up chairs to sit around Tonya. Tony said to the guys, "Tell us about this nigga Rick." King began talking, "Rick is one of them slick well-dressed pretty boy niggas. He is a smart nigga. As a matter fact, I have a lot of respect for the nigga in the way he run his house, but San Diego ain't big enough for the both Houses. Rick is a nigga with a heightened sense of disillusion of grandeur." JT looked at King in confusion, "Boss what that mean?" "It means the nigga think his shit don't stink, but his disillusion is such that not only does he think his shit don't stink, but he thinks his shit come out smelling like roses. Rightfully so because for a long time him and his brother Black Mike ran the streets of San Diego."

They continued talking, drinking, and smoking cigars until it got late. King looked down at his watch and said, "Damn, it's late; we got to go. Tony, do you and Tonya need a ride back to your hotel?" Tony and Tonya looked at each other before they laughed. "Naw! We good. We brought our driver and ghost with us, ahhh Damn! I didn't introduce you to our nigga Derrick, did I. Derrick! yo Derrick! com' here for a sec," Tony called out. A huge silhouette soon covered all three of them. King, Rainbow, and JT turned to see who or what was casting such a monstrous shadow over them. JT said "Damn! I got the driver part, but how is that big motherfucker a ghost?" "Ha. Ha. Ha. Ya, he is a big boy, but guys this is our driver and ghost Derrick. Derrick, this is King, Rainbow, and JT." Derrick reached out one of his tree trunk of an arm to shake their hands each. Derrick's hand was so massive that his hand completely covered theirs when he shook it. "So, King as you can see, Tonya and me are good, besides it's early; we still going to hit up the strip club." Tonya said, " Ya, we going to see who's fucking because somebody going to suck on this pussy tonight." JT took a deep breath, cleared his throat and swallowed loudly, "Hmmm ma', I don't mind helping you out with that. I'm down with handling that business for you." Tonya chuckled. "JT, you don't have but one good arm. Yo can't hold on to this bumpy ride with one arm." "Ya, ma', but it don't stop me from pushing the big stick." "Ha. Ha. Babe, let me stop this with you right now. I don't care how big the stick is, if you don't have a split, you can quit." King quickly interrupted, "Okay Tony and Tonya, hit us up anytime. We out of here, y'all do y'all." Tony said to King, "We will, you guys will hear from us soon. We will be dropping off a bag so we can pick up our cash." "Oh shit, I hope it's not a bag of thumbs." "Hell naw! That's Dee's crazy bullshit. We will have a bag of Nigga's nuts. A Nigga without nuts ain't no good to anybody." Tonya quickly chimed in, "No, a Nigga without nuts is the only good nigga." King shook his head, and said, "Wow! Aright then." King, Rainbow, and JT walked off toward the exit door. Once out of sight of Tony and Tonya, Rainbow said to King, "Bro, why the hell you didn't tell me one of the twins was a girl?" "Hell, I wanted you to be surprised like I was after Dee told me they were coming." "King, do you really think they can hanle Rick and his boys?" "Dee signed off on them. He said they are the best in the business." "Ya, Boss they are. I've been hearing about the Twins for years and the crazy shit they do to Niggas. I honestly never thought they were real, and I would have never guessed one of them was a fine ass bitch, but now all the shit I always heard about them makes sense. Those Twins have taken out some bad motherfucking nigga. Boss I'm talking about motherfuckers that no other hitter would dare to go for. Damn! They are real the motherfucking Twins from the "Four".... wow!!! Hey Boss, please can one of y'all tell me what color was they fucking eyes? I couldn't concentrate on what we were talking about for looking into their eyes." "Ya, King I'm like JT, I'm scared of them two motherfuckers." King just sneered without saying a word. King and Rainbow said bye to JT, and they separated.

Later that night, Tony and Tonya, with their driver Derrick, showed up at club Cleo's, a strip club. What King and Rainbow didn't know was, yes Tony and Tonya had been in San Diego for only one day, but Derrick, their driver, had been in San Diego for the past two weeks gathering information not only on Rick, but everyone in his house, from who he fuck to who feeds his dog. Them going to the strip club wasn't for pleasure but for business. A few of Rick's top runners hung out at this particular strip club. Derrick went into the club first, to secure a VIP table for Tony and Tonya. Once Derrick paid for the table, he then went back to the car. He brought Tony and Tonya into the club and to the host booth. On the way to the table, Derrick spotted Rick's runners. Once Tony and Tonya were seated, Derrick walked over to Tonya, leaned in to her ear because of the loudness of the music and said, "Boss, them Niggas there." Rick's runners were in the VIP table across from them with three dancers. Tonya called the bottle girl over, "Sweetheart bring us a bottle of Cris, Gold label Remy, and two cigars." Tonya then leaned over to Tony, "Tony, there I bet your ugly ass a thousand dollars you can't get them bitches attention from them Nigga." "Really, you should have just given me the thousand dollars. Anyway, when I do, those Niggas not going to pay your ugly ass any attention?" Tony and Tonya enjoyed being in competition and ragging on each other. The bottle girl brought the bottles of alcohol and cigars back to their table as Tony walked over to Rick's runners' table. He spoke to them, "Hey guys, what's up? Look over there; I came over because my sister wants to meet y'all Niggas. She wants y'all to come over to have a drink with her." The guys looked over at Tonya. "Damn, you mean that bad motherfucker right there?" "Yes, her right there." "Hell ya. We'll have a drink with her." "I'm gon' stay here to hold y'all table down. With these three fine ass women."

Rick's runners grabbed a bottle of crown from their table and headed to Tonya's table. Tonya introduced herself. "Hi, I'm Tonya. I am new in town and don't know nobody. I been bored hanging with my brother all night, but I want to have some fun; you guys look like the real ballers in here." One of Rick's boys jumped up, he spoke before the others had a chance to say anything. "Hell Ya' baby girl, we are ballers, well at least I am. These two Niggas here work fo' me. I'm the Boss." "Oh really.... yes, I can tell you look like you the Boss. Look at those big broad shoulders, muscular arms and that's an awfully large print in the front of them slacks. You don't mind if I smoke a cigar, do you?" "Hell no! I don't mind, you can do anything you want." Tonya told them, "Call some dancers over here guys, let's party. Mr. Boss man, I want you to know that it don't take much to get me drunk, so do you got me if I do? My brother is busy over there at your table with those girls; he won't be paying me any attention." "Baby girl, you damn straight I got you. Y'all Niggas get them girls over here. Here you go, Baby girl, have another drink of this Cristal you got right here."

After about forty minutes, the runner saw that Tonya's glass was empty again; he was pushing drinks on her. "Tonya, your glass is empty again. Here baby girl, have another drink." "No, I better not. Mr. Boss man, are you trying to get me drunk? You are, aren't you?" "No, but if you do, don't worry I got you." "I am already feeling the drinks I've had." Tonya leaned forward toward him with her hand rubbing up and down his thigh. She giggled. "Ahh I'm bout drunk, but you know what, you are a real Boss. I can tell and I like you. Do you like me?" "Hell ya! I do." "You sure? Cause you haven't attempted to touch me or nothing. You don't think I'm pretty?" "Baby girl', you the baddest bitch ooooh!! I'm sorry the baddest woman I ever seen in my life." "Then are you scared of pussy or something?" "Hell, no I'm not." Tonya put both of his hands between her thighs and squeezed her thighs together tightly on his hands. She knew that she had him going by the raised bulge in his slacks. She leaned forward once again and whispered into his ear, "Ooh these drinks got me. I'm telling you they really got me. Guess what? They got me horny as hell. I want to fuck, do you want to fuck me?" "Hell ya! I do." "You have a car here?" "Yes, but I have these Niggas here with me." "We can just go out for a few minutes then come right back. That way my brother won't miss me." "I'm good with that Baby girl. Let's go do this." The runner told his boys to stay there that he would be right back. Tonya picked up her Gucci bag, swung it over her shoulder as she unsteadily walked out leaning on the runner to steady herself. Shortly, Derrick followed them out as Tony watched them leave, he then slowly walked out behind Derrick. The runner opened the car door for Tonya. Tonya got in and by design, lifting up what was already an extremely short dress. As the dress rose revealing her pantiles honey pot, the runner couldn't believe what was happening to him. He thought to himself, "This bad ass woman that's not a stripper going to fuck me in the car and it's gon' cost me nothing." Tonya was teasing him, she got pleasure from his reaction to her tease. The parking lot was active with people going in and out of the club and that damn food truck. Tonya said to the runner, "There is too many people out here walking around, drive to a more secluded place." "What secluded mean?" She shook her head and said, "Where there's no people."

The runner nodded and quickly drove out of the lot. After a few minutes, he stopped on a secluded dark side street. Tonya asked, "Baby, can I see it?" "Hell ya, you can see it." The runner quickly began to unzip his slacks when Tonya said, "No. No. Baby not in here. Come around on this side of the car, stand in front of me." The runner jumped out of the car and went to the passenger side, he opened the car door. Tonya widely stepped one leg out of the car, separating her legs, giving her honey pot to the moon light. The runner stood looking and shaking as if he was suddenly struck with Parkinson's as he excitedly unbuckled his slacks. Then he whipped it out. He was so focused on Tonya and what he thought was about to happen that he didn't see this giant of a man walk up beside him. Tonya looked up at Derrick and said, "Get this stupid piss ant out my face." Derrick grabbed the runner. Tonya reached back into the car; she grabbed the keys from the ignition, stood up, and threw the keys into the darkness. She looked at him as she walked away, "The big Boss man hmmm." "No. No. Not me. Please no, I'm not no Boss. I work for somebody." While the runner continued to beg, Tony stepped up into the illumination of the car interior light with a three-inch serrated knife wearing surgical gloves. Seeing this caused the runner to start crying like the little bitch that he was. "Shut this bitch Nigga up." Derrick held his hand over the runner's mouth as he screamed in pure pain and horror. Tony castrated the runner, and he bled like a stuck hog. Derrick then threw the runner back into his car and closed the door knowing that he would bleed to death before he could get any help. Tony got back into their car where Tonya was sitting waiting. Derrick got in and they drove off.

The next day, Derrick, Tony, and Tonya were to meet for an early dinner in the hotel's restaurant. Derrick came late because of double checking on information he had gotten about who Rick's bitch was. When he got to the restaurant, Tony and Tonya were already eating. Tonya asked Derrick, "Where were you? Everything cool?" "Yes, just checking on some stuff that's not adding up yet." Tony rolled his eyes and smacked his lips playfully. "Nigga you weren't checking on nothing. Yo' big hungry ass probably was somewhere eating before you came here to eat." They all laughed as they talked about Rick's Lieutenant Sean and how they were going to put his ass in a box. After they ate, they drove across town to the Red and White Super Foods Market. This was one of the largest grocery stores in the New Town area. It also was the grocery store that Rick's lieutenant's girl worked at. Derrick pulled into the parking lot near the front door. He got out and walked into the Market looking around as he walked from aisle to aisle. After about ten minutes, he went back to the car. "She's in there working on aisle six stocking groceries." Tony and Tonya got out of the car and headed inside the grocery store. When they made it to the shopping cart area, Tony said to Tonya, "I bet you I can beat you down to aisle six." "You on." Tony and Tonya got themselves a shopping cart. They then raced the carts over to aisle six, as they turned the corner to go down the aisle Tony ran his cart into a mac and cheese display. The girl that was stocking the display yelled at Tony. "Sir! Look at what you did!" Tony quickly began to apologize, "Ma'am, I am so sorry; let me help you get this up. Tonya, you help too, it's your fault. If you weren't trying to race, this wouldn't have happened." "Tony, don't blame me because your ass is blind out one eye and can't see out the other one." Tony, Tonya and the stock girl restacked the boxes of mac and cheese. When they had all the boxes restacked, Tony reached out his hand to shake the stock girl's hand to apologize again. "Ma'am, again I am so sorry. Wait a minute, I know you, don't I? Give me a minute. I'll get it, I know! I know! I saw you in a picture the other night on that guy Sean's what-not stand, you remember Sis?" "Ya Tony, I do. You are right, this is her. We had a good time over there. I really enjoyed talking to Sean's fiancée." The stock girl became noticeably upset. She snapped at Tonya, "What you mean Sean's fiancée? I'm Sean's fiancée." "Oooh, excuse me. I must have been mistaken. Maybe they said Sean's friend." "No! No! Who was this bitch Sean had at his place?" "I don't know them like that. We went by for a minute to do some business with

Sean. So, forgive me if I misspoke by saying something I shouldn't have, but I tell you what, you are a beautiful girl. I wouldn't let no Nigga play me like that. You can get any Nigga you want, ain't that right Tony?" "Oh yes, you are a beautiful girl. He doesn't deserve you. You out here working gettin your owe. I can tell you are a good woman and that's something hard to find. I would love to have a woman like you. Some guys are so lucky and don't even know it. What a stupid man cheating on a woman that looks as good as you do plus got a job. See Tonya, this is why I can't find a good woman cause of sorry men like this nigga Sean, they get all the good ones." "Ya Tony, I see what you been talking about. Girl! There's no way.... you are a good one. If it was me, I would be going through my phone book right now calling me a new nigga up." "Come on Tonya, let's leave this woman alone. You have already messed up her day with your big mouth." " I haven't messed up her day. She is a pretty girl; she don't deserve to be mistreated. I helped her out, if anything, by letting her know her man ain't shit."

"Sweetheart, please forgive my sister. A cheating man is a touchy subject for her. Anyway, it was nice literally running into you. We will leave now and let you work." "Oh no, you guys are fine. You not bothering me or stopping me from working. I'm glad y'all ran into me. Now, I know, right?" the stock girl said. Then she began to cry, right on the mac and cheese aisle. Tonya reached out to console her with a hug and said, "Honey, everything going to work out for you." "Do you really think so? If it was you, what would you do?" "You don't want to know what I would do." "Yes, I do. Really, what would you do?" "Well, like I said, I would invite me a man over to my place and have a ball. If Sean called or came by, I'll tell him I am busy. I have company just like you did. Now that's what I would do." "Really, you would do that?" "Yes, I sure would." Tony stood listening waiting for his turn to jump into their well-laid plan at the right time. "Tonya, come on. Stop giving this woman your crazy advice." "Na! It wasn't all that crazy. I like what your sister said. I very well may do what she said." "Okay then, that's going to be a real lucky guy that get to go out with you. I sure wish it was going to be me." "Really? Would you go out with me?" "Hell yes, in a minute." "Will you?" "Will I what?" "Go out with me tonight?" "Yes, I will. Tonight, would be great." Tony got the stock girl's name 'Diane', number and address, then they both said bye to her. They continued down aisle six, then back to the front of the Market, right out the exit door, and back to the car.

Later that evening, Tony went to Diane's apartment. He knocked on the door. It took a minute before she came to the door. When she did, she didn't open it with the intent to invite Tony in; she kept the safety chain on the door. Tony looked at her with a concern look on his face. "Baby, what's wrong?" "I can't do this, I thought about it all this afternoon especially after Sean came to see me at the Market right after you and your sister left. He told me he loves me and that he's coming over tonight after ten o'clock." "Okay baby, no problem. I do understand he is such a lucky guy, but baby listen, it's only eight-thirty now. Can I come in, so we have just one drink together?"

"I don't think so, that would be so wrong." "No baby, it wouldn't be wrong. Remember, he is the one that did you wrong with the other girl, plus it would be an honor for me to just have a drink with you, or is it that you are afraid of me, or maybe you just don't like me? I know I don't look as good as your guy Sean. I'm sure he even smells better than I do. I'm asking that you give me a break and have one drink with me." "No, I am not afraid of you, at least not in the way you think. I do like you, oooh my God, I like you. You do look way better than Sean. I thought about how handsome you are when you ran into my mac and cheese display and you smelled so good at the store, and you smell hella good now. The person I am really afraid of is Sean, he would kill you and me both if he comes and you are here." "Baby, let me ask you, does he pay your rent?" "No, I pay my own bills." "Well, Sean need to sit his ass down in a corner somewhere and shut the fuck up. You said he's coming at ten o'clock. One drink, then I will be long gone by that time. I'm hoping this will be the start of a good friendship between you and me."

"Alright. come on in." Diane closed the door to take the safety chain off. She then opened the door and Tony walked in. Diane offered him some wine. "I have a bottle of Merlot I just opened. Would you like a glass, or can I get you something else?" "No baby, wine is just fine for me, but you do know, it's more about me being in your presence if not but for a moment.... right?" "That was so nice of you to say, but I need you to stop saying those types of things to me."

"Why baby, the things I'm saying is true." "I understand that, but you are getting all in my head. That's what I was talking about when I said I'm not afraid of you like you think. I am afraid that you will get in my head and have me twisted over you as you are doing now. You gon' make me do things I shouldn't be doing" "I still don't see what's wrong with that. It's a free world, and he ain't got no papers on you so do whatever you want to do." Diane walked out of the room to get the wine. Tony was sitting on the couch looking around at all the ghetto art hanging on the wall. A zodiac sign picture with the different sex positions, a velvet picture of Foxy Brown and next to the front door, three pictures that all Black folk have, their idea of the father, son, and the Holy Ghost. JFK (the father), MLK (the son), and Jesus (the Holy Ghost). Tony also noticed that her door was ajar. Diane brought back two glasses of wine. She sat down on the couch next to Tony and handed him one of the glasses of wine. Tony took the glass and took a drink, he then pointed over toward the door. "Sweetheart, your door didn't completely close." "Ya, it's that door thingy." "The latch." "Ya, that thing. It's been sticking for a few days now. I called management about fixing it, but of course, they are taking their dear time coming to fix it. I'll get it in a minute, but don't worry this is a good neighborhood." Tony refocused, he started to do a lot of teasing and flirting. The more flirting, he did, the more Diane would drink. It wasn't long before they had gone through two bottles of wine. Diane became touchy-feely as Tony took a glance at his very expensive time piece. " Is that a Rolex?" "Yes, it's a Rolex Explorer II." "That watch is beautiful just like you are. Tony, I like you and damn you really, really smell good." "Thank you, baby, but I better get ready to go?" "Really already Tony?" "Yes, your man, remember?" "Ooh ya. Right, him. Could I please kiss those wet juicy lips of yours before you leave. Tony, I have to ask, what color is your eyes. I looked into them at the grocery store; you and your sister both have funny color eyes." "I don't know baby. I think they are grayish blue or bluish gray, I don't know, but it is getting late." Diane pulled herself up close to Tony for a kiss. As she began to tenderly kiss Tony's lips, Tony slipped his right hand around her waist stopping at her lower back area and lightly pulled her into himself. As he pulled her in, he began to kiss her back. The combination of wine and their lust was the perfect recipe for a good fuck. Tony's right hand moved down to her pulp ass. He gently squeezed, rubbed, and patted it. Diane began to moan as Tony's left hand moved slowly up her long slender legs through her hefty thighs until he made his way to her clit that protruded through her pussy lips. Tony used two fingers to massage her clit.

He massaged it until he saw her hips begin to move and her moan turned into a pant. Then he took his two fingers and finger fucked her wet pussy. Diane began to bite down on Tony's bottom lips. The faster and deeper he fingers fucked her, the harder she bit down. Tony finger fucked her until he could feel thick silky cream on his fingers. While they were still tonguing each other, Tony took his now cream filled fingers out of her pussy and put them in her mouth as they continued to kiss each other, licking his fingers clean. This only made them more aroused. Tony leaned back, he looked at her, and then the front door, he looked at his watch again and said, "Wow, it's getting late baby. I got to go before your man come." "No, no, please don't go yet. Stay just a few more minutes, besides you can't leave me like this. You started this fire, now you got to use that enormous hose I felt pressing against me to put this fire out." "Okay, if, you are sure." "Yes, I'm sure.... please." Tony laid her back on the couch and slowly unzipped his pants. He thought to himself, "Fuck, I was trying not to do this, but I guess I'm going to fuck up my two-hundred-dollar pants on this ghetto bitch." He got his pants zipped down and cleared his dick from them. Diane grasped at his belt trying to get his pants off. Tony knew that Sean would be walking through that door at any time. A door that was not even locked. There was no way he could be caught with his pants down, restricting his ability to move quickly if he needed too. Even though Tony knew that Derrick and Tonya were outside waiting for Sean to show up, he also knew that anything could go wrong.

Tony pulled one of Diane's legs up and over his shoulder. This separated her thighs allowing him to push his hard throbbing dick into her juice box. By her reaction to the dick, she knew he knew his way around a pussy. He instantly began to pound her pussy with everything he had almost like he had a point to prove. Tony was laying down some fucking. This fuck had no feelings or emotions in it. Although Diane felt her and Tony was making love indicated by the way she kept crying out his name while experiencing multiple orgasms, Tony ignored all that non-sense. He was just trying to bust a nut before that fool Sean got there. The fact that Tony thought that anytime was the right time to bust a nut, may have been one of Tony's biggest down fall especially in the type of game he was in. Tony continued to pump her until he could feel himself about to cum. She looked up at him, and said, "Is it good baby, is it the best you ever had?" Tony looked back down at her and thought to himself, "RIGHT! What's wrong with this bitch? Hell No! and how in the hell would you think you was the best I ever had? Bitch, I'm trying to get this nut before that nigga of yours fall up in here. I'm doing this because I never been one to turn down a nut." he said to her, "Ya baby. It's good, you the best I ever had." Tony put his hands under her ass and lifted her hips giving him access to pure pussy. This made him cum in no time. Tony pulled out just before ejaculation and came all over her pelvic area. As he had his dick in his hand delivering a hell of a load, he felt another person in the room with them, out of his peripheral; Tony could see a shadow on the floor. As he looked at the shadow, a larger shadow consumed that shadow. Tony never turned around or looked up he said, "What's up nigga?" "Was it good Boss?" "It was a nut." Derrick had walked in behind Sean with his pistol in hand, he had it pointed straight at Sean's head. Tony got up from between Diane's legs just as Tonya stepped up beside him. She looked over between Diane's legs and said, "Hmmm! Nice, but Tony, I see you made a mess down there with your nasty ass." Diane jumped up, trying to quickly pull her dress down. "Naw! Naw! Bitch don't get ashamed and hide now; leave that motherfuckin dress where it is," Tonya yelled this with her Nine in hand. "What's all this about?" Diane asked. "Your Nigga Sean is a member of the wrong House, and you just fucked the wrong Nigga. That wild cookie of yours got you fucked twice tonight." "Please! Can I go clean myself up?" Tonya looked over at Tony and Derrick. Tony said to Diane, "Ya, you can clean up. Your Nigga right here, let him help you. Sean come over here, help your bitch clean herself up." "I need a wash cloth, a towel or something." "No, hell, you don't Nigga. Get your monkey ass over here and lick my cum out of your bitch pussy." "Say what? Fuck you nigga!" Tonya cracked Sean across his face with her Nine. Then Tony said, "Nigga can you hear me now? I said clean your bitch pussy up and you got ten second to get over here or eleven seconds before your ass is dead." Sean immediately got down on his knees between Diane's legs. Just as he began to lick up the mess, Tony and Tonya started to walk toward the door. "Bang!" "Bang!" It was two to the back of Sean's head. Neither Tony nor Tonya looked back to see the scene; they walked out of the apartment. Derrick stepped over Sean's body and out of the apartment. Together, the trio drove off. When they got back to the hotel, Tony asked Derrick, "Are we good for tomorrow or what?" "I don't know yet. I am still waiting on a piece of information that I should get tonight." "Alright Derrick, hit me as soon as you get it so we can do this last piece of work and get the fuck off the West Coast." "Gotcha Boss, as soon as I get it." They separated and went to their rooms. When Derrick got to his room, he saw that the message light on the phone was flashing. He called the front desk for his messages. It was the information he was waiting for about their next job. Derrick made a phone call after getting the message from the front desk. As soon as his call ended, he got off the phone and at once headed to Tony's room. "Boss, that Nigga Rick got a girl Zoey and the bitch is pregnant," Tony let him inside his room and said. "What the fuck we care if she pregnant or not? We don't have to pay for her crumb snatcher." "No Boss, we don't, but Mr. King do." "Mr. King who! Nigga make sense." "Boss Mr. King, the Nigga we are working for is fucking the bitch Zoey too." "Naw! Can't be Derrick, are you fucking sure?" "Boss, I checked it out twice. Mr. King and the girl went to dinner together last night." "Damn!" "Boss, what are you going to do? Are yo' going to tell Mr. King?" "Hell no! I want to keep my motherfuckin thumbs. Because just as sure as we tell King this shit and he don't believe us, King will send Dee crazy ass for us, and I don't believe in borrowing trouble, and we don't need to go to war with King or that crazy ass Dee. Hmmm, I tell you how we gon' to play this. We gon' do some of that fake shit you see on T.V., we gon' snatch that Nigga up, and throw him in the back of a van and have King and Rainbow help us with killing him. We will let that Nigga Rick tell King they are both fucking the same bitch." "Damn! Boss, that's some smart ass shit." "Ya, Derrick you go tomorrow rent us a van. I will call King and Rainbow. Derrick stop by Tonya's room and fill her in, also let her know that she can chill on this one." "Okay Boss, gotcha."As ssoon as Derrick left Tony's room, Tony called King. "Hello." "Hello King, this is Tony, look, we are going after that Nigga Rick tomorrow. I thought that you and Rainbow would want to be there when we do that motherfucker." "Hell Ya! We do where and when?" "Okay, tomorrow night. Let's use one of your Trap houses." "Okay cool Tony. That will work. I will close a Trap down for a few days." "Cool. Meet Derrick and me here at the hotel tomorrow night." When they hung up, Tony went to take a shower to wash that ghetto hoe Diane off him. While showering, he couldn't help but wonder how all this mess would play out. He shook his head, and said to himself, "Fuck, the heads of two different houses sharing the same back yard all but crossing swords." The next day, after Derrick picked up the van, he came back to the hotel to meet with Tony and Tonya. Tonya saw Derrick when he walked into the hotel lobby. She walked over to him to get the details on their hit. "Hey Derrick. You picked up the van?" "Yes, I did." "So, what's the plan? Where are you and Tony going to try catch that Nigga Rick slipping?" "That Nigga Rick like to go to one of those massage spas. We are going to catch him coming out." "That's smart; catch him right after he has busted a nut and weak." "Ya boss. This will be one happy ending that won't end some happy." Tony joined them. "What y'all two fools laughing about?" "Nothing! Derrick was just laying out the plan for tonight. You think Rick will tell King they are fucking the same bitch?" "Ya, I know he will, not only that, I know that nigga Rick will brag about fucking King's woman." "That's fucked up; I need to be there for this one." "No Tonya! You don't. We don't need King to get embarrassed about this shit. You being there Tonya, may cause King to become embarrassed. We don't know how King will react. We just trying to get our cash from King and get the fuck out of San Diego. It would be nice if we can do this without pissing King off and him having Dee breathing down our necks. That crazy motherfucker Dee will have every hitter from Miami to Maine coming for our ass. Derrick, you ready to go do this tonight?" "Yes boss, can we eat dinner now; I'm hunger." "Nigga you always hunger." They all laughed and ordered their food. Once they were finished eating and outside of the hotel's restaurant, Tony looked outside of the hotel and saw King and Rainbow pulling into the parking lot. Tony looked down at his watch. Then him and Derrick went to meet with them. King asked Tony, "What's the plan?" "You guys are early but we are going to roll up on that fool outside of the Imperial Spa where the Nigga goes three times a week to get his dick jacked off. We will let Rainbow drive King; you ride in the back of the van to help pull Rick inside once Derrick slap him in the head with his pistol. I will be outside the van with Derrick to drag him up to the van. We all good with that?" "I'm good Boss," Derrick said. "Yes, I'm good," Rainbow said. "Why the fuck don't we just drop that motherfucker right where he stands instead of going through all this bullshit?" King asked Tony. "Well King, we want to bring him to the Trap house and make that motherfucker talk. That way you know if anyone else in Rick's house will be coming for you. If so, we can go ahead take care of them while we are tearing his house down." "Ya Tony, you are right. Let's do this." The guys jumped into the van and headed for the dick jacking joint. They waited outside for hours; they knew that he was there. Derrick had paid a little youngster to fellow Rick to keep an eye on him. They were already very impatient and frustrated when Rainbow said, "How long do it take a nigga to get his dick jacked off away? Derrick asked Tony, "Boss you want me to go in?" Tony quickly said, " HELL NO! Nigga if you get in there, we'll have to send somebody in to get your ass out. We gon' to sit right here until this pussy buying motherfucker come out. Rick finally walked out. Derrick spotted him first, he yelled, "There Mr. Rainbow, the motherfucker is over there. Pull up over next to them cars and let us out." Rainbow pulled the van between a row of cars and the building. Tony and Derrick jumped out of the van just as Rick got to his car with his keys in his hand. He was finding it difficult to find his door lock in the dark with a poorly lit parking lot. While Rick was trying to get his car door unlocked, Derrick walked up behind him and smacked him in the back of his head with the butt of his Forty-five. This dropped Rick, hard to the ground. Tony waved for Rainbow to bring the van. Rainbow quickly pulled over to Derrick and Tony as they dragged Rick half way across the parking lot to the van. King opened the side door of the van. He stepped out to give Tony and Derrick a hand with Rick. Rick wasn't a small nigga at all; it took all three of them to get him in the van. Once in the van, Rainbow headed to the West Boulevard homes trap house. Once there, they all dragged Rick down to the basement of the Trap house where they tied him to one of the support beams. Tony told Derrick, "Slap that fool to wake his ass up." Derrick slapped him so hard that spit and blood flew from his mouth. Rick came around and began to shake his head from side to side trying to clear it. "What the fuck!! Who the hell are you niggas?" King stepped up into Rick's line of sight, "Motherfucker now do you know who the hell we are?" "Ya! You that nigga King the nigga that's been fucking with me and my house, but what I don't understand is why you got such a hard on for me? I know it can't be about that five-dollar hoe Zoey." "What the fuck did you just say Nigga? I'll cut your fucking tongue out of your fucking mouth, put her name in your mouth one mo' gain." Tony was standing off to the side with his serrated knife in his head and wearing rubber gloves waiting as he watched as King and Rick went back and forth with each other. "Motherfucker, I ain't did motherfucking thing to you or your house." "Yo' a fucking lie, Rainbow show this motherfucker I'm serious about this shit." Rainbow pulled his Nine from his waist band and popped one in the back of Rick's knee. King walked up nose to nose with Rick, "Now motherfucker, do I have your attention?" As Rick moaned and groaned in intolerable pain, he shouted out, "Alright. Alright. Damn motherfucker! NIGGA, I never touched you or yours even after all that shit you did to my house. You fucked with my runners and my fucking lieutenants, it wasn't because I didn't want to. If it was up to me, I would have burned your fucking house to the ground and had both you motherfuckers in a pine box with your dicks shoved in your mouth like the dick sucking bitch you are but I was ordered not to lay a hand on you by the Columbians. The night you and your Nigga Rainbow thought y'all was ripping my brother Black Mike. You two stupid amateur bitches fucked up twice that night. One was when you were seen by Zoey, she was sitting in my car that night waiting for me, she heard the shooting and saw both you niggas go in and come out of the stash house." "I knew it, King! I fucking knew it! I knew I had seen her somewhere before. King, she was the one sitting in that car with the loud music playing that night," Rainbow blurted out in relief of something that had been nagging at him for a time. "Yes Rainbow, yes you said it. Now let this Nigga finish saying what he got to say." " Zoey didn't tell me about what she saw until after that night I had to handle that business at Black Mike's. When I let you two Niggas live that night. If I knew you were the ones that pulled that rip, I would have dead both you stupid motherfuckers, it would have been doing you a favor. The second mistake you made; you didn't know who you were ripping. Y'all dumb motherfuckers not only ripped money belonging to the Columbians, but money that belonged to the Guarida de lobo Cartel. The darkest, immoral, evil minded motherfucker in South America. Their fucking name means, 'The Wolf Den' and a wolf don't kill, they lame then pull you into their den, so that they can feast on your rotting corpse until it is completely devoured. So, in a word, you both are fucked." "Fuck all that Nigga. Finish telling me how Zoey fit into this bullshit." "Zoey was my ten-cent hoe after she told me what happened at Black Mike's stash house that night, I put her on your ass to get close to you to get information, but that bitch crossed me talking about how she fell in love with your ass. You might kill me tonight, but you, and your Nigga Rainbow and even that bitch Zoey are marked for a slow pain staking death. So, fuck you, you, you, and you. You do know, I was shoving dick all down that bitch hoe throat of yours way before she became your girl...Right! So let me ask you; how do my dick taste, yo' second hand dick sucking motherfucker?" This angered King to the point of fury and rage. He grabbed Tony's serrated knife and cut Rick's throat from ear to ear. He did it so fast you could see the white meat before you ever saw any blood. Tony was smiling as if he was impressed by what King had just done. He said to king, "My Nigga. That's what I'm talking about, that's how you fuck a motherfucker up. So, what are you wanting me to do about the girl? Do we go for her too?" King looked up at Tony with blood shot eyes and steam coming out both ears and said, "Hell no!!! Don't lay one motherfuckin hand on her. I will take care of her myself." King left the basement and out the front door of the Trap house like the police was after him. Rainbow followed

King out the door and into the yard trying to get his attention. "King! King! How are we going to handle this shit with Zoey? Who did she really cross? You or Rick?" King walked away without saying a word. "Damn it! I'm out here breaking sound barriers trying to get to this girl's apartment, but what the fuck am I going to say or do when I get there? I love this fucking girl, what the fuck king? How did I get so fuckin twisted like this? Most of all, how did I let someone play me like she did? You know what? Fuck this. I'm going to fuck this motherfuckin girl up as soon as she come to the door, no questions asked." "Boom!" "Boom!" "Boom!" King knocked on Zoey's door like he was the police. He yelled for her as he knocked, "ZOEY!!! Open this damn door." Zoey ran to the door and quickly snatched it open. "William, what's wrong?" King paused for a second or two, Zoey had thrown him off guard by coming to the door wearing a see though night gown showing all her blessings from God and lord knows he had been good to her. She smelled of Charlie Blue perfume. She had a glass of what King thought was white wine in her hand. All of this put King in an even bigger tail spin than the one he was already in. Zoey called out to King to get his attention. "William! William! What's wrong?" King snapped back to his self, his anger and voice had softened just from the sight of her. "Nothing. Just nothing at all, but Zoey we do need to talk." King said while scratching his head. "Well William, come on in and take a seat while I go get you a glass of wine. I would give you this glass, but it's not wine; it's only sparkling water." King said to himself, "I don't want no fucking wine." In the past, King couldn't say no to Zoey, but he was about to tell her no tonight.

Zoey had already turned to walk away. He stood there hypnotized by her beauty as she left the room. King took a seat on the couch trying to pull himself together, but he knew how he felt about her and how she made him feel whenever he was in her presence. King began to give himself a pep talk. "King, come on. Get your shit together. This girl has crossed you, played you and downright lied to you. She got to get dealt with." Zoey walked back into the room. She came over to King handed him the glass of wine. "William, you seemed upset at the door. What was wrong?" "Zoey, we need to talk." "William, I need to talk to you as well. It's concerning something very important." "What is it Zoey, but after you tell me what you have to say then you are going to listen to me." "Okay William, I will." Zoey reached over and she took the glass of wine from King's hand. She laid it down on the coffee table. She then straddled King and began to kiss every inch of his face until she got to his mouth. She inserted her tongue into it, inviting his tongue to an intense game of tag. Zoey did this while gazing into his eyes as if she was trying to see his soul. She kept her hands busy by rubbing the crotch of King's slacks. When she felt that they were in tune with each other and that King really wanted her, although she had no idea that King was warring with himself trying hard as hell to resist everything, she was doing to him, but he was doing it with complete failure. Zoey raised her head from his lips while continuing to stare into his soul. "William, I love you more than life itself. You are the true flame to my wick." She placed his hand on her stomach. "William, baby look at me, I found out today that I am having your baby." "WHAT! You are what...having my baby?" "Yes King, your baby." King put his free hand on the back of Zoey's neck and looked into her eyes. "I love you too Zoey, and I will love our baby. I will give my life to protect you both." King pulled her head forward to his mouth as his other hand moved from her stomach to her pelvic area. He softly, tenderly massaged her pussy while Zoey worked his belt and zipper loose; she reached down into his slacks to find what she needed and wanted at that very moment, a physical expression of their love and what best could convey that feeling better than a wet pussy and a hard throbbing dick. Zoey guided his dick up into her wetness and rode it like she was an equestrian. She bounced on his hard lap until she knew it was about to explode. Then she jumped off of it to watch King's cum ooze out like lava coming from a volcano. As she watched it slowly run down the shaft of his dick, she couldn't help, but taste his creamy goodness. Zoey licked the shaft of King's dick, removing all the lava. With King's cum on her tongue and dripping from her lips, she looked up at him, in the most loving and endearing way. The way that any woman would look at the man that she truly loves. King couldn't resist himself in that moment of intense feelings of love and passion but to tongue kiss Zoey, filling his mouth with his own cum. Zoey, had just fucked all the fight out of King. King, now docile taking in the fact that Zoey is carrying his child, he sat on her couch in a daze. Zoey brushed her hand across his cheek, "William, are you excited about the baby?" "Yes, I am Zoey, overly excited." "William, you said you needed to talk to me about something." "Never mind Zoey, it wasn't important. Anyway, how are you doing and how is the baby? What did the doctor say, oh ya! Zoey will you Marry me?" "King, what did you say? Are you serious?" "I asked you to marry me and yes, I'm serious." "Yes King, oh my god, yes I will marry you."

King and Zoey spent the rest of the night talking about the baby and their future together. The next morning King called Rainbow to meet him at Denny's for a talk. King first had to meet with the Twins to finish up his business with them. He met them at the airport with sixty thousand dollars in cash, gave it to them and then he walked them to their departure gate. They all said their goodbyes. King drove back across town to tell Rainbow something that would make no sense to him. Like why Zoey was not dead, why he couldn't kill her and why he's not going to let no other motherfucker lay a finger on her neither. King arrived at Denny's at the same time as Rainbow got there. They met at the front door, greeted and walked in together. The host seated them immediately Their waitress was there to take their order right away. They both sipped coffee until their order came. Almost half through their meal, neither of them had said a word about anything, but not only was a big ass elephant in the room, this big motherfucker was obviously sitting on the table eating peanuts and throwing the shells into King and Rainbow's lap. Rainbow broke the silence to address the elephant. "So King, talk to me." "About?"

"King! You know what about, about that bitch Zoey!" "Watch your fucking mouth, Rainbow." "Wow King, what the hell? I take it she is still breathing?" "Yes, she is, and she better stay that fucking way, or somebody will answer to me." "Calm down King. Looka here King, you and I are brothers. All I care about is that you are good." "Yes, Rainbow. I know. I'm sorry I snapped at you. Man, I tell you what, dealing with all the issues that goes with selling cocaine and heroin, even with motherfuckers that always come for us, it is much easier than dealing with affairs of the heart. I love Zoey, Rainbow, and I know that she loves me too. I am at my happiest when I am with her. Rainbow or should I say uncle Rainbow." "Say What...no fucking way?" "Yes, Zoey is pregnant, Rainbow! She's having my baby and I asked her to marry me. Bro, she said yes." "Wow! King, that's a lot, but bro I got your back. King, for real though, I have to be honest. I still don't trust her, and I will be watching her, but I will show her nothing but respect.

Congratulations bro. I will be there with you every step of the way."

The house of King and Rainbow had become a force to be reckoned with, not only in the city of San Diego, but all up and down the West Coast. This made them a target for every wanna be in the city but no matter how hard of a target they were, they were niggas still stupidly came for them. It's said, "That a dog only barks at a moving car." Well, King and Rainbow were cars that stayed on the move.

There was one proud Saturday evening; Rainbow's oldest child James Jr. was going to his first sleep over. Rainbow's wife Debra Ann was to drop James Jr. off that evening at one of his classmate's home and Rainbow was to pick him up mid-morning on the next day. Debra Ann dropped James Jr. off around five o'clock that Saturday evening. James Jr. got out of the car and waved goodbye as his mom pulled off. Debra Ann waved back at him, she said, "Love you son, have a good time." When Debra Ann returned back home, she walked through the door and into the living room calling for Rainbow. Rainbow was at home with Brenda Ann when she left to drop James Jr. off, but there was no answer. She walked back up front to lay her keys down on the key table near the front door. There was a note from Rainbow laying there on the table. "Debra Ann, I had to leave to go meet King. There were some problems at work. I may be gone the rest of the night but will pick up James Jr. in the morning from his sleep over. Babe, Brenda Ann is next door with the baby sitter. Love you babe, have a goodnight."

Rainbow and King had gone to meet JT and some of the boys at the Sutton Park Trap house. The information that they got was that the cooker somehow burned down the house and himself half to death taking two blocks of their product with it. When they arrived, the fire department, the EMS and police Department were already at the Trap house. After standing around for more than four hours, King and Rainbow finally got to speak with their cook who the police had been questioning. King asked, "What the fuck happened? How you lose my shit?" "Mr. King, yes, I'm alright." "I don't give a damn if you are alright or fucking not, NOW I ask you again, what happened to my shit?" "Ahhhh! I don't know Sir, but it wasn't nothing I done and there was nobody inside the house but me." As the cook continued to explain what he thought happened, JT walked over from talking with the fire Chief. "This wasn't an accident. This was arson. Boss, somebody set this fire." "JT, do they have any idea who did it?" Rainbow asked. "No Boss. They don't, but that the fire was set by a professional." "Let's all go meet at the stash house." Rainbow and King got into the same car. They left to go meet JT and the boys at the stash house. On their drive to the stash house, King and rainbow conversed, "So Rainbow, James Jr. is out for his first sleep over." "Wow, how time fly. What is he now, about eleven?" "No King, he is twelve." "Ya, that is right because William Jr. is three." "But you are right, time does fly. Your son three and my son at a sleepover, and that Brenda Ann is four going on Forty. Mmmh! I almost forgot; I have got to pick James Jr. up before noon tomorrow. Anyway King, do you think this shit we do ever get any easier?" "Naw! Rainbow, I don't think so, but if it was easy everybody would be doing it. I'm going to tell you something that will be repeated for years to come, even famous singers will even sing these lyrics "The mo' money yo' make, the mo' problems you have." "Wow King, that's deep, and the truth."

When they pulled up to the stash house, JT and the boys were already there. King walked into the house barking out orders. "JT, I need you to send the boys to clear out all the Traps. Bring all the shit back here and when it all gets here, I want this place guarded like Fort Knox. Since this will take the rest of the night, most of the morning and Rainbow has to go pick his son James Jr. up from his sleep over JT you stay here with me." "Na King! I'm good. I'm not going to leave you here with JT one arm ass. Ha. Ha. Na, for real JT, you go pick up James Jr. from his sleep over and take him home for me. I will stay here with King until the boys get back." "Okay Boss, I can do that." Rainbow gave JT the address and time to pick James Jr. up. All the boys headed out, to the Traps. Once all the boys left, King went to the room he used as his office phone. He picked up the phone to check in with Zoey. "Hi Baby. How is everything? As you can see, it's been all night and going to be part of the day." "Yes baby, I see. So, what's going on?" King and Zoey talked for about thirty minutes or so. King told her about the fire at Trap house, and the need to clear out all the Traps. They also talked about Rainbow's son James Jr.'s Sleep over. King would often talk to Zoey about what's going on with his business as well as get her feedback on the details of his movement. King glanced at his watch and saw that he needed to go so he said, "Zoey love ya baby, but let me go. I will see you whenever I make it home."

A few hours had passed; the boys began to return with blocks of sugar and cash. They all made it back except one, Tim Lane. He should have been the first back because the Trap house he went to was the closest to the stash house. As King, Rainbow and some of the guys were about to ride out to look for Tim Lane, JT came crashing through the front door in a panic. "Boss! I went to pick up James Jr. like you told me, but he wasn't there. I waited outside for an hour before I went up to the house. I knocked on the door, I asked the lady that came to the door was James Jr. still there. She said no he walked out with the rest of the kids, and that they were all out front playing while waiting for their ride. Boss, I rode around the neighborhood, but I didn't see him anywhere. Boss, where could he be?" Rainbow said to JT, "Calm down. I'm sure Debra Ann went by to pick him up when she saw that I didn't make it back home last night." King asked Rainbow, "You good bro.?" "Ya, I'm good. Let's go find Tim Lane." They left JT and two of the boys there guarding the stash house. Rainbow, King and two of the other boys got in King's car heading to find Tim Lane. They drove for about forty minutes when they spotted Tim Lane's car in an empty lot off Walkup and Sutton Park Drive. They pulled up next to the car. They saw Tim Lane slope over the steering wheel with blood running down from the bullet hole in the side of his head. King became angry instantly, "Look at this shit right here! Damn! Somebody has already been in the fucking trunk. How the fuck did whoever did this know that our shit would be in the trunk of Tim Lane's car?" King walked around to the trunk while the others looked over the inside of the car. When King opened the trunk, there were blocks of sugar and cash lying all over the bottom of the trunk. There was also something lying on top of the blocks and cash that gave King a sinking feeling in the pit of his stomach. It made him pause. He took a step back. He couldn't believe what he was seeing. King yelled to Rainbow to come to the trunk of the car. King opened it so that Rainbow could look inside. Rainbow looked inside. He immediately started to vomit; he vomited up food that he hadn't even eaten. It was the bloody arm of a child, but the question was whose child's arm, was it? King and Rainbow shoved the blocks and cash into a bag. They hurried back to the stash house. Rainbow jumped out of Kings car into his own car to rush home. When Rainbow got home, he ran into the house almost knocking the front door off its hinges, an action that brought Debra Ann running downstairs and into the foyer where Rainbow was frozen in his steps. Debra Ann saw Rainbow, he was sweaty and out of breath, she said, "Rainmond, what's going on?" She looked around and behind Rainbow, knowing what type of business her husband was in, Debra Ann quickly became emotional. She yelled, "Where is James Jr., Rainmond? Where is my baby?"

At that very moment, what had been just a sickening feeling that Rainbow had become his worst nightmare. He couldn't do anything. His whole body became totally numb. Debra Ann was delirious. She was yelling and crying uncontrollably. King wasn't far behind Rainbow after Rainbow left the stash house. So, it wasn't long after Rainbow arrived home that King pulled into Rainbow's driveway. He could hear the yelling and crying as he stepped out of his car. King took a few steps toward Rainbow's house before he had to stop to sit down on the front of his car, his legs became weak. He was overwhelmed with a few different emotions and thoughts. The idea of his godson being murdered, and the slight but real possibility that it may have been his wife that caused

James Jr.'s death. King mustered up enough strength to make it into the house to try to comfort Rainbow and Debra Ann, he hugged both Debra Ann and Rainbow. He said to them, "We are going to find out who did this shit. I promise you and they will pay." "King, who and how, what kind of person would come for a child? King please can you leave now to let Debra Ann and me be alone?" "Okay Rainbow but know that I am here for you. I will come back tomorrow." "Okay King, please just go for now." King left upset that he was asked to leave but he did understand because he was sure if it were him, he would feel the same way. James Jr.'s body washed up in the bay a few days later.

It's been six weeks since James Jr.'s funeral. Rainbow and King had little to no contact with each other and very few words since the funeral, but Rainbow called King wanting to meet with him at Denny's. King was happy to hear from his best friend, his brother, his family, Rainbow. King has missed Rainbow over the last few weeks. Immediately King went to Denny's, he went on inside and got a seat. He ordered a cup of coffee, as he sipped the coffee, he couldn't help but wonder what frame of mind Rainbow might be in. Would he come in pointing fingers or what? When Rainbow was escorted to the table, King jumped up to greet him, he was excited to see him. What people didn't understand was that King and Rainbow's relationship ran deeper than still waters. "Rainbow, how are you doing? How is Debra Ann and Brenda Ann? Are they okay?" "Yes King. Everyone is good. I mean, it's hard at times, but they are all good." "That's good to hear. So, Rainbow, I'm sure you are ready to get back in the groove of things. So let me fill you in on the shit that's been happening over the past few weeks." "King! King! No, no, hold up. Slow your roll. I didn't come here for that. I came to talk to you." "Okay Rainbow talk. What's going on?" "King, you know this to be true. I love you like a brother. You and I have been together and family all our lives, but now, King, we both have our own families. Families that we must care for and protect. King, No, No, 'William Saint King', my brother, my family. I tell you this with a heavy heart and nothing but love and respect. I am done, I'm out." "Rainbow, What? Done? Why? What's up?" "Nothing's up. It's just this shit aint me King, it's all you, this wasn't never me. You built all we have; I have just been along for the ride. I was barely holding on to your back bumper. I knew this the night at Black Mike's stash house. I most definitely knew it the night at Black Mike's Trap house, when Rick let us go, I shit all over myself that night, but you, you were cool and calm in both those situations. Hell! In all situations." "No Rainbow don't leave me. I need you." "No, you don't King. You don't need me. Debra Ann is pregnant again. She needs me, her, Brenda Ann, and soon the new baby will need me. Besides King, I'm not leaving you. I will always have your back, but over the past weeks with the death of James Jr. and Debra Ann's pregnancy, my priority must shift. So, I had to put my priorities in order for me and my family. Whatever that may look like, and I honestly have no idea what it does look like, but I do know it ain't the life you and me been leading. This hunting and being hunted and always looking over our shoulders. Naw! King, this ain't it."

"Wow Rainbow, you have said a mouth full, but bro. I gotcha. I do understand where you are coming from. I promise you this, you never have to worry about a thing. I got you and your children forever. Rainbow, my brother, you go in peace. I love you." "King, you act as if this is goodbye. It's not. I still want you, Zoey and William Jr. to come over for dinner on Sundays although it will be a longer ride. I am moving the family out to Compton" "Bet bro. It's only an hour's drive. We will do that as long as you don't help Debra Ann cook." King and Rainbow laughed as they embraced each other.

As the years passed, King became the most talked about and feared man in the City of San Diego. It didn't take long for him to gain "King Pin" Status. Eventually, King and Rainbow's relationship became totally monetary; once or twice a month, King would send one of his boys to Rainbow's home with a big bag of cash. When or if any trouble was brewing with one of King's rival drug dealers, King would send his most trusted man JT and his boys over to protect Rainbow and Rainbow's family. King was still having some of his loads jacked and his men getting killed. As hard as King tried to keep his load information close to the vest, and his circle tight but the load information still was getting out. After King's last large load was jacked, JT went to see King at his home. JT pulled into the driveway, he walked to the front door and rang the doorbell. King came to the door before William Jr. made it completely down the stairs to the door. He let JT in. As he stepped into the house, William Jr spoke to JT, "Hey JT. What's going on with you?" "What's up Will.?" "Nothing." "Boy Will, you are tall like your pop." "I'm taller than Pops. Plus, I can play basketball." "Ya right. I bet you your lunch money that I can beat you with one hand." King jumped in, he said to JT, "JT, you don't have but one good arm. Bring your ass on, let's go to my office. You, William Jr., I heard your mom yelling at you about that water hose at the back door and your nasty bedroom. So that means she is being a female today." "Emotional.

Right Pops?" "Yes! So, go roll that water hose up and get to cleaning that room before she comes and jump on me about something that you're not doing." "Okay Pops. I hear you." William Jr. went back upstairs. King and JT walked toward King's home office. As soon as they walked into the office, JT said to king, "Boss, Will is old enough. Now ain't it about time for you to teach him the game and bring him into the House?" King snapped at JT, "HELL NO! It's not. It never will be. I'm keeping my kids as far away from this shit as I can. They don't know what I do, and they won't never know, and I will kill any motherfucker that come out their mouth to my kids about anything I do." "Sorry Boss, but I got you." "So, what was so important that it couldn't wait until I came into the office. JT, you know I don't do business at my home." "Yes, Boss, I know, but boss we got jacked again for half of load from Tampa last night." "Damn!!! How, when nobody knew about that shit coming in?" "I know boss, that's why I wanted to come here instead of talking at the office. Boss, it has got to be someone close to you, it can't be no one else. Boss, don't get upset with me when I say this, but Boss, the day you planned that delivery was the day that Mr. Rainbow was in the office waiting to talk to you." "So, what are you trying to tell me JT? Are you saying to me that you think a man that I have known all my life, a man that has always had my back, a man that is my children's godfather and I'm his kid's godparent and JT this is the same man that took your ass to the doctor the night you almost bled to death after you got shot in the arm. That man is crossing me that's what you saying to tell me JT" "Well, I guess not boss" "JT you are batting a thousand in pissing me off today." "Boss what are yo' gon' do bout these rips, it's somebody." "You think! Hell yes!! JT, I know it's somebody. I need y'all motherfuckers to find out who the fuck it is. Take your eyes off Rainbow. He was there at the office that day to get me to talk William Jr. into taking his daughter Brenda Ann to the senior prom. JT, what we got to do is keep our eyes open and our mouth shut until we can catch and kill the rat that's running around our house."

Brenda Ann ran downstairs to Rainbow's office. She was excited wanting to show him her gown she was going to wear to the senior prom. "Papi! Papi! Look, Look! How do you like it?" "I like it a lot sweetheart. You look beautiful." "Yes, I do. Don't I... Justin is going to love it too. PaPi, he's picking me up in a limo." "Who is Justin?" "Papi, he's the boy I'm going to the prom with." "Sweetheart, we need to talk about that. Your mom told me that you asked to go to the prom without a bodyguard. Sweetheart, that won't happen." "PaPi, I don't want to go to the prom with some big old man following me around. What will Justin think? I know it will scare him to death. Papi, if I tell him we will be escorted, he probably will back out on taking me." "Well sweetheart, I'm sorry. Your mom and I have talked it over. We feel the bodyguard would be best." "But Papi! I will be the only one there with someone following them around. Why do I have to have a bodyguard anyways?" "Sweetheart that's a long story that happened a long time ago." "Well then, I don't want to go. I'll stay home and die." "Brenda

Ann, stop being so dramatic. You are such a drama queen. I told your mom not to send you up there to that white school. I tell you what Brenda Ann, you want to go to the prom without an escort right?" "Yes Papi. I do." "Okay, then you must go to the prom with somebody that I trust." "Oooh Papi PLEASE." "PLEASE! Nothing. You can go without an escort if you go with William Jr." "Who? You mean Will, Uncle King's son? Papi. No! No! He got bucked teeth, and a runny nose plus I'm older than him." "Brenda Anne, only by five months and you haven't seen him since y'all was five and Six. Anyway, I'm sure your uncle King has had William Jr.'s teeth fixed by now and he has wiped his nose." "Papi, you are being funny. I'm serious. I'm up for Prom Queen." "Brenda Ann. You heard me. So now it's your choice. You go without an escort; you go with William Jr. or stay home and die." "Alright Papi, I'll go with Will." "Good sweetheart. That's my girl. It won't be so bad. I will get you a limousine and I even reserved a room for you at the convention center's hotel in case something happens or if it gets late.

Brenda Ann, if anything goes wrong, you go to that room alone, lock the door, go straight to that room's phone and you call me, stay there until I come to get you." "No PaPi! I don't need all that. I will be home early that night, and I would rather drive and meet Will at the prom. Can I at least drive myself to the prom, Papi?" "Yes, you can, but you have to go straight there and straight back with no stopping anywhere." "MAN! This sucks, that's going to be the longest night of my life." "Poor lil baby girl. You are going to have a great time and you will be the prettiest girl there and you'll win Prom Queen."

It's the day of the prom. William Jr. was in his room preparing for the prom when there was a loud slam of a door. A few seconds after that, William Jr. could hear yelling. King his Pops was yelling through the house from his office, "Zoey, that's not what I was saying!" William Jr. came downstairs just as Zoey, his mom, went into his Pop's office. William Jr. could hear his mom yelling at his Pops. "What are you saying then William? What are you asking me?" Zoey stormed out of the office right past William Jr.

and out the front door before King had a chance to answer her. William Jr. heard King say, "Damn! That didn't go so good at all." William Jr. knocked on his pop's door. King Yelled, "Come in!" "Pops, is everything okay with you and mom?" "Oh yes Son. We are good, she misunderstood the question I asked her, in other words son, it's her being a female." King and William Jr. both said, "Emotional" at the same time. They both laughed and king said, "Don't worry about it, your mom, just needs some air that's all. She'll be back and I will take her and your brother out for dinner tonight. I will get her some flowers and apologize to her. So, you go tonight and have a good time. It's been almost thirteen years since you've seen Brenda Ann, do you even remember what she looks like? Junior, I will tell you, what if she has taken after her mom, she is a beautiful girl. Son, you know how close me, and your Uncle Rainbow are. Right? So, please promise me son, that you will take care of and look out for Brenda Ann no matter what happens?" "Yes, Pops I will, I promise." "That's good Son, thank you. Now go finish getting your Mack on. Ha. Ha. Je T' aime fils." William Jr. responded back in French as well, "Je t' aime qussi' Pops. Hey pops, I would love you even more if you let me drive your new car tonight." "Ha. Ha Ha. Alright Son, be safe tonight and put gas back in my car!" William Jr. excitedly ran back upstairs to finish getting dressed.

At this point, in the story that William is telling his sons Hakeem and Saint, Hakeem looked over at Saint and then he raised his hand toward his father. Their father William asked Hakeem, "What is it Hakeem?" "Pop, when I go to my senior prom, can I drive your new car, like your father let you drive his?" "What? Boy, by the time you go to the senior prom, cars will be driving themselves." "Ya right pops," Hakeem said. "After all I have told you and your brother, the only question you have is about driving my car to the senior prom?" William shook his head and said, "Alright, where was I? Oooh ya. Me getting ready for the prom." William started to continue with the story when Saint yelled out, "Pop, I do have a question." "Yes Saint, what's your question?" "Pop, you were a boogie nose, ill pop?" Everyone started to laugh, even William and Brenda laughed. William stopped laughing, he said, "Ha. Ha. Funny! Anyone else got anymore crazy questions or corny jokes?" William continued telling Hakeem and Saint about Brenda and his family.

Brenda was in her room unsuccessfully trying to do her hair when she began to scream at the top of her voice, "Ma'! ma'! ma'! WHERE ARE YOU MA'!!!'?" Brenda Ann went through the house screaming and looking for her mother. Debra Ann stepped out of the kitchen. She looked down the hall at her crazy screaming child and said, "Brenda Ann!! Is someone dead or dying? If not, why are you screaming?" "Mom, my hair! Look at it, I can't get it right." "Brenda Ann, go up to your room. I'm coming. And please stop all that screaming." Rainbow came out of his office as Brenda Ann was heading back up to her room. Rainbow asked Debra Ann, "What's wrong now with our resident diva?" "No James Rainmond, our resident prom queen," Debra Ann said as she curtseyed. Debra Ann and

Rainbow laughed at her gesture. Debra Ann said, "I tell you what James Rainmond, I will be glad when this night is over. That daughter of yours…" "Oh, now she, my daughter?" "Yes, James Rainmond your daughter, you have that girl spoiled to death. She has worn me out and gotten on my last nerve." "Oh, poor Debra Ann. Ha. Ha." Debra Ann playfully pushed Rainbow away from her. "Stop it. I'm serious James Rainmond." "Alright baby, I know. I know. I tell you what, I will take you out to dinner tonight." "You forgot about your son, didn't you? What are we going to do with Matthew for the night?" "Honey, give me a little credit, I didn't forget about him. Since JT is not going with Brenda Ann tonight, he can stay here with Matthew. You know how much JT likes playing with Matthew." "Yes, JT is a big kid." "Right honey. So, I will let him keep Matthew while we go to dinner."

William Jr. had just left his house on his way to meet Brenda Ann at the Compton downtown convention center where the prom was being held. He was driving his father's brand-new 1983 Convertible

Cadillac Coup Deville. The car was clean, and William Jr. looked like new money wearing Yves Saint Laurent and Halston from head to toe. Brenda Ann had just pulled up to the parking Deck at the convention center. She parked as close to the parking Deck elevator as possible. She got out of her car and got right on the elevator and took it down to the main floor of the convention center. Across the huge lobby area, she saw the information board. She walked over to it to see which ballroom their prom was being held in. Her prom was being held in ballroom D2. She walked down the hall toward ballroom D2, as the information board directed her to do so. As she passed ballroom D1, she saw a female restroom sign hanging against the wall. Brenda Ann quickly turned right to walk into the restroom so she could touch up her make-up. William Jr. pulled up toward the front entrance where a man was collecting money to park your car at the front entrance parking spaces. William Jr. paid the man to park his father's expensive car right up front so everyone could watch him get out of it. When he got out of the car, he swaggered across the parking lot as his two hundred dollars Halston Ellie Chestnut Leather shoes clicked against the pavement like they were making music. William Jr. walked through the sliding glass doors that opened automatically, like the ones you would see on TV commercials. The doors made William's entrance even more dramatic. He was clean as hell, and he knew it and he wanted everybody else to know it. William Jr. did everything coming through the doors to get attention but strike a pose. He walked over to the information board to find out where the prom was being held. He got the information he needed and headed toward ballroom D2. When he walked past ballroom D1, he saw the male restroom sign. He turned left to go use the restroom just as Brenda Ann was coming out of the restroom to the right. Brenda Ann got to Ballroom D2 and walked up to the check in table to get her name tag, but she left her guest's name tag at the check-in table for him to pick it up. Then she walked into the prom looking breathtaking. She was wearing an Emilio Pucci long flowing designer gown; Maud Frizon designer high heel ankle straps snakeskin shoes, and a matching designer clutch. She knew she looked every bit as gorgeous as those T.V. models and that there was nothing that could make her night go wrong except her guest, the bucked teeth, runny nose boy that not only would embarrass her but ruin her chances of winning Prom Queen. "Why didn't I tell my father I would stay home and die because that's what I want to do right now," she thought to herself. As Brenda Ann was in a corner pouting, a commotion was going on at the front of the ballroom. This drew her mind away from her thoughts and she went closer, trying to see what was happening, but she was still too far back. She inched even closer to the commotion, wondering why everyone was gathered there. She quickly noticed it was coming from where the thirsty girls were standing. These were girls that would take all boys no matter who they belonged to. Brenda Ann worked her way through the crowd to the thirsty girls' side of the room. When she got to that side, she saw there was someone standing in the middle of the thirsty girls. She couldn't see who it was as there were too many people blocking her from seeing who it was. Eager to see who demanded such attention, she stepped to the side where she could get a better view into the center of the crowd. At first, she blinked hard, trying to convince herself she wasn't dreaming. She looked at the person again and her mouth nearly dropped. She couldn't believe her eyes. "Why does this person look so much like Uncle King, a man that I have always thought was a handsome man?" she asked herself. William Jr. looks just like his father. He had his father's big broad shoulders, tallness and was just as hella fine. Brenda Ann pushed her way through the sea of thirsty girls to get into William Jr.'s line of sight. When William Jr. saw her, he gently walked away from the swarm of girls swooning over him and toward her. By the time he got to her side, her mouth was hanging open. William Jr. took four steps past Brenda Ann, then he turned around looking at her back. Brenda Ann in disbelief whipped around in Williams Jr.'s direction and saw that he was smiling. "You thought I didn't remember you, didn't you? How can I ever forget the little bossy girl that always reminded me that she was five months older than me, and I had to do what she says because she was the oldest. I also remember we had to play every game you wanted to play and went everywhere you wanted to go all because you were the oldest. Brenda Ann, Uncle Rainbow's little spoiled brat." "William Jr., the little buck teeth, runny nose boy." "Are my teeth still bucked and is my nose still runny?" "No, it's not. You look good." "So do you Brenda Ann. It's been a long time Brenda Ann, let's go and dance." "Yes, we can only if you call me Brenda." "Okay then, like when we were kids, you call me Will." Brenda Ann and William Jr. went to the dance floor and all eyes were on them. Brenda Ann couldn't believe how good William Jr. looked. She thought to herself as they danced, "Not only does he look like a million dollars, but he smelled like a million." They danced, talked, and laughed all night. The ballroom lights came on, they both looked at their watch and couldn't believe it was twelve o'clock. That meant the prom was over. Brenda Ann and William Jr. joined everyone else in walking toward the exit door and out to the main lobby area. William Jr. turned and ran back to the table they had been sitting at to get Brenda Ann's Tiara, which she won for being Prom Queen. After giving the Tiara to Brenda Ann, William Jr. glanced at his watch again. He said to Brenda Ann, "I can't believe how quickly the night went and that it is over with already." "I know, right. It seems like we just got here an hour ago. Will, are you hungry?" "Sure. Would you like to go get some food?" "Well actually, what I was thinking was that my father reserved me a room here at the convention center in case of an emergency. If you want, we can get the room, order room service and talk. We can even have a drink if you like." "Okay Brenda. I'm good with that." Brenda Ann went to the front desk to pick up her room key, then they both went up to the room. They ordered half of the stuff on the late-night room service menu. It was like Brenda Ann and William Jr. not only had known each other all their life, but there was a connection as if they had been together their whole life. Brenda Ann asked William Jr., "Will, do you believe in love at first sight?" "I don't know. I never thought about it until now that you asked." "Will, I have had the best time of my life, and I don't want this feeling to ever go away. It's like you have been my best friend all my life. I can't explain what I'm trying to say, so I know I sound silly, don't I?" "No, Brenda, you don't, at least I don't think so, but of course I have had a crush on you forever even though you didn't do anything but pick on me." "I know I was so mean to you, wasn't I?" "Yes, you were, but I will get over it one of these days." "How about I help you get over it by kissing your nose and kissing your mouth." "That sure will help." William Jr. didn't know how he felt. He has had his share of sex for an eighteen-year-old, but somehow the feelings he got when she kissed him, or he touched her was different from any other times that he has been with a girl. Her kisses felt so much better, so much more tender, and so much more loving. As Brenda Ann has always done since she and William Jr. were kids, she took control. Within seconds, her kisses became so much more; it was breath taking as she slid her tongue into his mouth. She kissed him like kissing was going out of style. Brenda Ann pulled her head back to look into his eyes. She stared at him in the eyes for a full two minutes without saying a word. This happened while William Jr. was trying to process the way he was feeling. Brenda Ann broke her stare as well as her silence to say to William Jr., "I asked you about love at first sight Will, because as little as I know about love, I know that I love you. I knew it when you walked toward me in the ballroom; it felt like there was something that I had been missing in my life that kept me from being happy and you just walking into the room and filled it with joy." She rose up from the couch where they were sitting, walked over to the bed, while gathering her long gown up in her hands and exposing her legs as she did so. She sat down on the edge of the bed and then she sent a personal invite to William Jr. by fanning her legs open and closed. This was an invitation that William Jr. could not and was not going to turn it down. As he rose up to walk toward the bed, there was a knock at the door. William Jr. turned and went to the door to answer it. It was the food that they ordered. He pulled the food cart into the room, he tipped the server, and sent him on his way. With his back still turned to Brenda Ann, he looked at the food cart, with all the food they had ordered and said, "Brenda, are you still hungry?" "Yes, I am, but not for food." He turned to look at her and saw an undressed prom queen, sitting on the edge of the bed showing off God's perfection. An athletic body, long legs and an ass to kill for, she was sitting on the bed reinforcing her earlier invitation for him to join her by finger popping her clit with her index finger. This attractive invitation set William Jr. thinking, "Wow! Why do I have this feeling in the pit of my stomach like I was a virgin and never done this before? Why does my excitement feel like fear? Most of all, why is it that this beautiful girl is sitting on the bed in front of me, booty butt naked and playing in her pussy, begging me to come over to her, but my legs won't move, nor will my dick? It has not moved one inch since she started playing with herself. Any other time with any other girl, if a light breeze had hit it, it would get hard as a brick, but tonight, it won't even jump. It has hidden its head like a turtle does when it's scared. Am I scared of Brenda or maybe even intimidated by her? I may have to concede to Brenda's thoughts of love at first sight. That is the only thing that would explain the butterflies in my stomach, my sweaty palms and the failed erection." William Jr. stood still beside the food cart where his legs refused to work. Right then and there was where he decided to answer Brenda Ann's question about love at first sight. "Brenda, you know the question you asked me earlier tonight about if I believed in love at first sight or not? Well, yes I do because I love you and I mean that from the pit of my stomach as well as my heart." William Jr. could see tears gathering in the wells of Brenda Ann's eyes and for some reason, after he revealed this revelation of his feelings to her, his legs began to work. He didn't have the butterflies anymore and his dick was so hard it was throbbing to the point that it hurt. William Jr. made it over to Brenda Ann on the bed and began to softly kiss her moist lips until he had her whole mouth covered with his mouth. Brenda

Ann fumbled with William Jr.'s clothes trying to get them off him as he continued to kiss her. She got his shirt unbuttoned, his belt unbuckled, allowing his pants to drop to the floor revealing his Halston under shorts with an impressive bulge in the front of them. As her attention was still on the bulge, William Jr. took her hardened nipples softly between his teeth, nibbling on them like a Savory snack. A moan escaped her lips, just then William Jr. applied more pressure with his teeth on her nipple and she lost it. She quickly worked William Jr.'s Halston under short down around his ankles, giving her full exposure to his fully erected penis. It stood up in her face like a springboard and she began to massage it. Whenever she would pull it down, it would bounce right back up as a springboard would. Taking her attention away from his dick, she put her hands on both sides of his face directing his head so that his eyes was looking into her eyes. She softly, lovingly, kissed him on the lips. As she continued to look into his eyes she said, "Will, I do love you, and I want you to know I have never been penetrated by anyone. You will be my first. This is a gift that I want to give to you, so, please promise me if you take this gift that not only you will make me a woman tonight, but that you make me your woman for life." "I promise you Brenda, it's you and me from this day on." Brenda laid William Jr. down on his back with the springboard pointing North. She began to massage his nuts with her tongue, licking them up one side down the other. This drove William Jr. insane; Brenda Ann watched as his toes curled each time, she sucked his nut sack into her mouth. She moved to the head of his dick without missing a stroke with her tongue. She traced the out-line of his hat, making sure to only stop to lick away any pre-cum. William Jr. couldn't help, but to think, "Damn! Brenda may have never been dicked before, but she must have had a lot of practice on her head game cause her head is out this world." Brenda said to William Jr., "Baby, I want you to just stay laid back, I want to ride you." William Jr. nodded, and Brenda straddled his legs, with his dick sticking up between her thighs. She played with it some more by squeezing her thighs around it, before slowly climbing on to the dick. Slowly, she navigated it into her uncharted territory until she could feel him in her stomach. She moved around looking for a softer spot to sit. There were no soft spots, everything up there was bone hard. When she became comfortable, she began to move up and down slowly and carefully at first. Then things changed once she was overcome by pleasure. It was as if she was going for first place in spring boarding. William Jr. asked, "Brenda, are you okay? Am I hurting you?" "Yes! But it hurts good." Brenda Ann moaned and groaned in pleasure, "Oooh God Will, it's getting bigger and harder. I can feel it all the way in me." Brenda Ann went from moving up and down to bouncing on it. William Jr. grabbed both of her ankles; he held them up as he thrust his hips upward, pushing his dick even deeper into her walls opening her pussy up. She shouted, "Will, do that again, harder. Will go faster. Oh my God Will, it has gotten so hot in here. Will, I'm so hot, Oh God, oh God I'm hot, but please don't stop. Please Will, don't stop. Will! Will! Will! Oh My god Will, what's happening to me?" Brenda Ann quickly laid on his chest, shaking and moaning. William stayed inside of her, filling her virgin pussy up with a man-sized load. When he pulled out, she fell over on the bed in pure satisfaction. "Wow! I have never felt anything like that before. Will it be like that every time?" she asked. "I promise that it will feel like that every time, because I will love you every time. Now can we eat something?" They both laughed and jumped up to race to the food cart. Brenda Ann and William Jr. talked, played and enjoyed the love they discovered that they had for each other for the rest of the night.

The next morning, Brenda Ann woke up before William Jr. It was late morning, about ten-thirty. "Will, wake up, get up Will! Get up! I got to go. How did time go so fast? My parents are going to kill me. I haven't called them all night. I got to hurry home." "Brenda, Brenda, calm down. You forgot you are with me, your father's best friend's son, they know you are alright." "Yes, you are right Will, but I still better hurry. My Papi may not say anything, but my mom is going to hit the roof if she hasn't already. She will have me washing dishes and mopping floors until I'm an old grey headed woman." "Yes, I guess you are right. I better hurry too. I have my father's new car." "Ya, really when are you going to take me for a ride in it?" "As soon as my mom lets me drive again, that should be when I'm about hundred. That's if she doesn't kill me first because I didn't call my parents either." "Okay, Will, I'm ready to go I will call you later?" "Okay. Call me Brenda, don't make me come hunting you down." Brenda Ann, and William Jr. rushed out of the hotel to their cars, both were smiling at each other as they got into their cars to head home. They left the hotel room so fast that they didn't see the message light flashing on the phone. Brenda Ann had left the keys in the room, so she didn't go to the front desk to checkout. She had no idea that she had a massage. When she arrived home, she pulled in front of her driveway she saw fire trucks all over the place. She began to panic not knowing what had happened. The fire trucks had the driveway completely blocked. Brenda Ann, parked beside the street jumped out of her car and frantically ran toward her house. There was a fire man that stopped her and said "Young lady where are you running to" "I am Brenda Ann Marsh; this is my house. What happened? Where is my family?" "Yes, your father, Mother, and little Brother. Brenda I am so sorry,

When William Jr. was pulling up to the driveway of his house. He saw an Ambulance unit pulling out of the driveway with its emergency lights on. There was a police officer standing at the end of the driveway directing William Jr. over to him. William Jr. pulled over to the officer and the officer asked, "Are you William Jr.?" "Yes I am. What's going on? Has something happened to my family?" The office started talking on his radio as William Jr. continue to ask, "What's going on where is my family."

The Twins

From The "Four"

Short Story

Volume One

Born in one of North Carolina's smallest and quietest towns; a town that time has forgotten. The town hasn't changed much in over forty years. It laid its claim to fame on two things, not three as it should be. One, it's the hometown of "Randy Travis", two, it was the place where the movie, "The Color Purple" was filmed and three, the town doesn't want to acknowledge or even talk about "The Twins." The twins are two straight hard-core contract killers. It's rumored that they have bodied more people than high blood pressure or heart attacks. Other than that, it is a town that when you get old enough, you get the fuck out. The town is forty-five miles or so east of the Queen City, if you leave one of the smaller towns surrounding the Queen City. The Queen City is where everyone runs to. If fortunate enough to leave for school as the Twins did, when you return to the area, you would go no further east than the Queen City. The Queen City is the home to a lot of famous people. People such as actors, singers, authors, pro-ball players, and now hitters. The Twins are hitters with the working title of professional contractors.

Most people think the Twins are a myth. You know, like stories told to put a small town on the map or the ones where an old lady or man with their teeth in a glass sitting on the Mantelpiece. Tell while sitting around in a rocking chair at the fireplace surrounded by children, the story that starts off with "Once Upon a time."

I thought The Twins were not real, that they were just some made up bullshit, until I found myself soaked in my own piss and minutes from defecation, Oops! Mmmmm well not minutes, now with shit filled draws shaking like a wet dog in the back corner of a closet with the Twins breathing down on me. I saw what they did to one of my boys; it was insane. They cut this nigga's nuts off, then they drove him and dropped him off in front of the E.R. so he could live nutless. Who does that type of bullshit? So, this story I'm about to tell you didn't start off with no "Once upon a time" bullshit or any fucking toothless old people in rocking chairs with some snotty nose ass kids sitting around a fireplace.

"Ring" "Ring" "Hi Sis!" "What's up Tony. You forgot how to get home, or do you have one of them trifling tricks of yours out in front of your condo showing their ass again?" "No Tonya and you didn't have to remind me of that crazy shit plus you know I moved downtown to Sky View because of that. Anyway, that's not why I called you. Dee hit me up from Tampa. He got a personal job he wants us to take care of for him. He said he got a Nigga that somehow slipped through his fingers, that the motherfucker got up out of Tampa still breathing. Dee said, "he got word that the motherfucker has set up in the ATL with the money that he ripped from him." "Oh, hell no! Tony, you know how much I hate Atlanta, plus I'm still tired from that long ass flight from San Diego." "Okay then Sis. I'll let him know we will pass. He can give that half mill' to somebody else."

"Tony. Hello Tony! Did I hear you right? Did you say a half mill'? "Yes! A half mill." "Fuck it. Hit Derrick up and get his ass over to Atlanta." "I thought you hated Atlanta Sis?" " A half million dollars' I don't hate it that fucking much." "That's what I thought with your ugly ass." "Fuck you, Tony, that's why one of them tricks is going to be at your place when you get home, and I hope she get your ass kicked out of your condo again." "Tonya, don't say that shit, it ain't funny" Tony and Tonya went back and forth ragging on each other for five more minutes. When Tony got off the phone with Tonya, he hit up Derrick to see how the drive was going as he was coming back from California. "Hello boss. What's up?" "You Nigga, what's good with you?" "I'm good. I am actually making good time." "Good, 'cause I need you to go straight over to Atlanta. I will text you the info. It's one of Dee's jobs so, he's paying a grip." "Good that way I can afford to quit this shit." "Nigga you ain't going to quit shit. Anyway, you could afford to do a lot of shit if you stop trying to buy up all the pussy." "Ha. Ha. Boss! I'm not trying to buy all the pussy, just my fair share. Send over the info boss, Peace." "Peace." Tony was laughing and shaking his head as he hung up with Derrick.

"I know good and damn well this motherfucker not spraying water on my fucking windows. Look at this here, he's gon' to wipe my windows with that dirty nasty ass rag he got in his hand. Yo'! Yo'! Don't do that shit. Motherfucker, if you wipe my windshield with that dirty ass rag, I'm getting out of this car and stomp a mud hole in your ass," Curtis said to the man at the stop light who was trying to earn some change by cleaning car windshields. Curtis had figured out quickly that Atlanta was totally different than Tampa. This was a city known as mini–New York. So, there is something always going on and it's full of crime, stoplight windshield cleaners, homelessness, and hustlers. Curtis ran to what he thought was out the reach of Dee, he ran from Tampa to come to Atlanta for its lure to a hustler because of the peach bottoms, the hoes, the streets, and the strip clubs. Atlanta is big enough that a nigga can blend in and make some real Nigga money. After getting to Atlanta, Curtis didn't waste any time getting into the mix of things. Immediately he settled into the city, he set up a meeting with his Mississippi connect. "Niggas sleep on them Niggas in the Ssipi, they move more dog food than anyone in the south, and that damn Dee didn't know he was gon' be the one to set me up here in Atlanta. I knew if I stayed close to him long enough, I would catch that motherfucker and his weak ass goons slipping, giving me the opportunity to go deep into that motherfucker's pocket. Now I got to get my niggas Lewis and Charles, down here. They are two of the baddest goons a mother fucker can have rolling with them plus them niggas are out of New Orleans. I got to get them down here in a hurry so we can get this shit popping. These Niggas in Atlanta ain't gon' know what the fuck hit them," Curtis thought to himself.

"Hello Tony. What are you up to tonight?" "Nothing. What's up Sis?" "Let's go over to Kings and Queens tonight. I want to play some poker." "Okay. I'm with that. I'll meet you there at about eleven-thirty." "What? Why so late? I want to go at Nine." "No Tonya, that's too early. I'll go at Eleven." "Wow really! Then I'll meet you there, you call to get us a table in the club because I'm going to be in the poker room until you get there with your lazy ass." Tonya enjoyed playing poker, rightfully so, she was good as hell at it. When the time came, Tonya showered and got dressed to head over to Kings and Queens to play poker. Standing in front of her mirror, she slid into a glove fitted just above the knee Prada dress, then she bent over and strapped up her knee high strapped red bottom stilettos with a matching Louie carry all bag. Checking the mirror once again, she whipped her hair, placed her nine inside her bag, and then headed downstairs to the concierge desk in her building. As she walked up to the desk, her Uber black that she had ordered pulled up out front. It was a black extended Escalade SUV; the concierge walked her through the doors, opening them for her. When they reached the Uber, the driver held the SUV door open. Tonya got into the SUV, the driver closed the door, and then went around the car to get into the driver seat. Tonya could see a grin on the driver's face; he was grinning like a Cheshire cat. Looking at her through the rear-view mirror, the driver said,

"Good evening, ma'am, if you don't mind me saying, you are a beautiful woman and you look good tonight." Tonya said, "Thank you" and she put her ear buds in her ears to politely ignore him.

"I want this motherfucker to drive! This is an Uber black which mean he has no business talking to me, so why is he? Hell! I know I'm beautiful and I don't need no non-English-speaking, red dot on the forehead motherfucker to tell me that."

The Uber driver pulled up to the front of the club and got out to open her door. She said, "Thank you", and walked over to the host booth. She told the girl that was standing there her name. The host said, "Ms. White, your VIP table in the club is ready. Would you like to go in now or wait for the rest of your guests?" Tonya said to her, "No sweetheart, my brother Tony will use the table in the club. I want to go to the poker room and could you please have a bottle of Remy Martin Black with a setup, and two of your hand rolled cognac-soaked Cuban cigars sent to me there.

The host signaled to the girl at the VIP door. The girl came down to the host booth to escort Tonya to the poker room. When Tonya walked through the entrance door and down through the club, you would have thought that "Sza", or somebody just walked into the building. She turned heads of men and women alike as they watched her move through the crowd. Tonya was escorted to an empty seat at the poker table where she sat down and was dealt into the game. Over the next few hours, Tonya was enjoying herself, until the man that was playing in the player's seat opposite her got out of pocket. Tonya had been whooping some ass at the poker table; the man became downright indignant and started shouting at Tonya. "What the hell lady? How is it that the cards keep falling your way? Bitch, there is no way anybody is that fucking lucky. You have had three full houses, two royal flushes. How is that shit even possible? You and these two bitches beside you are sitting there drinking on your second fourteen-hundred-dollar bottle of Remy and puffing on those expensive Cuban cigars distracting everyone. Who the fuck is you with your fine cheating ass and what color is your fucking eyes, I been trying to figure it out for the last two hours had me fucked up while I was trying to play?" Tonya laid her cards face down, took her cigar out of her mouth and placed it in a nearby ashtray. She looked at the beautiful poker room girl sitting on the left arm of her chair and at the one sitting on the right arm, she said, "Excuse me sweethearts. Y'all stand over here behind me for a minute." As the girls stood up to move, one of the male poker room attendants walked over to the indignant man who was still shooting off at the mouth to Tonya. The attendant leaned down to whisper in the man's ear. "Sir, excuse me but that's one of The Twins and Sir, you may want to calm down and maybe even check yourself." The indignant man looked up at the attendant and said, "Get the fuck away from me, I don't give a fuck who this funny color eyed, cheating bitch is." Tonya calmly leaned up in her seat toward the indignant man. She was careful not to wrinkle her thirty-five-hundred-dollar dress. In a mellow tone, she said, "I see you are one of those disrespectful niggas running around out here, What? You didn't have a daddy or a man in your life that would climb off your hoe of a momma long enough to teach you how to be a man and treat a lady with respect? I don't mind you disrespecting me so much. I know how to handle bitch niggas like you but disrespecting these beautiful ladies, who I'm sitting with, well that's where I draw the line." "Fuck all that! BITCH!! What did you say about my momma?" "She called your momma a hoe. Now make a move so your hoe momma can come to your closed casket funeral because I'll cut your fucking head clean off and throw it into Lake Norman," Tony said. He had been in the room long enough to see what was happening. He stepped up behind the indignant man and placed a three-inch serrated knife at his throat. By then, Tonya was standing beside the man. She leaned into the man and with that same mellow tone in her voice, she said, "You stupid motherfucker, you have a tell. Your right eye twitches whenever you get a good hand. So, yo' twitching eye ass paid for one of these fourteen-hundred-dollar bottles of liquor you were so concern about and the rest of these fools here paid for the other one with their no poker playing assess. One more thing, the next time you call me a bitch you better put some respect on it. It's 'Hella Bitch' to you." With the knife still pressed against the indignant man's Adam's apple, Tony stood him up and said, "Now it's time for you to go or do you have something else you want to say?" The indignant man shook his head "No". Tony let the man go. Tonya quickly put her arm out, stopping the man from leaving. "You need to thank my brother and your god for your life tonight." Then she moved her arm away, letting him walk away. Turning to the two beautiful poker room girls, Tonya invited them to their VIP table in the club. One of the girls gave Tonya a kiss on the cheek and said, "Thank you for putting him in his place. He is in here all the time disrespecting all the girls. Last week he kept us with him at the tables all night so we couldn't go to any of the other players. He even won big that night, but he stiffed us on the tip." Tonya looked over at the girl and said,

"Really?" "Yes, he is a friend of the owner so he will fire us if we complain." "You talking about that Nigga named Range Rover, he's the owner, right?" "No, he's not the owner. He just manages the poker room and club for the owner. The guy that owns it is a white man." "Hmmm! Okay sweetheart. You don't have to worry about any of that tonight. I gotcha. Let's go have some fun," Tonya told the poker room girl as they walked into the club area. Tony and Tonya partied only one way, "hard." It was almost time for the club to close when Tonya leaned over to Tony to ask, "Did you drive?" "Ya, why?" "Give me your keys. Catch a cab, Uber, walk or whatever." As Tony gave her his keys, he said, "Really? Walk? Ha. Ha. you got to be joking."

Tonya walked over to one of the club security who was familiar with The Twins, most real hitters, ballers and hustlers were. It was the very reason why there was no response from security regarding the incident in the poker room even though they were there. Tonya asked the club security guy for some information on the guy that her brother had to put back in pocket earlier that night in the poker room. After asking around, the security guy got the information that Tonya had asked him for. If there was one thing that Tonya couldn't abide with, it was disrespect from a man to a woman. So, the stuff that the poker room girl had told Tonya about the indignant man, who is also a friend of the club owner stayed in the back of her mind all night. More than that, it pissed her the fuck off. The information Tonya got was the indignant man's home address. Tonya rode by the man's house and around his neighborhood. This was something that Derrick would do for The Twins once they had marked someone, and Tonya had marked this disrespectful motherfucker. But since Derrick was in Atlanta setting up The Twins for their next job, Tonya had to check out him for herself. This was one that she didn't mind doing because it was personal. The next day, Tonya made a lunch meeting with Shantel, their computer geek. Tonya met her at the Cheesecake Factory at South Park Mall. Tonya pulled up to the

Mall's valet right at one o'clock. The valet opened the door of her champagne color 500L Lex. with gangster tinted windows and 22 inch blacked out feet. The car had a vanity tag on the back that said, "Hard Candy." Tonya is 5-foot 8-inch, with pecan brown skin tone, Meg the Stallion thick, with ass and legs for days, her tag "Hard Candy" describes her best. "Hard" She is a woman about her business and her business is about not giving a damn and will body a motherfucker just because it's Monday, but that goes for any other day of the week as well. "Candy" A woman that is a female in her walk and in her dress which borders between super sexy and just before the line of slutty but never trashy. She is the woman that all the men want, and women want to be. She answers only to herself, making no apologies for nothing. Tonya stepped out of her car on feck as she always was. Her hair whipped, she was wearing a fendi thigh length sports dress, channel strap up stilettos, and a Louie tote with her Nine strategically placed inside of it. Tonya drew everyone's attention as she walked toward the restaurant. This is something that just happens, so it wasn't done by design, but done naturally. She had an interactive walking style; hips noticeably sway every which way. Tonya walked up to the host desk. Shantel saw Tonya as she entered the restaurant and began waving her hand left to right in an attempt to get Tonya's attention. Tonya scanned the restaurant as she spoke with the host. She spotted Shantel's waving hand from a corner table toward the back of the restaurant. She excused herself, "Excuse me sweetheart, I see who I am looking for. Thank you for your help." Then she walked over to Shantel's table. Shantel stood up as Tonya approached the table to greet her with a hug and a kiss on the cheek, as their server walked over to take their order. They both ordered the blackened Salmon with a blue cheese wedge and a cocktail as well. Shantel ordered a top shelf Margarita while Tonya ordered, as you would expect, an unusual drink. This made the server look at Tonya strangely, "Could you repeat your drink order please?" "Yes, gladly. I would like a half of a flute of champagne, a splash of orange juice, topped with Grand Marnier, with a strawberry kissed sugar rim." The server looked up from her order pad at Tonya as if she just ordered a glass of human blood, but the server smiled and said, "Okay, ma'am got it. Will there be anything else?" Tonya shook her head 'No"; Shantel did the same. The server walked away from their table. Once she was out of earshot, Shantel looked over at Tonya, she paused for a fraction of a second before saying, "Damn girl! With yo' bougie ass, it couldn't been just a regular drink." They both laughed and began to talk as they waited for their food and cocktail to arrive. By the end of their lunch, Shantel had given Tonya everything she needed to know about her no poker playing, eye twitching, disrespectful indignant man. Shantel told Tonya, "I found out his name is Hank. He's a wanna be. He ain't racking for real, he is just out their crumb snatching. Getting a hustle every now and again. When he does rack, he gambles it all away at the poker tables. The club owner who is his friend is an Italian man from Virginia Beach. His name is Chris, and he owns a few other businesses other than Kings and Queens Poker room and club. The other business he owns is in Virginia Beach, a fishing charter and a strip club sugar and spice." After receiving the information from Shantel, it set Tonya to thinking. There were a hundred and one thoughts going through her head about how she was going to teach that Nigga Hank some manners. Tonya continued in deep thought even after she and Shantel stepped outside of the front door of the restaurant where she gave Shantel a smooches and said goodbye. Then she walked back to the valet stand to retrieve her car. As she stood waiting for her car, she continued to ponder on what she considered a major issue. "A disrespectful Nigga!" Tonya said to herself. She shook her head in frustration not understanding why Tony let the motherfucker live. "AND WHERE IS MY FUCKING CAR!" She said out loud. Her car was there immediately. Her outburst made her think about her girl Mel. "Hell Ya! Mel my bitch." And Mel is that bitch! Banging ass body and she can throw hands and don't mind laying them on a motherfucker. She will slap a Nigga just as quick as she would a bitch. "Ya Mel! She is who I need to teach that disrespectful Nigga Hank some respect, let me call her right now." Tonya picked up her iPhone to call her girl Mel and at the same moment, she was getting an incoming call from Tony. "Hi Tony, what's up?" "Nothing, I just got off the phone with Derrick, he said that he will be ready for us to come down to Atlanta week after next." "That's good Tony, okay I'll talk to you later." "Hold! Hold! Tonya don't hang up. Tonya, what's up with you? There is something going on. You are my twin; you think I don't know when something is going on with you? You know you can't hide anything from me." "Ya Tony, I know, but it's nothing." "Yes, it is Tonya, and I bet you it's about that fool from the other night, you are still mad about his disrespect and probably madder at me because I didn't drop that fool. Tonya, we are at home, and you know we must stay low key when we are at home." "Yes, it's that fool from the other night, I tried but I can't let that shit go. You are right at home; we need to stay low key. So, I understand why you didn't dead that fool, but I got to teach that motherfucker some respect." "I knew it. I could tell there was something up with you. Tonya, you do need to let that shit go, but I know you're not. So, what you need me to do?" "Nothing, I'm good…. better yet Tony, I do need you to do something, how do you like Virginia Beach?" "I don't know. I only been there once. I went to the Neptune festival, but it wasn't what I thought it was. I thought it was a big beach party, but it was a bunch of white people playing in the sand bullshit making Sandcastles, why you ask?" "I need you to go there and go fishing." "What am I doing? Catch and eating (body that fool) or catch and release (bring him back, let her deal with him)." "Catch and eat. I'll text you the details." "Okay cool." Knowing they didn't have much time to deal with this no moneymaking bullshit, Tony went to Virginia Beach the very next day. He called one of his boys as soon as he hit town. "Hello Greg, it's Tony." "What's up my Nigga?" "Greg, I need you to call whoever you know in Virginia Beach to get me some info on some Italian motherfucker named Chris, they say he have fishing charters and an ass shaking spot named sugar and spice. See if that's all he's got going on. Hit me back as soon as you find out, alright Greg, peace." "Peace." "Greg, Greg, I forgot, also get one of your boys to get me a table at his strip club." "Why didn't you tell me you were turning up? I would have set up the turn up." "Naw, I'm out here working." "Oh, okay cool. I'll take care of that right now." As Tony got off the phone with Greg, he was thinking to himself, "I think I'm gon' make this motherfucking Chris Nigga rack up before I body has ass. Tonya is taking this shit personally. This guy has really pissed her off. So, ya I got to into his pockets before I send him swimming." Tony checked into the Auberge Resorts Collection Virginia Beach; he was going to take a nap before going to the club. It was about two hours into his nap when his phone rang. "Hello." "Tony, it's me Greg, I got your info. That Italian nigga Chris is also pushing that white boy candy." "Hmm, he's pushing Meth." "Ya and he's pushing a hell of a lot of it too. Not only that Tony, he's married, but hitting this bad ass bitch that's his bookkeeper at the strip club." "Okay, she will be my way into his pockets. Cool Greg, thanks." "Okay then. Oh Tony, they don't have VIP at that club." "What the hell! They don't? Okay man. No VIP, wow." After he ended his call with Greg, Tony began to get dressed to go to the club. He decided to go casual, so as not to stand out. Which for him would be hard to do a 6 feet 5 inches nigga with a muscular build, brown skin, and curly hair and funny colored eyes so he most definitely would draw attention no matter where he went. Tony went through his Dunhill 1893 harness hold all bag to find something casual to wear. He went with an Armani V-neck Tee, Prada slacks, Hammetts belt, and G.H. bass loafers. He checked the mirror one last time before he called the front desk to ask that his car be brought around; then he went down to the hotel valet to pick up his awaiting car. After a twenty-five-minute drive, he pulled up to a hole in the wall of a strip club with no VIP and saw there were no valet parking either. The good thing about the club was that it had a decent crowd standing outside waiting to get in. Tony parked his car in the club's parking lot. He had to park in the back of the parking lot away from the club and any working streetlights which pissed Tony off. "This back wood half ass strip club don't even have valet parking. Who does that? Not only do I have to walk back across this long ass parking lot, but I have to park my 2024, S63 AMG Benz in the dark and these Niggas around here look like they'll steal from their owe momma. Tonya better be glad as hell her ass is my Twin. Ain't no way I'll do this bullshit for no other motherfucker. Damn! I just brought these twenty-fours on this bitch." Tony got out of his car to walk across the parking lot back over to the club. He took a few steps before he looked back to see how dark it really was back at the car. It wasn't as dark as he thought. The streetlight of the adjacent parking lot to the club's parking lot slightly illuminated the back side of the club's parking lot where Tony parked his car. Looking back again, he could see how the light shimmered off his pretty black on black Benz and how it made the chrome edge that went around his blacked-out rims shine. He couldn't help but say to himself, "Damn! Look at that bitch, that motherfucker is clean as hell." Tony smirked and continued to walk to the club. When he got to the line of people waiting to get inside, he knew that he was not planning on waiting in no line. He looked around and said to himself, "This bullshit here ain't what the fuck I do." Tony walked up to the club's security and slid the security guy a hundred-dollar bill. The security guy escorted Tony straight into club and up to the bar.

Tony stood there looking around for a few minutes. He didn't see anything or anybody that was overly impressive. As Tony shook his head at the unimpressive surroundings, the bartender walked over to the end of the bar where Tony was standing. He asked, "Sir, what would you have to drink?" Tony turned to face the bartender to tell him what he wanted to drink, but over in the corner behind the bar area, he saw a slender woman, with dark chocolate skin and carrying a nice bump on her. She had a pen and pad in her hands counting liquor bottles. Quickly, Tony thought that she must be the bookkeeper that's fucking Chris, the Club owner. He stood looking with his attention drawn toward the woman counting the liquor bottles. The bartender asked Tony again, "Sir! What can I get you to drink? I'm sorry it is a two-drink minimum here?" "Oh Yes, let me have a double shot of Patron and a red bull, and I would like the young lady over in the corner counting bottles to get it for me." The bartender looked over to the corner at the woman then turned back to Tony. "She is not a bartender." As the bartender was telling Tony that it wouldn't be possible for her to serve him, the woman counting the bottles stepped up to the bar and said, "It's ok I got him. You get the other customers." She then asked Tony, "Sir, what did you say you wanted to drink?" "A double shot of Patron and a Red Bull. Can I buy you a drink as well?" "We can't drink while working." "I am not talking about now. I am talking about when you get off work." "I'm sorry I can't do that." "What you got a man or something?" "That's beside the point. I just can't." "Okay then, but listen my name is Tony, What's your name?" "Why?

You don't need my name." "You are right. I don't need it. I want it that way I at least know the name when I tell my boys about this fine ass girl in Virginia Beach, that shoot me down." "Ha. Ha. Mr. Funny Man. My name is Tammy, but everybody calls me Tam, anyway I didn't turn you down. I told you I couldn't go out for a drink after work. I don't get off until three o'clock in the morning. I don't drink at that time of the morning." "You are right Ms. Tammy." "You can call me Tam." "No, I will call you Tammy. I don't want to call you what everyone else calls you. As I was saying, you are right and you made a great point that it is too late or early for a drink, so I apologize. So, let me try again. How about going to lunch with me tomorrow once you are up moving around? You can name the place." "Now, that I can do." As Tony and Tammy stood at the bar talking, Tammy waved at a group of dancers that was standing near the stage across the room. Tony turned his head to see who she was waving at. Tammy saw that he looked, so she quickly said, "That's my younger sister, she just started dancing here." "Okay.

That's good." Tony didn't know which one of the girls she was saying was her sister. The thing was that Tony didn't give a damn which one she was talking about. He only looked just because he didn't want to get caught slipping knowing that she had a Nigga. He didn't need her man or any of his boys walking up on him.

"Hello Mel. It's Tonya, Girl, you didn't get the voice mail I left you yesterday?" " Ya, I got it. I was going to hit you back, I had to take care of some of this and that." "So, what's been up with you Girl?" "Nothing, but I'm about to fuck this bitch right here up, if she don't get out of my way. Hold up for a minute Tonya." Mel yelled out of her car window, "Bitch get the fuck out the way. You see me looking at that fine ass Nigga. So, what if he's your Nigga. Hell, he was looking at me first, you awe get your nigga in check?" "Girl! Yo' stupid. I see you still the same crazy ass Mel." "You know that's right! Girl! So, what's up with you Tonya? What's good in yo' world?" "Bullshit, that's all. Mel, let me tell you what happen GIRL! I was over at Kings and Queens the other night and Tony and me had a run in with a disrespectful motherfucker that I want to teach some manners." "Wait a damn minute! Tonya, you trying to tell me that a Nigga disrespected you while you and Tony was together, and they didn't find that motherfucker floating in Lake Norman? How the fuck is that shit even possible? I know you and I know tony, but both of y'all Twin motherfucker together. I am hella surprised y'all didn't burn King and Queens to the ground with that Nigga still inside." "Ya! You know that's right girl, but you know how it is when we are at home, we try not to blow no smoke. That nigga got out of pocket because I was killing his ass at the poker table. His ass got quickly snatched up, but I later found out he is a friend of the owner of the club which he thinks gives him the right to go to the club and disrespect the girls that work there. He talks to them crazy and stiff them on their tips after he keeps them from any other customers all night. I had two of the poker room girls sitting with me while kicking ass at the table. He talked to them crazy. Mel, you know how I feel about a man disrespecting a woman, especially in my presence, but for some reason this disrespectful motherfucker really rubbed me the wrong way. So, he got to learn a hard lesson, are you up for teaching a Nigga some manners?" "Hell ya, I am. You know I can't stand that bullshit myself. What do you need me to do?" "Okay Mel, I need you to go to work as a poker room girl and take that motherfucker for a ride." "Bet baby girl."

The next day, Mel went to Kings and Queens club. She talked to the manager about a job as a poker room girl. The manager quickly took a liking to Mel, he couldn't keep his tongue in his mouth. During the interview with Mel, he salivated like a dog that had just got a piece of meat on a tray. Although Mel was applying for the open poker room girl position, the manager wanted her for a bottle girl; it may have been because they worked closely with him. Mel refused to work as a bottle girl and declined to work there all together. When she stood up to leave, the manger stopped her and offered her the job as a poker room girl, as she wanted.

Mel had been working at Kings and Queens for a few days waiting on the Nigga Hank to come through. During her days working, the manager whom she now know as Range Roover would ask her out. He had already asked her out a half of dozen times. He was a short balding man with a gut, he got women because he ran the club and that impressed the women. Mel didn't give a damn about any of that bullshit, she got and can get her own. One thing about her is that other than dick she didn't need a Nigga for nothing and even the dick part was questionable as long as Adam and Eve continue to sell bullets. So, neither the club nor Range Roover impressed Mel in the slightest. Mel is 5 foot eight inches, and thick as hell, she reminded people of "Black China," but with more attitude and confidence. As Mel was turning Range Roover down for the thousand and one time, she thought to herself, "Anyway, why would anyone call themself something as stupid as Range Rover, hell, his name should be Volkswagen beetle this short fat dumpy fucker." The Nigga Hank had just walked into the poker room. Mel moved away from Range

Rover and around to the other side of the room. She positioned herself so that Hank would notice her. Hank came in harassing one of the poker room girls, but it didn't take him long before he noticed Mel. He tried to get Mel's attention by yelling, "Hey!" from across the room. He continued trying to get her attention by calling her like she was his pet. Mel turned her back to him, she played hard to get. Hank had to walk over to her, he tapped her on the shoulder and said, "Hey Ma' I was trying to get your attention. What's yo' name?" "It's Mel." "Well Mel, I want you to come sit with me over at the poker table. You look like you can bring me good luck." "I'm sorry, I am already sitting with a customer. I came up to the bar to get him a drink." "Looka here ma', I know you are new here so I'm going to excuse you and give you a pass for not knowing who I am." "Is this motherfucker fo' real? I see why Tonya wants to fuck this nigga up," Mel said to herself before she responded to him. "Ya really! Well then, you tell me who you are." "I am Hank, your boss's best friend and I almost own part of this place." Mel paused and said to herself, "What the hell! How do you almost own part of something? Listen here, this wanna be motherfucker. Ain't got shit going on for himself other than the fact he's cute." Seeing that he had lost her attention, Hank brushed her arm with his fingertips. She turned to face him and looked him in the eyes. "Well then, it sounds like if I want to keep my job, I need to be sitting with you, don't it?" "Yes, you do." "Let me take these drinks back to my customer, then I will excuse myself and get one of the other girls to sit with him. I'll be right over to sit with you." Mel turned to go back to her customer when Hank said, "Okay, but hurry don't keep me waiting." Mel looked back over her shoulder at Hank, she had to catch herself. It took everything in her not only to curse him out but to lay hands on him. Mel was just like her girl Tonya, it irked them both to no ends to be talked down to and be disrespected by a Nigga. They both have fucked a motherfucker up for much less. Mel kept her composure and smiled as she reminded herself why she was there, but she said to herself, "If this motherfucker come out his mouth sideways one moe time, I'm going to have to apologize to my girl, cause I'm drop this motherfucker right where he stand with two to the side of his doom." Mel made her way to the poker table where Hank was playing and sat down on the arm of the seat that he was sitting in. Hank instantly placed his hand in Mel's lap and began to rub her thigh. After about thirty minutes of Hank playing, he said he needed a drink. Mel asked, "What would you like?" "No, No! I don't want you to move, you stay right there." He then began to yell at one of the other poker girls who was passing by the table. "Hey, Hey, you girl! Go get me a Henny and Coke." "Sorry sir, I am already getting drinks for my customer." "I don't give a fuck, go get me a Henny and coke now!" "Yes sir." The girl went to the bar and waited on her turn to order her customer's drink from the bartender, plus Hank's Henny, and Coke. She grabbed her drinks from the bartender and placed them onto a waiter's tray. She brought over Hank's drink first; she laid the drink on a napkin and then placed it at the edge of the poker table. She stood back up from bending to place the drink down and said, "Would there be anything else?" Usually when that phrase is said, it indicates the completion of a task and the server is waiting on some type of gratuity, may it be verbal praise or monetary, but Hank, only said, "Next time don't let it take you so damn long." He raised his arm in expression of his anger, knocking the poker room girl's tray with the drinks on it to the floor. The girl became noticeably upset, but she did not say a word in the fear she may get fired if she did. She bent down to clean up the mess Hank had just made. Once she finished cleaning the mess up, she stood back to her feet. Mel grabbed the napkins the drink was sitting on and stuck out one of her arms to give the girl a hug. As she reached the girl the napkins to wipe her tear-filled face Mel said, "Don't let this motherfucker get to you hold your head up." While still hugging the girl with her right arm, Mel took her left hand, went down into her skirt pocket and took out some folded twenty-dollar bills. She placed them on the girl's tray. Then the girl walked away to go back to the bar to replace her customer's drinks that Hank had knocked over. Meanwhile, Mr. Personality's hand moved from Mel's lap to her ass. He rubbed her ass with the one hand, which wasn't all that bad, but every few seconds, he would pluck at her skirt. It began to get on Mel's nerves, she was thinking to herself, "What this fool doing? He acts like he is trying to find something; I know goody damn well this stupid motherfucker not looking for my panty line. I do believe that's exactly what this dumb Nigga is looking for. Tonya told me this motherfucker is married, something really got to be wrong with that dumb bitch married to this fool. Let me put a stop to this shit right now." Mel leaned over and whispered to Hank, "What are you looking for back there?" "Nothing, I was just wondering why I didn't feel a panty line when I was rubbing your ass." "That's cause I'm not wearing any." She startled him to the point he almost choked. He said, "Are you serious?" "You don't feel any, do you?" "Damn girl, you are so damn sexy." Hank continued to rub her ass and play poker; he played to almost midnight. He did pretty good; he won about twenty-five hundred dollars and was really feeling himself so much that he said to Mel, "Come go to the bathroom with me." She looked over at him with a blank naïve look on her face and said, "And why would I do that?" "Cause you are fine as hell, and I want to fuck the hell out of you."

Thump, Thump, was the sound Tony's car doors made when he and Tammy closed them in the driveway at Tammy's house. Tony was dropping Tammy off from their second date. They stood outside of Tony's car in the driveway talking. It was a nice winter night, the sky was clear, the stars were bright, and the moon was full. After standing on the driver side of Tony's car for a few minutes, Tammy leaned back against his car. "I know she didn't! PLEASE! Tell me I'm not seeing what I think I'm seeing. There is no way in the hell this girl with this long ugly ass church dress on that has some kinda fringes, shiny buttons, or what the hell ever those things are on that dress is leaning against my paint job. Who the hell does that?" Tony thought to herself. He gently but quickly reached out his hands and grabbed her hands. He pulled her off his car and into his body as he said, "Come here girl, come close to me; I want to look into your eyes." She abruptly interrupted Tony, saying, "Speaking of looking into someone eyes. I wanted to ask you this since the first time I saw you. What color are your eyes? They are a funny color." "I don't really know, just a funny color is all I can tell you, but anyway, I was saying that I really enjoyed myself with you tonight, and may I say, you look amazing in that dress. Girl! I mean that dress is killing it, and you are wearing the hell out of it." "Oh please, but I thank you for saying so. I enjoyed myself with you as well." Tony held on to her right hand with his right hand and slid his left arm around her waist; he then began to walk her toward her house and away from his car where she had planted her ass. As they walked side-by-side up the driveway, they came up along the side of a gray Dodge neon which was parked in the driveway, Tony stopped beside it. He turned her toward him and backed her up against the Dodge neon. "Here, plant your ass on this car, instead of mine, crazy ass woman," he thought to himself. While she leaned back against the Dodge neon, Tony moved in close for a kiss. He was tonguing with Tammy, when out of the corner of his eye he could see someone peeking out of the house through the curtains at them. He quickly pulled back from the kiss. Tammy said, "Wow! I didn't expect that." "What? The kiss?" "No, how good that kiss would be. Short but good." In his head, Tony said, "Short! Hell, next time use a Tic-Tac or some type of breath mint, it felt like forever to me with your tart ass breath." Tony said to Tammy, "Yes, it was short because we have an audience. Someone is looking out that window at us." Tammy turned to look at the window. She saw one eye looking around the curtain and out at them. She smirked and said, "That's my sister, the one I waved at the other night when you were at the club, do you remember?" "Really! Hell no, I don't remember your peeping Tom ass sister," Tony said in his head. "Oh, ya okay, yes, I remember that. So, your sister lives with you?" "Yes, we live together. My sister and I are close." "That's good; are you guys from here in

Virginia Beach?" "No, we have only been here for the past six years, we are from up top."

When she told Tony where they were from, Tony paused and said in his head, "Nigga Plezzz! Yo' country ass ain't from no New York. Hell, you probably got a slip and bloomers on under that long ass church dress you got on." He continued to talk in his head, "From up top... Really, you even talk country as hell! This hoe country as a bucket of slop." Tony shook his head in understanding to what she was telling him. "Yes! I knew it that's why I asked where you were from. I could hear that New York accent and you carry yourself like a real city girl." "Thank you, Tony you are so nice and such a gentleman." "Baby, it's easy to be a gentleman around a classy lady like you. So can we go to dinner again tomorrow night?" "I would love too but I'm sorry, I have something to do tomorrow, also I have to go in to work about midnight to take inventory so I can make my liquor order." "Okay, I understand; maybe another time." "I tell what, I don't have to be at work, but for about an hour or so. So, if that's not too late for you, we can do something right after that." "No! It's not too late. I will come by after the club closes." "No, don't do that. Come early and hang out. Have some drinks and even a few lap dances. The girls would really appreciate the tips. Wednesday night is a slow night." "Okay then. I will come early and have some drinks and support the cause." Tony walked Tammy up to the front door of her house. He gave her a kiss and said goodnight. Then he walked back down the driveway to his car while Tammy stood in the doorway watching him until he got in the car and pulled off. As he drove away, Tony looked in his rear view and saw that she was still standing in the door; she stood watching until his car's taillights got clear out of sight.

Tammy sighed as she shook her head thinking about how nice Tony was as well as how hella fine he is. She stepped into the house and closed the door behind her, her sister ran out from the back and began bombarding her with a bunch of questions and statements. "Oh Sis. He is so cute; do you like him? Who is he, where is he from, does he have any bothers?" "Girl! Calm down, yes, I like him, his name is Tony, he's from down South, and I don't know if he has brothers or not, and GIRL! yes, he is fine, ain't he?" Tammy and her sister stayed up for hours talking about Tony and how much Tammy liked him.

The next day, when Tony got up, it was after twelve noon because he never got up before twelve. Reaching over, he got his phone to give Tonya a call. "Hello Tonya, what's going on?" "Nothing bro. Have you caught that fish yet?" "No not yet, but I will soon. I have been going out with his side piece. I'm going to have that country bumpkin put me in that Nigga Chris pockets before he falls. It's almost Christmas and I thought it would be nice to give his mistreated employee a Christmas bonus" "Hell ya, I like that bro. I put Mel on that Nigga Hank." "Oh hell! That means he's dead by now." "Naw! I told her not to body him. I want that fool to live with this lesson he is going to learn." "Alright, but if that's the case, you better keep a close eye on Mel. You know Mel, that Nigga's heart can beat too loud and Mel, will clap that fool." "Ya, I know, but she is good." "Alright, then I will see you in a few days." "Tony! Tony!" "Ya sis?" "Oh, I thought you had hung up. Have you heard from Derrick?" "Ya, that's right. I totally forgot about that. He called me yesterday. He wants us to come to Atlanta for New Year. He got us a table at the Gold Room for Jugs big New year's party." "Okay. Cool, that will work." "Alright Sis. Talk to you." "You too Bro. Bye."

Tony laid back down to get a few more hours of sleep. He slept and laid around until seven o'clock, then he took his time in the shower, and got dressed. The scent for the night was Polce and Gabbana. The dress was Armani shirt and trousers, Giuseppe shoes and a Vacheron overseas self-winding watch. The more he tried not to stand out, the more he stood out. Checking out himself in the mirror, he counted, "One-two-three-four-five." He did this all the way to twenty. This was something that he always did to push back any caring feelings that he may have deep inside. The Tony the twin had to make sure that the Tony who doesn't give a good damn about nothing or nobody is the one that hit the streets. After getting his physical and mental together, he headed out the door. The hotel valet had brought his Benz up, he tipped the valet and got into his car and headed for Sugar and Spice strip club. He got there around ten-thirty and saw there was no crowd or a line waiting to get in like it was the other night. "Wow! Tammy said tonight was a slow night, but I didn't know she meant it was a funeral procession," Tony said to himself. There were only a few cars in the parking lot, allowing him to be able to park his car upfront close to the club in a well-lit parking space. He took his time getting out of the car, surveying the landscape. Tony knew that Chris had come back to town earlier that day, according to his boy Greg. He was still unsure what type of a relationship Chris and Tammy had. He wondered how close they really were, was that Italian motherfucker jealous over her or what? He had to be on his toes so as not to have that motherfucker pull up on him slipping. When he was done pondering, he got out of the car and walked into the almost empty club. He went straight to the bar and sat down, shaking his head as he thought to his self. "This is a true ratchet strip club; it smells like sweat and booty. I bet the dancers have knife and bullet wounds on top of all them stretch marks I see coming from under those full swimsuits the dancers have to wear." The bartender walked over to where Tony was sitting, he asked, "what yo' have?" "Let me have a bottle." "A bottle of what?" "Ace of Spades." "Ha ha ha good joke, now tell me what you want to drink." "A bottle of Ace!" "Really… that's a Fifteen-hundred-dollar bottle of liquor, look around you, do you think we have Aces up in here?" "Alright then, give me a bottle of patron and a bucket of red bulls. Have it brought to that table over next to the pole." "Alright." Tony got up from the bar and walked over to a table that was closest to the strip pole. The bartender brought over his bottle and bucket of red bull. When he sat the bottle and bucket down, it was like ringing a dinner bell calling in the hungry workers for dinner. The girls swamped the table, they drunk, rubbed, and grinded all over Tony. There was one cute little dancer that was paying extra close attention, or at least more than the others were, she asked him if she could give him a lap dance. Tony nodded "Yes", a few minutes into the lap dance the dancer noticed that she was arousing Tony, he was given away by the bulge in the front of his slacks. The dancer concentrated the movement of her ass at the bulge. The more she moved, the more the bulge grew. The cute little dancer sat down in Tony's lap, covering the bulge with her phat ass and wide hips. She leaned back against Tony's chest and whispered, "Baby, can I take you to the couch to give you a private lap dance?" "Yes, you can," Tony said. Standing on her feet, she reached down, took hold to one of his hands she led him to a couch which was tucked over in a corner. It had a make shift half wall in front of it. She directed Tony to sit down on the couch. Tony looked down and then around the room, he thought to himself, "Damn, this couch is nasty as hell, but I guess when in Rome." Tony sat down on the couch as the cute dancer instructed. She straddled him, with her knees up on the couch as she waited for the next song to come on. Once the song began, she concentrated her efforts once again on his already erected dick. She twerked, pulled, and rubbed until she felt that she had a full erection. Then she climbed down between his legs and slowly zipped down his slacks with her teeth. Once she got his zipper completely down, Tony's dick jumped right out like it was a jack in the box toy. He had on Gucci boxers with the peekaboo slit in the front, so he had nothing to hold the erection down. The cute dancer was surprised by the pop-up, but not afraid of it. She started plucking at the head of his dick and running her finger up and down his shaft. This was driving Tony crazy, as she felt his body tense up, she bowed her head and licked the head of his dick. This made him jump; she looked up with a smile on her face because she knew she had him going. She once again bowed her head, taking the head of his dick into her mouth. This made Tony push back hard against the back of the couch; again, she looked up with even a bigger smile on her face. The cute dancer repeated her performance of taking the head of his dick and going to work. A couple minutes into the fellatio, she could tell that Tony was really enjoying it. She looked up and asked, "Do you like that baby?" "Yes." She took another pull on the head of his dick and said to him, "You do know that Tammy is my sister." "Say what?" "Tam is my big sister. I seent y'all in our driveway last night. She really likes you." "Girl! You are crazy, you know you are so so wrong for this, but go ahead and finish this time but you are dead wrong." The cute dancer went back down on Tony; she was bobbing her head up and down like she was a bobble head doll. It wasn't long before Tony felt a load about to be released into her mouth. He thought to himself, "I have a difficult decision to make. Should I be nice knowing I'm 'bout to cum and lift her head up off my dick so as not to cum into her mouth, but if I do, I will mess up my three hundred dollar slacks or do I let go of this load dead into her mouth. Well, as I think about it, that wasn't really that difficult of a decision to make. I am not going to mess up my slacks." He let it go she took the whole load without spilling a drop. "Damn! Impressive," Tony said to himself. The cute dancer stood to her feet and said, "That was fun, we got to do that again." Tony was in disbelief, he just didn't know what he was more in disbelief about. Was it the fact that it was Tammy's sister that just sucked his dick or the fact that it was so damn good? "Oh hell," Tony said looking at his watch. He got up from the couch and gave the cute dancer a big tip. He then headed to the bathroom to get himself together. He was supposed to meet Tammy, the big sister of the cute dancer that just sucked his brains out through the head of his dick there at the club at Twelve. Tony made it to the bathroom and cleaned himself up as best he could. He straightened his clothes up, took a look in the mirror, and then walked out of the bathroom. When he got almost back to the club area, he saw Tammy standing in the middle of the floor talking to her sister. He stopped just before the end of the hallway from the bathroom where they couldn't see him. He stood watching their interaction. One of the dancers walked over to Tammy and her sister, Tammy reached over to her left to give the girl a hug. This also gave Tammy a clear view down the hall where the restrooms and Tony were. When she saw him, she grabbed her sister's by the arm to drag her over to meet Tony. Tony didn't know how this was going to play out, but he was ready if it went left. When Tammy and her sister got over to Tony in the hallway, Tammy said, "Hey Tony, I want you to officially meet my sister, Little Angel. Lil Angel, this is Tony, Tony, this is Lil Angel. She is my girl; I look out for her, and she look out for me. As I told you, we are really close." Tony and Lil Angel both paused for a minute not knowing what to say. Lil Angel reached her hand out first to shake Tony's hand. She said, "Hello Tony, I have seen you a few times from a distance. So, it's nice to meet you and see you up close." "Damn this chick is cold bloody," Tony thought to himself. "Yes, it's nice to meet you too," Tony reluctantly said. "Did you enjoy all the attention you were getting from the girls earlier tonight?" Lil Angel asked Tony. "Yes, I did. It was quite the ego boost." "I'm sure a man like you don't need your ego stroked especially by anyone in here." Tammy interrupted them and said, "Tony, are you ready to go?" "Yes, anytime that you are." "Okay Lil Angel, Tony, and me are going to leave now. You be safe on the highway to D.C. in the morning." "Okay Tam, I will. Bye Tony, hope to see you again soon." Lil Angel walked up to Tony and gave him a big hug. She whispered into his ear, "And dance for you again too." Tony quickly stepped back from her. He thought to himself, "If I give a damn about either one of them, this situation would be sad, sense I don't. I find it amusing." He nodded his head at lil Angel without speaking.

Tammy and Tony then walked toward the exit door, as they walked, Tony asked Tammy, "Do you know where we can go get something to eat this late?" "Well, if I would be honest, I would like for you to follow me to my house. We can get something to eat there. We will be there alone. As you heard Lil Angel is going to D.C. after work with some of the other dancers. They are going to work at one of the D.C. clubs for All Star weekend." Tony looked over at her and said, "If that's what you want to do. I am game, I'll follow you." "Although I was more excited about going to your house when I thought of the possibilities of both you and your sister being there," Tony said to himself. Tony and Tammy arrived at Tammy's house. Tammy got out of her car before Tony. Tony quickly sent Tonya a quick text, "Tonya, call me in two hours. Don't talk, just listen to me talk." Tonya texted Tony back, "Okay." By the time Tony exited his car, Tammy had walked over to him. When he got out, she was standing right in his face. "Damn girl! Stand back. Shit, give me some wiggle room," Tony said in his head. Together, they walked up the driveway to the front door of her house. Tammy already had her house keys in her hand. She unlocked her front door and invited Tony in. "Come on in and have a seat over on the couch. Please make yourself comfortable. Tony what would you like to drink?" "A glass of Red Wine if you have it." "Yes, I do, but would you mind if I get out these clothes and put on something more comfortable before I get the wine?" "No, I don't mind, do what make it easy and comfortable for you." "Tony, I have to ask, are you really real? Can't no man be as nice and considerate as you seem to be." "Well, I am real. You can pinch me if you like." "Ha. Ha. Ha. No. That's not necessary." Tammy left the room to change and get the wine. Tony sat on the couch looking around the room. He saw her bookshelf with several books on it. He got up from the couch and walked over to it. He saw that she had a lot of urban novels. It seemed this guy 'Muhammad X' was one of her favorite writers. She had quite a few books of his. While scanning through her collection of books, he noticed one that had an interesting title, "My Silent Loud" which was also by Muhammad X. As he continued to scan, he saw a Steve Harvey book, "Act like a lady; Think Like a Man." When he saw that book Tony, began to say to himself, "Damn! Damn! Damn! That stupid ass ninety-day rule bullshit of his. One day, I'm going to write a book putting women up on true game. I'm gon' name it "Hell, if you think like a man; you better act like one to." Women do not realize two things off gate, one is that Steve Harvey big lip ass wrote his book after he found and married who he says is his soul mate. This book would never have come about if he was still out there hounding. Two, yes you may wait for ninety days before you fuck the man YOU WANT, he may even hang around for the ninety first day to fuck you, but you can bet your bottom dollar he didn't wait no ninety days before he fucked. These Niggas kill me with their instant religion, enlightenment, or whatever in the hell they call it. I call it Holy Than Thou, but anyway, all I know is now because of this damn book, I got to tell this girl I love her to get her to break that ninety-day rule. Just so I can get her panties off. Well in this case, get her bloomers off, in order to make this bitch fall in love with me." "Here we are Tony, your glass of Red wine," Tammy said as she walked back into the room with a glass of wine in each hand. Tony turned to look at her as she went toward the couch to sit down. He walked back over to the couch, as he got there, Tammy reached up and handed him one of the glasses of wine. Tony took the glass and sat down on the couch next to her. He took a sip, "Hmmm, this is good." "Yes, it is, ain't it? I see you took notice to my collection of books. Did you find any one of the titles intriguing?" "Yes, I did. Two of them actually, the one by Muhhamad X "My Silent Loud." and that one by Steve Harvey, 'Act like a lady; Think Like a Man.'" "Yes, both of them were a good read. I learned a lot reading them both." Tammy walked over to the bookshelf and picked up both of the books. She brought them back over to the couch and laid them on the coffee table that was in front of the couch. Then she sat back down beside Tony, she looked over at him and asked, "Are you familiar with either one of these books?" "Yes, the Steve Harvey book and that thing about women waiting for ninety days before being intimate with the person that they are interested in." "Okay, you do know the book, so what do you think about his ninety-day rule?" "It's fucked up," he said in his head. "Well Tammy, I tell you if it is a man, you want and you are the woman that that man wants. He will gladly comply to any imposed requirement or rules like the ninety-day rule, now for me, I like when a woman imposed the ninety-day rule, because I am one of those guys that easily fall in love and intimacy only make me fall even quicker and harder, so waiting helps me to know who I'm dealing with and see if she is really worthy of my love or if she might be a little cray cray." They both laughed at the 'cray cray' comment, then tammy said, "See right there is why I say you can't be real." "Well, my offer still stands, you can pinch me if you like." "Naw, but what's up with you and this pinch thing, let me find out." "Ha, Ha, No nothing like that." Tony wanted to know what she thought about the rule. "Tell me what did you get or learn from the Steve Harvey book." Tony, picked up the book from the coffee table and begin thumbing through it as Tammy, answered his question "what I got from it was that women shouldn't be driven by pure emotion. Acting or reacting, emotionally is the same as acting crazy or as you put it "cray cray." It's acting without the benefit of Intellect, without intellect is the same as without understanding and who want to be in a relationship without understanding." "Wow! impressive I love a girl with a head on her shoulders, especially one that's not overly emotionally charged and fine as hell like you." "Thank you. Would you like another glass of wine." "No, I better not… girl if I didn't know any better, I would think you are trying to get me tipsy." "Maybe" they both laughed as she headed out of the room to the kitchen to get Tony, and herself another glass of wine. Tammy was wearing a long house dress that dragged the floor when she walked. It didn't take her long to come back with two glasses and a bottle of red wine. She gave Tony, one of the glasses, then poured him a full glass from the bottle of red wine. She then poured herself a glass and laid the bottle down on the coffee table. She then walked back over to the bookshelf to take the two books back. Tony watched her walk with that long ass house dress dragging the floor. It was getting on his last nerve to the point he had to comment on it. "That is an interesting house dress you got on and it is really long and flowing" "it look like a house coat my grandma use to wear" Tony, said in his head. Tammy smiled, then laughed as she propped her arm up on one of the shelves on the bookshelf, she then said "yes, I know it is long isn't it. It took me a minute to find it in the back of my closet. I wore it because I didn't want to come out here in anything that would give you the wrong impression of me. That I am easy or some kind of hoe or something. I already invited you here to be alone with me at my house after only a few dates. That itself made me feel, that you would think that I'm easy." "Oh no you shouldn't feel that way. I don't think that at all." "Thank you, Tony, I'm glad that you don't, and by the way this is not a house dress. It's a house coat worn over something like this I got on see." Tammy, had zipped down the house coat showing off a above the thigh length black lace teddy

Tony, sat back on the couch with his eyes fixed on her reveal. All Tony could say is, "Damn ma! Com'on over here a little closer, I got bad eyes I can't see you that good from way over there. "Tammy, dropped her open house coat to the floor and walked back over to the couch where Tony, was. On her way over to the couch she was thinking to herself, "I want him so bad. I want him to throw me on that coffee table and fuck the shit out of me." Tammy, smiled as she sat down by Tony, thinking about what she wanted Tony, to do to her. Tony, turned to face Tammy. He looked at her up and down in a way that made Tammy's clit jump and her pussy wet. He moved towards her gently, seductively and swiftly before she could even catch her breath his hand was under the front of her teddy softly tickling her dark chocolate silky legs. He started at her knee moving his baby butt soft hand up too and through her thighs with his fingers finding her silky wet bladed pelvic area. With his large hand he cupped her pussy with the middle finger inserted inside of her as her eyes rolled to the back of her head. He was doing exactly what she wanted him to do, and he was doing it well. His head moved in close to her looking her in the eyes as if he was staring into her soul. He paused for a second and just stared at her before he kissed her, his tongue caressing each and every corner of her mouth. When Tony, kissed her he was trying to give her the illusion that he was kissing her like he had never kissed anyone else before. He took his free hand and held her behind her neck. He held her tight but gentle close into him so that she couldn't back away. Tammy relaxed her body and submitted to him giving her what she had been wanting from him since the first time she seen him in the club. With his eyes still piercing through her soul he said to her, "I want you so damn bad right now." "I know you can tell I want you too Tony. So please take me." When she said those words, he embraced her even harder holding on to her like she might fade away. Tammy, melted against Tony, with a lifetime of built-up passion. For the first time in her life, she felt like she was with someone that wanted her and not just her body. This was a learned skill of Tony's, making a female feel as though she is the only woman in the world, and that she is the only one he wanted or even that he loved. This is what made Tony, the best at what he does. It's all a planned and practiced act. Tony slid her silky black panties down her long slender legs as he giggled to himself and said, "I know. I know I was wrong. I'm sorry they are panties, not bloomers." Tony guided the panties over her bare feet and tossed them across the room. He leaned her back from the sitting position on the couch. He positioned himself on top of her. He began kissing her ear lobe, her neck and her erected nipples as Tammy, moaned and groaned at each and every kiss and touch. Tony slowly and gently opened her legs, he ran his tongue up and down her inner thigh, left thigh, right thigh, back and forth, up here and down there. He had her body reacting to him in pure ecstasy. Tony took his index finger from each hand and spread her labia open giving him direct access to her yum yum. Tony, licked her clit like it was a tootsie pop and he picked that day and that time to answer the age-old question of "how many licks does it take to get to the center of a tootsie pop." Tammy, laid back on the couch with her back arched gasping at air until wrapping her hands up in Tony's Two hundred- and fifty-dollar Armani shirt. Tony pulled his shirt over his head and came out of his slacks faster than shit through a goose. He continued to lick, suck, and inject his tongue in and out of her wet hot pussy. When Tony, thought he had her at the point of eruption, which was indicated by her bucking and moaning, Tony, began to kiss and lick his way back up her body until he came face to face with her again. Tony, reached down to grab his throbbing dick to guide it into the bark hole of bliss, once he felt her warm wetness on the tip of his dick, he removed his hand knowing that muscle memory would take over. It did just that as he pushed into her sending his pulsating dick deep into her snug fitting pussy. He completely filled her up as he intensely stroked her. He went In-n-out never completely pulling from her wetness or tightness. Tammy wrapped her legs around his torso and clamping them in place around him. She wrapped them around him so tight that when he went up and down, he would lift her from the couch, while his hardness caressed every inch of her inner walls, Tony reached under her Armpits, bringing his hand up onto her shoulders, pulling her down into his self. He was pulling her down and his hip thrust would push her back up. His body moved in and out of her faster and faster, causing mounting passion, Tammy, begging "please, please, don't stop." He grit his teeth as he pound the back walls of her pussy. She could feel him in the bottom of her stomach, but she loved every inch of it, he buried his face into the crest of her neck, biting down on it. His movements became more intense as Tammy, incoherently babble out an order for him not to move, as her body began to uncontrollably shake and shiver. He paused to watch her succumb to his passion. After a few seconds, he went back to intensively stroking her pussy until he felt a warmth rush from the top of his head to the tip of his dick, Tony, breathless shouted out "oh baby, I'm cuming damn you feel so good." Tony, give up the ghost and collapsed on top of her with sweat pouring from his whole body. Tony, laid beside her with their sweaty bodies, press tightly together. She looked at Tony, and asked "was it good to you baby? Was it the best you ever had." that question made Tony, shake his head and say to herself "she was doing good until she asked that bullshiting stupid ass question. Right there is why women always get their feelings hurt because they love to invite a nigga too to lie to them. Damn what a crazy ass questions what in the hell did you do different than anyone else to make you come close to asking are you the best I ever had, hell no yo' stupid ass." Tony, looked her straight in her eyes with passion and love he said Tammy, it was better than the best yes you are the best I ever been with." Tears formed in Tammy 's eyes as she looked at Tony, Tammy, said "Tony, I got something to tell you." Mel, shocked the hell out of Hank, when she said "Alright." "what! Really." "Yes, come on let's go." are you dead ass." "Dead ass come on." Mel got up to walk toward the bathroom. As she headed that way, she thought to herself. "Let's see if this Nigga is a real Nigga or a wanna be bitch Nigga. Hank, got up after Mel, and followed her to the bathroom. He was still in disbelief. "Damn, is she really going to do this? She's ain't going to do it. I know she's not. She better be glad she's not going to do it, I would have fucked the hell out of her in that bathroom, she don't know who she fucking with cause I am the man they call me Mr. Long stroke. I would got in that pussy and stayed there all night." When he went through the swinging doors that was at the beginning of the hall where the bathrooms were. He saw Mel standing in front of the men's bathroom with one hand on the door. when he got close to her, she pushed the door open and said to him come on let's go in. Mel went in the bathroom in front of Hank. Mel didn't look around to see if anyone was in the bathroom or not. She didn't really care. Mel was a woman that didn't think about what others had to say or how they felt about her. Not only she didn't think about it, but she didn't give a damn. Hank, slowly, hesitantly walked into the bathroom looking around and under all the bathroom stalls. Mel said "you happy no one is in here. Now let's see what you working with. Mel, reached out to his belt buckle to unbuckle it. Hank, pushed her hands away and said "No, no I will do it let me do it." "Okay baby I'm sorry you go ahead and do it. I was just trying to help you out." "Well! I got it." Hank, slowly unbuckle his slacks and zipped them down. When he got his slacks open, he put his hand down into his underwear, and got this look on his face of disappointment, or like somebody nun stole his candy. He pulled out a flaccid wet dick. He was so excited that he pre-ejaculated on the way into the bathroom. Mel, looked at it, then looked up at him, and said to herself "this motherfucker right here. look at this bitch ass Nigga all that walking around here like he is the man. For now, on I'm calling his ass quick draw." As she looked at him, she said "that's Okay baby I understand that can happen. Don't worry I will give you another chance but maybe next time it can be somewhere with a bed" "Okay bet how about tomorrow at my hotel room?" "Well, I am off tomorrow, so I guess that will work. My number is 704-777-9311 call or text me where and when" There was a man that came into the bathroom as Mel, and Hank, was standing in the middle of the bathroom floor talking, they both looked over at the man who had stopped in his tracks in confusion when he saw them. Hank, said "maybe we better leave." They walked to the Bathroom door and pass the guy that had just came in. When Mel, got to the man, she padded him on his ass and said "make sure you wash your hands when you finish." Mel and Hank left the bathroom without saying another word to each other. In embarrassment Hank headed for the exit door of the club. Mel had a few more hours to work. When she got back into the poker room from the club area. The poker room girl that Hank had knocked the tray out of her hand spilling her drinks. Walked over to Mel and gave her a big hug she said "Thank you so much." "No problem honey." The folded Twenty dollar bills that Mel laid on the girl's tray was actually one Twenty and five One Hundred Dollar bills. Mel got up the next morning and made herself some toast and a cup coffee. While sitting enjoying her coffee, she picked up her phone to hit Tonya, up. Rang, rang, rang "Hello" "Hey girl" "Hi, Mel, what's up." "I tell you what's not up." "What's that Mel." "That Nigga Hank's Dick." "Mel! don't tell me you cut it off." "Tempted, but no. Tonya, that fool took me in the bathroom last night at the club and couldn't get his dick up. Look like he came all over his self." "Wow! Mel, that limp dick motherfucker. So, how you gon' to work this." "Tonya, you told me what you want to do to that fool, but I want to go into his pocket first." "But Mel, I was told that nigga ain't Racking." "He's not, but I found out from some of the girls at the poker room, that the address you give me was not his house it was a friend's. He comes to town from Virginia Beach, twice a month to do a drop and pick up. I want to catch him slipping before the pickup. when he's still holding his reup cash." "How you going to catch him slipping like that." "Tonya, you already know. The same way we catch every other nigga slipping." "Trying to get some pussy." They both said it at the same time. Tonya, said to Mel, "I am with that. Let me know when you are finished playing. Mel, please don't get mad and body that fool I need this fool to hurt for a long time." "I will try not. alright, Tonya, I'll let you know when I have hit his pockets." "Okay Mel, do that." When Mel, hung up with Tonya, she noticed she had a text. It was Hank, with a time and which hotel that they were going to meet. Mel laid her phone down on her kitchen table to go get dressed. She had some errands to run before she was to meet Hank, that night at the Midtown Marriott on Trade Street. She threw on her,

Victoria's Secret pink sweat pants with matching jacket, and knowing that one of her errands was a mani-pedi she stepped into her Gucci slides and she headed out. Mel had been out running around for a few hours and while she was sitting in the chair at the nail shop. She got a text it was Hank, texting her again "you are coming tonight right, and don't be late." This text pissed Mel, the hell off. Mel can't stand an insecure man, but she hates an insecure man that have the nerve to be demanding. She was thinking to herself "This motherfucker here got to go, fuck the rip. I got to turn him over to Tonya, before I body this fool. I know if I do my girl and me will fall out and Lord knows I can't afford to fall out with Tonya, because if you fall out with one twin, you fall out with both of them. Then you spend the rest of your short lived life looking over your shoulder. I am hittin Tonya, up right now." Ring, Ring.... " Hey Mel, what's good." "Tonya, tonight he's yours. I will text you the details." "What happened to you going into his pocket." "I'm scared I can't hold myself back from bodyin that fool." "I feel you girl, text me the info and I will see you tonight." Mel, texted Hank, back." Yes, baby I'm coming, and I will be on time. You think we can have some drinks first." "Yes, we can. I will meet you in the hotel bar at Seven o'clock instead of the room at Nine o'clock." "Cool baby, again I will be there, and I will be on time." Mel laid her clothes out before she got into the shower. After getting out of the shower, she oiled her body down and slid a Gucci Bodycon dress on. It was paper thin and left nothing to the imagination, the strapless dress was a task getting it over her head, but her oiled down body allowed the dress to ease down over her curvy thick body.

She slid her Chanel stilettos on and checked her Chanel bag to make sure her small .22 LR had a full clip in it. She touched up her lipstick and whipped her long lace front and headed to the parking deck of her building where she parked. Mel just had her black C30 Mercedes detailed, so she was ready for the night and as always, she was going to look good doing it. Mel, pulled up to the Valet at the Mid-Town Marriott hotel on Trade Street. Mel, looked so good when she stepped out of her car the three men that was standing at the valet booth waiting on their car, They all at the same time put out their hand to assist Mel, step up on the curb in her four-inch stiletto heels and skintight dress. Mel, walked into the hotel's lobby and went to the bar. When she got their Hank, was already sitting at a table looking country as hell. Mel took four deep breaths to calm herself, then she walked over to the table. When she got to the table, the country, gold front, uncouth nigga didn't even stand to greet her. She reached out her hand so he could take it He just left it out there hanging. Mel, said to herself with her teeth clinched, "I alter pop one dead in the side of this motherfucker's neck right here in this crowded bar." Mel, took a seat with a smile on her face and asked Hank "Have you been here long?" "Long enough." "Wow!" Mel said to herself with a raised eyes brow. Mel, immediately waved for the waitress. The waitress made her way over to their table she said "Good evening what may I get for you guys tonight." Mel, pleasantly said to her "Good evening sweetheart, could you please hurly let me get a double shot of Remy XO." "Hold! Hold! Girl, do you know that that drink is one hundred dollars a shot?" "Yes, I do know. Can you please bring me my double shot please and bring me the check. Thank you, Sweetheart." "Well, if that is the case you paying, I will have one too." Hank was a fucking jerk, and I don't think he even knows it. After one or two drinks Hank, had a better disposition about himself. He was actually kinda of funny. Mel, and Hank stayed in the bar for over an hour drinking and laughing. After about the fourth drink Hank, was twisted so much so he didn't see what every other man that was in the bar saw. This hella bitch had just walked into the bar. She was on fleek, and everyone thought she was some kind of model or movie star. She was wearing the average nigga's yearly paycheck from her Cartier CT sunglasses, all the way down to those bad ass Jimmy Choo shoes she had on. Mel was sharp as hell, but she even had to give this woman her props. She took a table that was two tables back from where Mel and Hank were sitting, after one more drink Mel asked

Hank, " Baby, are you ready to go up to your room?" Hank was so twisted he could only answer Mel, in a mumble. Mel, waved for the server to bring their check. When she brought the check Mel, told her to charge it to room 710 which was Hank's room. Mel, said to herself "you cheap fuck you gonna pay for these drinks anyway; that's what yo' punk ass gets for not being enough man to hold your liquor." Mel, scribbled a name on the room check and said to the server "Hon, I added a nice tip to the check, you have a great night." Mel, stood up from the table and said to Hank, "I'm ready baby, come' on." "I need some help. I can't get up by myself." Mel went over to give him a hand to get up from the table. As she was pulling him up Mel, winked her eye at the woman two tables back. The woman smiled and winked back at Mel. Hank draped his arm over Mel's shoulder, and they began to walk towards the lobby with him leaning against Mel. They took three steps when Hank, yelled, "Hold it. My bag. I had a black bag with me." By that time the server, had already picked the black bag up and brought it to them. Mel, grabbed the bag from the server, when she did the server leaned in close to Mel, and said "Thank you, and may god bless you." The tip Mel, added to Hank's room check was three hundred dollars. Mel said, "Hon, that's fine, and thank you for the bag." Mel, walked Hank, out and through the lobby to the elevators. Mel pushed the elevator button marked up and the doors opened right up, they walked into the elevator. Mel pressed the number Seven button; it lit up and the elevator began to move. When the elevator started its ascend Hank, yelled out, "weeee." like a little kid on a ride. Shut your twisted ass up. A nigga that's so big and bad when it came to bullying women but can't hold his liquor worth a damn just like a bitch nigga, Mel though to herself. The elevator got to the seventh floor. The doors opened up, Mel, assist Hank, to walk down a long hall to room Seven-ten. While standing in front of Hank's room door Mel asked Hank "Where is your room key." "In my back pocket." Mel went into the back pocket of his Jeans and got the room's key card out. She slid the card down into the lock a green light came on indicating the door was unlocked. Mel pushed the door open, and they walked inside." What would you like to say to me Tammy" Tony asked. "Tony please don't look at me like I'm crazy when I say this to you." "Hell with all the other crazy shit you nun said, how do you think I already look at your crazy ass" Tony said in his head. Tony sincerely said "Never Tammy, you can say anything to me." "Tony, I love you." Tony paused as Tammy, laid beside him waiting for a response from him. Ring, ring, ring, "right on fucking time" Tony said to his self. He then answered his planned call from Tonya, to farther draw Tammy, in by playing on her emotion, "Hello Greg, what's up." Pause "say what Greg you got to be fucking kidding me." Pause "It wasn't a real company, so it's all gone." Pause "All of it DAMN! I am going to lose everything. even the clothes on my back." Pause "I don't know what I'm going to do, but right now I'm here with my lady and I'm not going to let this crazy shit mess my night up with her. I will talk to you tomorrow." Tony, look back over at Tammy, and dropped his head, and said "I heard you and I want you to know I think I love you to, but I'm going to have to leave now." "Why Tony, why do you have to leave." "As you just heard I got some bad news that's going to leave me busted and, on the street, and I don't want you to think I'm a weak man by me crying in front of you." "No, no, baby, I would never think that about you. Please look at me Tony, come on Tony, hold your head up and look at me. Tony, tell me what happened, I love you I got your back." Tony, looked up at Tammy, and he began to tell her a straight face lie, as he told her a very convincing lie. A tear fell from his right eye. Tammy took her hand and wiped the tear from his cheek. she said to him, "Baby, that's alright go ahead and cry if you need to. I got you baby I promise." "No Tammy, I can't put anything like this on you. I'm talking well over Five Hundred Thousand Dollars in less than a week." Tony, I am embarrassed to tell you this, but when I met you, I was sleeping with my boss, as well as keeping his books and making bank deposits. I know all his codes, have all the keys, plus I know the combination to the safe in his office, where he keeps all his drug money." "Wow! who is your boss." "This Italian guy from right here in Virginia Beach." "Naw, I can't ask you to do that. Tammy, I love you too much to endanger your life like that." "Tony, don't you worry about that. There is nothing I wouldn't do for you. Give me a few days and I will have all the money for you." Tammy and Tony, laid together in each other's arms the rest of the night. Tammy rubbed her fingers through his hair as she kissed him on the forehead. As tears fell from Tony, eyes Ironically Tammy, had music playing in the back ground, it was the O'Jays cry together. Tony, eventually pretended as if he was sleep, so she would stop touching, rubbing, and kissing on him it was getting on his nerves. Tony and Tammy, slept to midmorning of the next day. Tony, said to Tammy, "baby, I have to go back to my hotel to take a shower and get dressed so I can meet with my business manager as soon as possible, but I will see you in a few days right." "Yes Tony, you will and don't you worry things are going to work out." Tony quickly got dressed and left Tammy 's house. He went back to his hotel room and laid down so he could get some sleep. Tony, really never slept as Tammy's, matter fact he never slept at anyone's house. He stays aware of his surroundings at all times, that's one thing about him that make him damn near impossible to caught slipping. Tammy, looked at the clock on her wall for the time as she tried to come up with a plan to take the money she believed Tony, needed from Chris. She needs to make it look like it was a rip, there were a lot of wanna be's in the area that try to come up by ripping other drug dealers, so that story would be easy to believe. Tammy, wanted to get the money for Tony, badly but she also wanted to continue to live once she does. Tammy, quickly slid on a white tee, a blue jeans skirt, and headed over to the club to look around Chris's office. Tammy, got to the sugar and spice club a little after 1 p.m., thinking that she would be there alone, she parked her car at the back door of the club. She sat in the car for a minute just looking around and thinking "this shit I'm about to do is crazy as hell. I am getting ready to go in here to steal a half million dollars from a man that will kill me dead as hell, if he catches me or think that I had anything to do with stealing his money. Then I'm stealing it for a man that I have known for less than a week, Tammy, what in the hell is wrong with you? Are you gone crazy or what? I know what's wrong, I love that man with all my heart. Yes, in other words, I am whipped, whipped like a bowl of cool whip. If Tony, told me he can fly, I would say take me flying sometimes Superman. That's how much I love him and believe him. Okay then let's do this Tammy." Tammy, leaned over to the passenger side of the car to her glove compartment she opens it. Once she got it open, she reached in and grabbed the club keys. Tammy, exit her car and walked up to the back door of the club, she uses the keys from her glove compartment to unlock it. She then opened up the door. Tammy, walked inside the club and turned to close and lock the door back behind her. It was dark inside of the club she could barely see her way around, but she didn't want to turn on any lights. Tammy made her way to Chris's office door and because it was so dark, she fumbled with the keys to open it. She finally found the key to the office door. She put the key into the lock, but she noticed that the door was already unlocked. Tammy, slowly pushed the door open and creeped in. As soon as she cleared the doorway she saw Chris, sitting behind his desk, writing on a pad. It startled her, she made a faint noise, which made Chris, look up at her as she stood looking like a deer caught in the headlights. Chris, immediately said "Tam." Tammy, couldn't find her voice to respond, but in her head she said "oh shit." Tammy tried her best to push out words from her mouth. The only thing she could get to come out was "Chris, what are you doing here." "it's my office hell it's my club." "Oh, ya that's right what I meant is I thought you was with a charter today." "Ya that's later it's going to be a one man charter at 3 o'clock, but I had to take my car to get detail. I went fishing last night and left my fishing gear in the back seat of the car. When, I got in the car this morning It smelled like fish, so I dropped it off at the car wash to be detailed, then uber over here to do some paperwork, while I waited for them to finish my car, but what are you doing here so early?" "I forgot my liquor order list here last night. So, since I was on this side of town, I thought I would come by and get it." "I'm glad you had to come by here because I was going to come by your house later. I have been calling and texting you and you have not responded. What's going on Tam? Where have you been?" "No where Chris, where do I ever go, but to work and back home to wait for you to decide you need a break from your wife, then you come to grace me with your presence for a few hours?" "What are you saying Tam? all of a sudden you got a problem with our arrangement? What Tam, are you seeing one of these jigs out here is these streets." "No that's not what I'm saying, and no I'm not seeing anybody." Chris, stood up and walked around his desk and over to Tammy, with one hand he aggressively grabbed and squeezed her jawbone and said "you better not be." "I'm not Chris, damn." Tammy took a step back to get her face out of his grasp. Chris, said to her again, "so Tam, why haven't you been answering my calls or text." "if you can remember Chris, it was you that said you were going to get me a new phone because last week the Liquor delivery guy laid all them cases of wine and Liquor on my cell phone, when he put the cases down where you told him to put them. It hasn't worked right since then." "Oh, ya that's right. I will get you another one tomorrow." "Ya, Ya, Chris, that's what you said last week. I bet if wifey needed one you would have been got it." "Tam don't be like that. you know I'm going to leave her as soon as my last daughter go off to college. Then you and I can be together. My wife and I don't even sleep in the same bedroom anymore." Tammy, dropped her head and said "Chris, you said that before your son went off to college." Chris walked up close to Tammy and started to massage her shoulders from behind her. He then said "Tam, I know, but I promise you I will this time." Chris, continue to massage her shoulders as he pushed her forward towards his desk. Chris, said "Then we can even get married Tam." Chris pushed her even closer to his desk until he got her up against the desk. He pushed her father forward so that she was bent over his desk with her elbows resting on top of it. Tammy said "CHRIS! NO!" Hank and Mel, walked over to the bed. Hank, sat down on the end of the bed. He said "wow… that walk did me good. It sobered me up so now that I'm good let's get it cracking up in here." Mel slid her strapless dress down onto the floor and stepped out of it. She was standing in front of Hank, in just a pair of four inch stiletto heels with her hands on her hips. Hank, looked up at her and said, "Damn!! You are a bad motherfucker." Mel dropped it, but not like it was hot, but like that shit was on fire. Hank couldn't compose himself he was going crazy. "God damn! You are the baddest looking chick I've ever seen." "Did this country motherfucker just call me a Chick?" Mel, said to herself. Mel, turned with her back to him and bent over again and touched her toes, then dropped her ass to the floor. Hank was about to go through the roof. Mel, turned to walk to the bed where Hank, was sitting. She put one knee up on the bed and got close to his ear and whispered "I'm going to the bathroom while you get undressed." Hank, said "Okay bet." Before Mel, could get off the bed Hank, started pulling and tugging at his clothes. Mel, walked into the bathroom and closed the door. While she was in the bathroom Hank, pulled out his phone to call his wife he said to himself "I'm calling home and tell my wife I ain't never coming home again. Hank, you still bout drunk. This ain't No "Helen Nights." Naw, it may not be, but Mel, sure is sunshine. I think my drunk ass better just text my wife and tell her, "Hey I ain't never coming home again. Should I hit send? Hell no! Delete, Delete, Delete. Hey, Honey I will be home in the morning. Got tied up with some work" as he pressed send Mel, walked out of the bathroom. "Damn" Mel, said to herself. Hank had taken all his clothes off and his freakish large dick was standing straight out literally like a flag pole. Mel, walked over to him and put his tree trunk of a dick in one hand, and she massaged his nuts with the other hand. Mel, looked down at it and said, "Very Impressive, but can you work with it?" "Hell, ya I can. You wait until I get up into that phat ass pussy. Girl you goin fall in love with me." Mel went down to one knee. "Calm down Tam, you know you want this." With one hand holding Tammy, over on his desk. Chris, used the other one to pull Tammy's, skirt up then unzipped his pants pulling out a fully erect penis. Chris licked the palm of his hand putting a heavy amount of saliva into the palm of his it. He then put his hand between Tammy's legs rubbing his saliva filled hand back and forth on her pussy trying to induce wetness. When Chris, felt that he had it wet enough he guided his dick between her legs pushing himself into her. Tammy, saw that it was going to happen whether she wanted it to or not, so she said to herself "the best thing I can do is go with his program and help him get his nut off and get his ass out of me." Tammy rose up on both of her hands and placed her right leg up on the desk. She licked her fingers on her right hand and put them between her legs rubbing her clit until fluid began to drop to the floor. This allowed his dick to easily slide into her now wet pussy. When she felt the head of his dick touch the lips of her pussy, she let out a moan and said, "Go ahead daddy get it. Fuck the hell out of it." Chris was pushing in even harder as he felt her juices run down the shaft of his dick to his nut sack. Tammy, reached back with her right hand and grabbed the front pocket of his slacks and pulled him in even closer to her. When Chris, pushed forward Tammy, pushed back sending his dick to the back walls of her pussy. This made Chris, weak in the knees now where Chris, was trying to fuck Tammy, instead Tammy, fucked Chris. She pushed back on him faster and harder still holding the front of his slacks, she took control of his program. Chris, yelled out "slow down Tam, slow down." Tammy, only got faster and more intense "Tam, slow down, no Tam, oh my God." Chris was finish, sweating, windless and weak so much so that his knee buckled sending him to the floor. Chris, looked at Tammy, and said "Tam, what the hell was that." "You just got fucked that's what you wanted wasn't it. Before he could answer or get his self together his phone rang. "Hello, yes I'm on the way out." It was his prescheduled uber, to take him back to the car wash to pick up his car. He quickly jumped up from the one knee that he was on and zipped up his pants, and he said "listen we will finish this talk later. I need to know what your problem is." Chris, walked out of his office and through the club area out the front door where his uber was waiting. Tammy followed behind him and watched him get into the uber and leave. She then went back into Chris's office opened his safe. She saw stacks of hundred dollar bills banded up in bands of Ten Thousand Dollars. Tammy grabbed the trash can beside Chris's desk and she stuffed it full of the Ten Thousand Dollar bands. Mel, had to repositioned her hands to hold his large dick with both hands. Mel, thought to herself "If he really knows how to work with this monster right here. He would be a dangerous nigga, he'll have a bitch strung, and out looking for a nigga in the daytime with a flashlight. Damn, if I ain't eager to find out for myself." She brought it close to her mouth, when she did, she could feel him jerking and shaking. Mel, looked up at him she said "NO! this motherfucker not. I know goodin damn well you are not." Mel quickly placed her hands over the head of his dick to protect her hair, Hank nut it into the palm of her hands. "Damn! This bitch, if he would had nut, in my Fifth teen Hundred Dollar lace front, I would have cut that Nigga dick slam off" she shook her head as she said, "This Nigga ain't shit and what a waste. He got a serious quit nutting problem, she said to herself. Mel, got up off her knee to go to the bathroom to wash her nut filled hands, and from the bathroom Mel, talked shit to him." Nigga all that shit you talked about what you can do then you got finished before you got started." Mel, walked back into the room from the bathroom to a pleading, excuse making, limped dick Nigga saying "please Mel, give me another chance. If you wait a minute, it will get hard again. Com' on Mel, you won't be sorry. You are so fine Mel, I couldn't help myself." Mel ignored him and walked over to the bed and sat down. While Hank, stood in the middle of the hotel room jacking his dick trying to get it up again. Mel got on the bed stacked up some pillows from the bed against the headboard. She then leaned back on them. She reached over to the nightstand where the TV remote was sitting. She picked it up turned on the TV to channel surf. As

Hank, continue to play with himself trying to get an erection. Mel quickly grew bored she was already mad and frustrated. She was ready to hit the ceiling, because has thought sure she would have at least got a nut off with a Nigga that had a dick that big. "Fuck it" she said. She reached over to the bottom of the bed, where her bag was hanging on the bed rail, she went into it and took out her phone and sent a text "in Ten minutes." Mel, looked over at this fool, still standing in the middle of the room jacking, beating, and praying trying to get his dick up again. Mel, said to Hank "com' on over here baby, let me see if I can help you get it up." He walked over to the bed and climbed up on it. He got up between Mel's legs and he leaned forward, while holding his self-up with one arm he grabbed his dick with the other hand. He began to slid his dick up and down Mel's, pussy lips, as a sweet smell, filled the air of the room. It smelled of expensive perfume. Mel had left the hotel room door a jar by turning the thumb lock to the door to the lock position before closing the door, when Mel and Hank first came into the room. Hank didn't pay the smell, any attention because of him, focusing so hard on getting an erection. He didn't notice anything until he felt a piece of cold steel between his legs pressing against his nuts. This made him quickly look down to see what was going on. In a soft, sexy voice Tonya, said "Nigga don't move. Cause if you do all that pretty pussy you see in front of you will be the last pussy you will ever see." Mel, slid back and away from Hank, she jumped off the bed and went straight for Hank's black bag. Hank, looked over to see the naked Mel, looking into the bag, Hank, yelled out towards her "you bitches don't know what you are doing. You are ripping off some powerful people." Tonya, stepped around in front of Hank, she asked "motherfucker, do you remember me." "Ya, I do. you that bitch from the poker room with the funny ass eyes." "Wow, you are a brave Nigga calling me a bitch with my nine pressed against your motherfucking nuts. I told you that I was going to teach, your ass some respect. This ain't no rip that bag is just a bonus. This is about teaching you how to respect women with your sexist motherfucking ass. Tammy, put all she could in the trash can and then went and found another bag to put the rest of the money in. In all Tammy, had Fifty bands of hundred dollar bills. Tammy took a hand full of the bills from the safe and threw them all over Chris's office. She even went up to the front door and threw some bands, when she flung the bands, they broke open causing the hundred dollar bills to rain all over the place. While she was up front of the club, she unlocked the front door. She then went back to the office to grab the trash can and the bag of bills and ran from the office. She left the building through the back door the same way she came in. When she left the club, she left the office door and safe open and there were hundred dollar bills scattered everywhere. Tammy, drove off nerves as hell, but when she got almost home. She sent a text to Tony, "Tony, we are good. I got that for you." Tony, text her back "That's great baby. are you Okay?" "Yes, I am I'm great I just miss and want to see you." "Okay baby, that's not a problem. I am in a meeting right now, but later tonight my love I will come to your place." "Later tonight that's great. I love you so much Tony." Tony had booked a Two-hour fishing charter for Three O'clock that day, that he was on his way too. Tony, drove down the beach line looking for Pier Twelve, after about Twenty minutes of driving he saw the Pier he was looking for. He pulled up to the parking area and parked his car. Tony was running a little late, which shouldn't be a problem. Since he rented the whole boat out to himself. It may have been possible that he didn't need to do that he may have been the only one on the charter anyway, since it was wintertime, and he was at the beach. It would be cold as hell out on the water, but Tony didn't want to take any chances of anybody else being on the boat with him and Chris. He needed that Italian motherfucker on the boat only. Tony, got out of his car and walked down the dock to Pier Twelve, this guy met him and welcomed him as he turned to walk up the pier to the boat. The guy that met him had on a white uniform, and on his white uniform shirt was a name tag that read "Captain Chris, so this is that Italian motherfucker that Tonya, want gone" Tony, said to his self. Tony, got on the boat with Captain Chris, he asked Tony, "How far would you like to go out? I must tell you Sir. the father we go out the windier it will get which means the colder it will get." "Okay then let's just go out a few miles, to be honest with you for me it is not so much about the fishing then it is about a few hours of peace of mind. That's why I rented out the whole boat." "Okay Sir, I understand." When Tony, was seated they launched off. It was about an hour of being out, when Tony, began walking up to the front of the boat to where the captain was. Tony, holding his nine in his hand he eased up the side of the boat. When he made it almost there Tony, could see another boat coming towards them. Tony, stopped to wait for the boat to pass. The boat did pass them, but it didn't seem to be getting any farther away from their boat. It seemed that the boat had anchored in place. It was a good distance off from where they had anchored, but Tony, didn't want to take the chance that they could hear a gunshot. So, Tony, changed his plan he called out frantically to the captain "CAPTIAN! CAPTIAN!

HURRY! come back to the rear of the boat." Captain Chris, quickly walked back to where Tony, was standing, looking over the rear of the boat and down into the water. Tony was also pointing down into the water as he if he saw something. Chris, hastily walked up to Tony, to see what was going on. Chris, looked down over the rear of the boat where Tony, was pointing. Chris couldn't see anything, so he got closer to the rear edge and leaned over, Tony, stepped up behind Chris. BANG!! Tonya pulled the trigger on her nine, and the bullet went straight through Hank's, nut sack and into the headboard of the bed. He screamed out, unlike any other scream that they had ever heard before. Blood sprayed everywhere it soaked the bed in the matter of seconds. Tonya, said to Hank, "I know your whole fucking family from your wife Marybell to your three kids Ashley, Danny, and Little Hank Junior, don't let them wash up somewhere because you can't keep your mouth closed. Com' on Mel, let's get the fuck out of here."
"

Gotcha let's roll GIRL!" "Ahh. Mel, are you forgetting something?" "What! Tonya." "BITCH! yo' naked, you ain't got a stitch of clothes on." "Oh, shit girl! I shu' hell don't. You know me I don't give a fuck especially when I got a bag in my hand. Hell, this is the first time my pussy jumped and got wet all night." "Ya Mel, a bag of money tends to do that to a bitch." Tonya, walked over to the nightstand and picked up the hotel phone. She pressed zero for the front desk." Hurry! Hurry! call 911, somebody been hurt up here." On their way out the door Tonya, left Hank, with one more demand. "Take your ass back up to Virginia Beach, and don't ever come back down south again." Tony took out his six inch serrated knife to cut Chris's throat. When Tony, walked up and grabbed Chris, Chris, yelled out "No! No!" "You should have picked a better person to be friends with, so you can thank that nigga Hank" Tony, said. As Tony, had an arm around Chris's neck about to cut his throat, a large wave hit the boat and violently rocked it back and forth. The harsh movement throw Tony and Chris off balance. Splash!! Chris went over the rear of the boat into the Ocean. Tony fell back into the boat knocking the beath out of him. It stunned him for a minute, when he came around Tony, jumped up to his feet and looked around. He didn't see Chis, so he ran to the rear of the boat and looked over, he didn't see him, there either, but he did see a lot of blood in the water. Tony, thought to himself, "I must have cut that motherfucker as I was falling backwards." The one thing that Tony, knew and that was they were at least Two miles out in the ocean, plus Chris, is cut and bleeding. There's no way he can swim that far back then he'll have sharks on his ass with all that blood in the water. Tony, drove the boat back to shore. When he got back to the dock, he jumped out of the boat, without tying off. He even left the boat at the dock with the engine still running. Tony ran up the dock, and across the parking lot to his car, he jumped in it and sped off. He didn't slow down until he reached the main street. Tony, was headed to Tammy 's house to finish up this business, so he can ghost Virginia Beach." Damn! Girl, it got to be at least Two Hundred Thou in this bag" Mel, said while her and Tonya, briskly walked down the hall to the elevators. Tonya, press the down button on the wall next to the elevator. As they stood waiting for the elevator to come Mel, continue to talk about how many racks was in the black bag. The elevator doors open Tonya and Mel walked in after about hundred motherfucking hotel staff rushed out and headed down the hall towards room Seven-Ten. The doors closed Tonya, pressed the lobby button. Mel, said to Tonya, "It got to be more than Hundred Thou for each one of us in this bag." "Naw! Mel, that's all you, Merry Christmas." "See! that's why I fuck with you. You are the classiest bitch I know." Mel and Tonya got out of the elevator at the lobby, and they separated. Tony knocked on Tammy 's front door she came to the door after Tony's first knock. She quickly opened it and invited Tony in. Tony looked in her face and could tell she was upset or afraid. It may have been a little of both upset and scared. Tony, said to Tammy "Tammy, let's go sit down so you can tell me what happened." For well over two hours, which seemed like a lifetime to Tony. Tammy, told Tony, step-by-step details on her days events. While rehearsing her terrifying experience she was noticeably shaking in fear. Tony, hugged Tammy, to comforted her and ease her mind. Tammy, was unaware that Chris, was dead and that she never had to see or deal with him again. As Tammy, continue to talk, Tony, caress the back of Tammy 's neck. Tammy, stood up from the couch that her and Tony was sitting on. She reached out her hand and told Tony, "Come go with me. I have something to show you." Tony gently grabbed Tammy 's hand as she laid him to the bedroom. Once in the bedroom, Tammy, lead him over to the nightstand that was next to the bed, on the nightstand was stacks and stacks of bills. Fifty stacks of Hundred Dollar bills to be exact. Tammy, sat down on the bed next to the nightstand with the bills on it. Tony, join her on the bed sitting down right next to her. He again began to caress the back of her head. She leaned over against him and moved her hand up and down his upper body as she gently pushed him back on the bed. Once Tammy, got him back she laid her head on the left side of his chest. She continued to rub her hand up and down his upper body until her hand became more focused. She focused on the tip of his right nipple, rubbing it softly with her thumb and forefinger. "Ahh girl" Tony, said. As he continued to rub the back of her head. She placed her lips on Tony's left nipple through his shirt. With her lips tucked between her teeth she softly bit and nibbled on his nipple, Tony, let out a moan of pleasure. Tammy, said to him, "I know baby just lay back and relax." Tony, caressed the back of her head more vigorously as Tammy, sent a tingling through his whole body. Tony, put his hand on her chin and lifted her head up, so that she could look at him. He said, "No baby please stop, this feel good and everything, but I was trying to comfort you and make you feel better after the day you have had." "Tony, you are comforting me and making me feel better by you being here with me and you allowing me to make you feel good. You do feel good don't you baby." "Yes, I do." She then brought her head up to the left side of his neck and begin to softly kiss and caressing it with her tongue. She raised up even more and begin to flick her tongue back-and-forth on his Adams apple "baby! Baby! hold you know I have to go take care of some business" Tony, said. "Wait, wait, Tony, please stay here with me just a little while longer" Tammy, said as she stuck her tongue down the canal of his ear. Tony, tried to talk again, but Tammy, licked his lips quickly Shutting him up. Tony, started thinking to his self "fuck it… a nut is always a good thing." So, he moved his left hand from her head and placed it on her back slowly moving it towards her thick round ass. Tammy arched her back making her ass easier for him to reach. Tony's dick came alive by swelling up when he palmed her phat round ass. As Tony, squeezed and rubbed it he creeped her skirt up getting to her waist. Tony, continue to rub and squeeze when he surprisingly discovered Tammy, wasn't wearing any panties. Tammy knew he had discovered that she didn't have any panties on by his long stern squeeze on her ass. Tammy smiled and giggled when he did. She looked up at him and said "for you baby." "Hmm I like" Tony, said as he gave her a soft slap on her naked ass. The blood continued to rush to his shaft, giving him a full erection. Tony moved his right hand from Tammy 's head, and he reached down to unbuckle his belt and zipped down his pants. He slid them down to his feet. He must have not been moving fast enough for Tammy. Cause Tammy, reached down over Tony's hands and grabbed his pants and pulled them over and off his feet. She then grabbed the tail of his tee and quickly pulled it up over his head and off his arms. She than stuck her tongue inside of his belly button. Her left hand slowly moved south until she found the south pole. It was throbbing and fully erected as Tammy, grasp it, and began to stroke it until passion filled the room. Tony moved his left hand from Tammy 's ass to reposition himself to caress her inner thighs, stopping his hand at the lips of her pussy. Tony, stroked the silk moist area with his index finger, causing Tammy, to shake and wiggle like he was playing her favorite song. "On my God Tony, I love you. Tony, you are on my spot." Tony had inserted his index finger even deeper inside her now dripping wet pussy and moved it in and out of her in a quick circular motion. With Tony's finger still inserted into her pussy Tammy, continue to lovingly stroke and rub his dick. Tammy, pulled back, leaving Tony's wet hand, laying between her thighs. She pulled back to reposition herself to get closer to his pelvic region. With one hand wrapped around his dick she inserted the head of it into her mouth. She clamped her lips down around it as she moved her head up and down. She could feel his dick pound in her mouth like it had its own heartbeat. Tony, wanted to take back control so he repositioned his self so that he could reach Tammy's pelvic area again. He gently stuck his fingers inside of her once again, causing her ass to clinch and fluid ran from her pussy like somebody turned on a faucet wide open. "Baby!!! oh my." Tony, smiled to his self in satisfaction and said "I got to put this girl to sleep so I can get the fuck out of here and out this damn state." Tony flicked his inserted finger back-and-forth making her quiver. Tammy, quickly pulled back again from the powers of Tony's finger. Tammy, said to herself "I'm gon' put it on his ass to make him not want to leave."

Tammy moved South again taking his pole into her mouth she bobbed her head on his dick in multiple direction, as the saliva from her mouth ran down his shaft on to his pubic hair. Tammy, remove Tony's dick from her shiny lips and begin tracing the head of it with her tongue. Both with their opposing plans Tony, trying his best not to explode before he put her to sleep so that he could sneak out, and Tammy, was trying to give the best head of her life, so he would stay. Tony knew that he had to get her off his dick with her mouth, or it was going to be an uncontrolled explosion happening up in there. Tony reached down and lifted Tammy 's head and brought her up eye level with him. He rolled himself over on top of her, holding his self-up with one hand, he picked up one of her knees with the other hand. Putting himself in between her legs. Tony quickly went down to find her clit with his mouth. He sucked on it long enough to get her hips moving, and her breathing became labored. He then would pop his head up, sending his dick straight up into her wet pussy. She tightly grabbed his upper body pulling him into her as if she was trying to give him his rib back and making them as one. Tony continued to stroke Tammy's pussy with a purpose. This was driving Tammy, insane she yelled out, "Baby! come here to me. I can't take this you are driving me crazy. Baby what are you trying to do to me." "Just trying to make you feel good." Tony went faster and harder in his pursuit to knock her ass out. Tammy, began to say every curse word in the book, calling him everything but the child of God. Through clinched teeth Tony, yelled out "I'm cumin baby, I want you to come with me." "Okay, Okay baby, go faster, yes right their baby I'm cumin. Ahhh baby, I'm cumin with you." "Damn Tammy." "Tony, what the hell was you trying to do make me have a heart attack or something." Both of them sweating, breathing hard, and panting, they fall over on the bed. Tony, turned to look at her he said "you are the best." "No, you are Tony. you got me on that one you wore my ass out." Tony, rolled Tammy, over to her side. So that he could spoon with her. He spooned her with his arms wrapped around her she rested her head on one of his arms. It wasn't long before Tammy, was in a coma like sleep. Tony gently and easily pulled his arm from under her head being extremely careful not to awaken her. Tony slid his pants and shoes on. He took his Tee and tied knots with both arms of the Tee. He then walked over to the nightstand next to the bed, he opened the tail end of the Tee and raked all the stacks of bills into the Tee. Tony, eased out of Tammy's front door and got into his car with the Tee full of the stacks of bills. He drove off and just before he hit the interstate, Tony, threw his burner phone out the window. He had Tammy's number programmed in the burner it was the only way he had of contacting Tammy, and the only way Tammy, had of contacting him. While on U.S. Route Fifty-eight East getting the hell out of town, he called Tonya, "Hey Tony, you still in Virginia Beach." "Ya, but I'm on the highway now heading back as fast as I can. My Fishing trip was good I caught a big fish, cooked and ate it too. I was even able to Rack up so maybe you can give the girls at the poker room a Christmas bonus from their boss." "Yes, that will work." "I will see you in the morning. Tonya, don't forget we have to be on the road to Atlanta, tomorrow." "I didn't forget I'm good. I closed school all lessons been taught, Shantel, been called to heck into the hotel security cameras to scrub me and Mel." "Cool see you tomorrow." When Tony, got back to town he also gave Shantel their computer geek a call to make sure he couldn't be found even if anyone googled him. The next morning Tony, drove over to Tonya 's condo, with Fifty Stacks of Hundred Dollar bills inside a black carry all Prada bag. He gave the bag to Tonya and said "Here with yo' ugly ass. Having me doing free shit that's crazy." "Well yo' ugly ass didn't have nothing else to do anyway. Don't no woman want you, so you better be glad I gave you something to do." "Ya, right, alright Sis. I'll see you in Atlanta, Love you I'm out." "Alright I called my girls, Marie and Regina, to pick me up from Hartsfield-Jackson International." "What!! why those two crazy ass bitches." "Bro. we may need them." Tony, walked to the door shaking his head. He knew if Tonya, was going to use Marie and Regina for the job in Atlanta, that meant Tonya, was planning on burning the whole city of Atlanta to the ground." Tonya, condescendingly said "Bro. Love you too See you there."

Made in the USA
Middletown, DE
05 February 2024